W9-ATD-580

SLOW DANCE IN AUTUMN

Other Books by Philip Lee Williams

The Heart of a Distant Forest
All the Western Stars

SLOW DANCE IN AUTUMN

A HANK PRINCE MYSTERY NOVEL

Philip Lee Williams

Peachtree Publishers

Atlanta • Memphis

Published by
Peachtree Publishers, Ltd.
494 Armour Circle, NE
Atlanta, Georgia 30324

A version of the first chapter of this book appeared in *Open City*, a newspaper published in Atlanta, Georgia.

Manufactured in the United States of America

10 9 8 7 6 5 4 3 2 1

Design and illustration by Paulette L. Lambert

Library of Congress Catalog Card Number 88-61457

ISBN 0-934601-56-9

This book is for
Laura Jane, Scott and John
and
Mark and Anne
and, as always,
for Linda

AUTHOR'S NOTE

I would like to express my appreciation to the Atlanta Police Department for its hard work, dedication and pursuit of justice. Policemen everywhere are over-worked and underpaid and deserve much more. This work of fiction portrays the good and evil sides of human nature, but does not depict any person who serves or who has ever served in the Atlanta Police Department.

SLOW DANCE
IN AUTUMN

VAN WILLIAMS BLACK LABEL SOUR MASH Bourbon Whiskey is the best in the world and I should know. I'd spent the past week trying to destroy my innards with four quarts, no glass and a photograph Wanda Mankowicz had given me back when I thought she loved me, the bitch. Finally, I'd finished off a bottle I thought had two gulps but had more like half a pint. After smoking a Camel and taking a Darvon I had left over from my foot trouble, I lay down and prepared to meet my maker. Instead, I dreamed about being a swan and lazily drifting across this fog-shrouded pond. Nothing else. Just a swan, the pond, fog.

I was starting to fly out of the pond when I awoke groggily and found myself staring into the face of my landlady, Myra Gunnerson. She weighed about two-fifty and had a face that looked like J. Edgar Hoover after having gone fifteen with Roberto Duran in his prime. She shook me, holding my shoulders with her fists as if I were a child. I wondered if my head would roll off and fall on the floor.

"What is it?" I managed to say, but the words fell apart in my mouth. Not that it would matter to Myra. She was from Finland or somewhere, had been raised in the Ukraine, and had a speech defect. I never could understand much of what she said.

"Meithsor Prance!" she said, still shaking me. I felt my eyes roll up, and I wanted to quack, honk or whatever it is swans do. "Iss a mun hyare!" I opened my eyes and sat up and backed off. She had turned and was looking at the photo of Wanda that was taped to the wall just over what had once been a dresser but was now a pyramid of clothes. Somehow it seemed smarter to pile them up than having to look through a drawer. The reason Mrs. Gunnerson was staring at the picture was that my Rapala fishing knife with the six-inch steel blade was plunged into Wanda's forehead through the sheetrock. I thought Mrs. Gunnerson was going to cross herself, but she merely turned back to me and dramatically placed her hand on her chest to remain calm. "Iss a mun hyare," she repeated.

"I need a translator," I said. She was trying to rephrase the sentence when the doorway darkened, and I saw Jack Railsback standing there looking at me, his mouth open in mild horror. Mrs. Gunnerson, rescued, nodded to Jack and repeated whatever it was she said and left. Jack came on in. I rubbed my face and felt I'd grown something of a beard. I didn't want to get up.

"My God," Jack said, looking around. I glanced around the room with him. The bottles of Evan

Williams Black Label Sour Mash Bourbon Whiskey were lined up neatly on the table. My room is small but it is also ugly: a table, a bathroom, a two-burner Hotpoint stove I'd bought at a yard sale. I didn't get up. Jack seemed close to gagging. "How can you live like this?"

"I'm trying to emulate Howard Hughes," I said. I motioned toward the pile of clothes. "Get me that pack of cigarettes."

My pack of Camels was on top. He stopped for a minute to look at the picture of Wanda Mankowicz and the knife in her forehead.

He brought me the cigarettes, and I lit one with my bedside Bic. It tasted good. I didn't figure this was the time to quit since my hands were shaking like I was being electrocuted. Jack was imperially slim, wearing white jogging pants with a thin blue line down the side, light blue Nikes and a T-shirt proclaiming his membership in the Atlanta Athletic Union. I was staring at his T-shirt wondering if they ever went on strike when he spoke.

"Anthony Browning's missing, Hank," he said. He struck a nervous pose in front of me. His face was lean, and his blue eyes glowed with health. His hair was dark, and he looked like he'd just come from the club. I didn't like clubs. I'd tried doing a bench press one time and dropped ninety pounds across my trachea. Some fun.

"I don't care," I said. I finished the cigarette and lit another. I was feeling better. Jack walked to the window and opened the Venetian blinds and raised the window, and the sounds of the day came in, the traffic below on the streets of Atlanta. I got up on toddler's legs and walked into the bathroom and stood over the john wondering how swans whizzed. I looked older than 35, say about 53. Maybe I should take up eating yogurt and live in the Urals. I slid on my pants, carefully selecting a pile from the arrangement under Wanda's careful watch, the bitch. How can you respect a woman who runs off with a salesman for the World View Encyclopedia Company?

"Sherrill is worried sick," Jack said. He looked like he wanted to sit, but there was no place but the bed. He stood. "She says it's different this time, that something's wrong. She thinks something's happened to him."

"What would you think," I said as I pulled on a shirt, "of a woman who ran off with an encyclopedia salesman?"

"I heard," he said grimly. "Would you please listen to me?"

"Why doesn't she call a cop?"

"She's afraid they'll bust Tony," Jack said.

I put on a pair of shoes, black tassel loafers. I seemed to have cut off all four tassels for some reason. "You know all about this. She wants you to find him. She'll pay. You know she'll pay. You look like you need some money."

"I'm getting out of the business," I said.

I'd known Tony and Sherrill Browning for years, and I didn't approve of what Tony did, but you learn to look the other way. I spent most of my time looking the other way with my friends, a courtesy I expected them to return. Jack was not much more than an acquaintance, but he wasn't turning the other way now, and it irritated me a little. Tony and Sherrill meant much more.

"Just go over and talk to her."

"You know what I thought?" I said. I lit a third Camel and was starting to feel like the bum I was. I wished Marlon Brando had been there. "I thought Wanda had been kidnapped by the Hare Krishnas. I was following the wrong damned car. Hank Prince, sleuth. Shit."

"Henry, just go over there and talk to Sherrill." He was holding his hands up and his feet were spread apart, and he reminded me of myself in my one and only acting attempt, when I was in *Arsenic and Old Lace* in high school.

"I'm going to become a Fuller Brush man to expand my sex appeal," I said.

"Goddamnit," he said, "would you forget about Wanda, huh? I'm telling you something's happened to Tony. And besides, you look like hell. You need something to keep you busy."

"Maybe Tony's been kidnapped by the Hare Krishnas," I said, warming to the idea. Mrs. Gunnerson came scuttling back into the room, hauling a vacuum cleaner behind her. Forget Roberto Duran. She looked more like she'd been pummeled by Sonny Liston.

"Sheem urna yaw fer disa tang!" she said. Jack looked at her as if he were watching a car wreck taking place.

"I think she just put a curse on the room," I said to Jack. I went into the bathroom and got my gun out of the medicine cabinet and clipped it to my belt and took my jacket from the pile of clothes and followed him down the stairs. He ran. I walked. I wish I could have flown.

Jack wanted to eat at Sandifer's, a trendy yuppie hangout where the men were slim, their gold necklaces were real and any hint that the meat might once have had blood was scandalous. I wanted to go to the Primate Haus, a combination hash hole and bar where they at least knew me.

I was surprised to be hungry. Atlanta didn't look so bad for my mood. But then it was October, and I had been in this sunny city for more beautiful Octobers than I remembered. I thought about food. I didn't think too much about Tony or Sherrill.

Tony was a low-rent middleman for the dope trade, but not such a bad guy, at least that's what I thought when I was drunk, and I wasn't sure how many times I'd been sober in the past year. Actually, I'd known Sherrill years before I'd known Tony. One night, a lifetime ago, we'd driven to the beach and made love, but it never worked out, though I thought for a long time I loved her. Maybe I still did.

The Primate Haus was about four blocks from Mrs. Gunnerson's, in the southeast part of town, and since it was midmorning and all the local winos had gotten hold of themselves, the place was nearly deserted when we came in. It had once been an Ace Hardware store and the faint outline of the words "lawn care" could still be seen on the wall behind the counter. There were four booths along the wall and a couple of tables, but the regulars usually sat at the bar. Jack and I sat there. The jukebox was playing Tony Bennett.

"I didn't know you had died," said Treena, the counter waitress. I never knew her last name. She always looked the same, like she had been remolded fresh each morning from some waitress factory. She had lacquered blonde hair, trowel-thick makeup and violet eyes. Her teeth were crooked so that when she smiled, she kept her upper lip down. She appeared to snarl even when she was happy.

"You're sweet," I said. "Give me and my friend Jack a coffee."

"Anything else?" she asked.

"Orange juice and two hits of speed," I offered. Jack looked ill. "You want anything?" Jack said he only wanted the coffee. The coffee came and I sipped it, and I almost thought I could feel my heart turn over once or twice like an old car engine, sputter and then begin to beat again.

"Why do they call this place the Primate Haus?" Jack asked, looking warily around. The wall near the rest-room still had the hole where Bull Feeney had put his fist after losing his ass on the first Duran-Leonard fight.

"Man who owns it works for the Yerkes Primate Center," I said. "I think he came in here once to see what his beloved business was really like, and it upset him so much they put him in a cage when he got back. You can probably go out there now and see him sitting there with electrodes in his brain."

"Hah," said Treena, scraping grease off the grill.

"Anyway, Sherrill is really down about it this time," said Jack, sipping his coffee carefully. "She thinks something bad's going to happen to Tony."

"She should sell that mansion and buy a wagon and be a fortune teller," I said. "You hang around people like he does, and sooner or later you're going to show up in poor health."

"You have no compassion whatever, Hank. None whatsoever. Jesus, I'm glad you're not president."

"Oh, hell," I said. "There goes the campaign." Andy Williams was singing "Days of Wine and Roses."

I don't care what anybody says, Andy Williams is a damn good singer. I was wondering what relation Andy might be to Evan Williams when Jack turned on his bar seat.

"You son of a bitch," he said, "do something useful with your life."

"There," I said. "All you had to do was ask me the right way."

Anthony and Sherrill Browning lived on the northeast side of town, which was not as rich as the northwest, but still a lot better than anything on the south side. If you cared about money. I did. I had gone back to my room late that morning and found Mrs. Gunnerson just finishing up. It smelled like a pine tree would smell if it were a mammal and had been dead a few days.

"It looks nice," I said as I surveyed her handiwork.

"Shrda luke data vey," she said. "Aw spit tyerrah ers." I nodded as if I understood perfectly. She had even folded all my clothes and put them in the drawers, though she had refrained from touching Wanda's photo or the Rapala. She looked better to me now. Maybe she looked more like Tip O'Neill than J. Edgar Hoover.

She left, pulling the vacuum, which scuttled along obediently like some kind of primordial beast she kept as a pet. I lay across the clean sheets and slept. I tried to dream about being a swan, but instead I dreamed of my baseball career. I had been good at Savannah, damned good, and I was about ready for the majors when I tore my hamstring. I dreamed about how it happened, how it hurt, and when I awoke, it was after five, and I felt like I'd been in a brawl. I showered and shaved and took out a pair of blue slacks and a brown sweater, dressed and left, feeling better.

My car, a 1968 Buick Electra with a 425-cubic-inch engine that kicked out 310 horsepower, got about three feet to the gallon, but I didn't care because it was comfortable. Try to get comfortable in a subcompact. Besides, I felt I accrued some prestige because the rear end was jacked up so high you could get a nosebleed just sitting in the back seat.

Tony and Sherrill lived on Eaglewatch Drive, an exclusive area in the far western part of DeKalb County, just inside the Atlanta city limits. I pulled into the driveway just as the sunlight was beginning to ease west over the Georgia-Pacific Building, beyond which no life as we know it exists.

The house was at the rear of a vast expanse of deep green lawn. A flagstone walkway curved to the front door. The light was on, a small Williamsburg lamp next to the door. I reached out to touch the doorbell, and the door opened as if it were one of those damned grocery store doors that opens when you get anywhere within thirty feet of the store.

"Hank," said Sherrill Browning. "Please come in." I followed her. She was wearing a long brown caftan with some kind of Indian brocade around the neck. No shoes. Classy. Her hair was piled up on her head in the kind of artful carelessness that takes hours to affect. I followed her into the den. I had been there many times. She walked to the mantel and turned and held on to it and stared at me. I looked past her to the head of the fourteen-point buck Tony had killed. I would rather go fishing than do anything but make love or drink, but I couldn't understand the allure of shooting a spindly-legged animal with what amounted to a shoulder-held mortar.

"Jack said Tony is missing," I said. Maybe if I got right to the point, she'd give me some money. It never hurt to try, and as I said, I like money unreasonably.

"Would you like a drink?" she asked.

"Sure. Evan Williams. Double." She walked around the heavily padded bar that ran from one end of the low-ceilinged room to the other. She poured one for me, one for herself. I watched her closely, and her hands were trembling.

"It's worse this time," she said. I took a sip and already felt better. Andy Williams should be so lucky to be related to Evan Williams. "I can't shake this feeling that something bad's happened to him, Hank." She sat down on the sofa and started crying. I finished my drink and sat beside her and put my arm around her.

"Oh come on, Sherrill," I said. "This has happened before. You have another fight? When did you see him last?" She sniffed and sipped daintily at her drink.

"Day before yesterday," she said. "It was late at night and he hadn't come in, and I was in bed reading that book by Stephen King. You ever read Stephen King? God, he scares the holy Jesus out of me. It's about this big slobbering dog."

"So what happened?" I was starting to feel the liquor. Good.

"He came running in, and he was scared," she said. "He was scared half to death. His hair was standing out all over, and he pulled a bunch of clothes out of his drawer and stuffed them in a bag." She got up and walked to the fireplace. Soon, it would be cool enough for a fire, for sweaters, for the smiles of lovely women.

"He started to leave, and I jumped up and I asked him what happened, and he only said he'd be gone for a day or so. And he went running out. Something was after him. Jack told me I should call you."

"I thought you told him to call me."

"Don't make me think about it."

"So what do you want?"

"Just find him for me," she said. "I can't stand this waiting. It's like waiting for Christmas or something."

"Sherrill," I said patiently, "I was thinking of getting out of the business. You know, going with a security firm or something. I don't have enough discipline to work for myself." She sniffed and waved away my objection.

"Oh, by the way, how's Wanda?" she asked.

"She was kidnapped by the Hare Krishnas," I said. "Can I have another drink?"

"Oh, I'm sorry," she said. She walked around the bar and thoughtfully handed me the bottle. "I've got plenty of money. I know you'll probably say this is just between us as friends, but I'd like to pay."

"Many friendships have been ruined by money," I said. "I will allow you to reimburse me at my regular rate."

"Oh, thank you," she said. And that's how I went back to work.

2

LOSING WANDA MANKOWICZ WAS NOT MY only major foul-up in the past two years. I seemed to be losing my touch. There was the Ailsman divorce case, when I'd confronted Mr. Ailsman about having an affair with a woman who turned out to be his elderly aunt. The young woman in the house was her nurse and a licensed Seventh Day Adventist minister or bishop or whatever the hell they have. So I was sloppy.

Then there was the horror with Mr. Casey. You never seem to forget the really bad times. I hope he never finds his damn Renoir. My foot has just now healed properly. How can a scion of the country club set get so much enjoyment over a fat woman washing her feet? My ideal of a real artist is Van Gogh. He didn't shoot himself in the foot with a .38 Police Special, but he did cut off his ear, for which I've always been fond of him.

The next morning, I sat in my room and boiled some water for a cup of coffee. I made a list of the places I could go look for Anthony Browning. Most of the places would not be pleasant, but Sherrill had given me $2,000 in cash from her safe before I'd left, so I was not in much of a hurry. If I ever turned to larceny, I knew where to start.

Tony Browning had started out as an importer in Savannah, where I'd met him when I was playing ball. He and Sherrill were, as they say, a cute couple then, not worldly-wise but naive and eager. Jack Railsback was Tony's right-hand man.

Tony had started out with a small office on the waterfront, a fondness for wicker and Indian ornaments, and an undying faith in the spiritual balm of The American Way. He got richer in the two years I was in Savannah than I could imagine, buying a Mercedes and a six-bedroom house for which he had little use. Jack started wearing gold chains around his neck even before it was certified as proper attire by wimps everywhere. I presumed Tony had not hit it rich with wicker, so one night I asked him, and he started laughing and told me about it, about the bales of marijuana he sold, about how easy it was. In those days, I liked being around both of them.

I think, little by little, I fell in love with Sherrill, though, of course, our escapade had been over for a long time. There was something about her shape, the way her eyes shone whenever I talked. She was a good listener, the kind who made you feel you mattered. She was excited by the life around her, its variety and richness, and I wanted to be around her, not for another secret affair, but merely to bask in her warmth. I wanted to talk to her, endless hours of talk and walking on the beach, gathering conch shells and periwinkles and scallop shells in all their splendid colors. Tony didn't mind. He knew I would never make a move on Sherrill, and there was something almost platonic about our friendship, she never crossing the lines of affection nor I. We went to museums, the three of us, and though I could tell Sherrill was crazy about Tony, she gave to me some of her feeling for life, and I felt warm and happy. If we drifted apart, that glow never did. She and Tony would come to the games and cheer for me and once, when I was five-for-five, we ate out later, laughing and drinking until the quiet stars hung over Savannah. I thought about what it might have been like if Sherrill and I had stayed together before she met Tony. But it was a pointless thing to care about now. Yet I was still strongly attracted to her.

I'd known Sherrill back when I lived in Atlanta and, in fact, had introduced her to Tony at a meet-the-players thing we had to do at a clam bar one Friday afternoon. I was hot at the time with Renee Vallon, who was not from Paris but from Spartanburg, South Carolina, so I didn't mind when Sherrill and Tony started dating, then living together. He gave her everything, jewels, money, maybe, sometimes, love.

Then I got hurt and eased out of the minor leagues. They didn't actually tear off my number or ask me to turn in my jock strap, but I was out and on the streets. I was large, six-three and two-ten, and so I hung up my spikes and moved back to Atlanta and opened a private investigative agency for which I had no experience and apparently little aptitude.

Still, I had been at it for nearly ten years when things started turning sour a year ago. During that time, I'd worked mostly on divorce cases and a few missing people. I liked divorce cases because sometimes I got to see people doing lustful things through my spyglass. I have always been something of a voyeur, which is not the kind of qualification you find in the bios of major league outfielders. For a time, things went well. I bought a Bass Tracker II boat and a $200 graphite rod, and the fish in Lake Lanier all cringed when they heard I was on my way. But then the cases started to dwindle, and I lost my interest as well as the boat.

And then there was Wanda, the bitch.

It was only when Sherrill and Tony got married and moved back to Atlanta due to Sherrill's homesickness that Tony realized he was not in control, that he was a pawn to much larger interests in Miami. Still, he held up his end and never told Sherrill the truth. I had more reason than Sherrill to worry about Tony. I never did trust Jack, even though he seemed to be a friend. He had not worked for Tony for several years, but I'd heard that Jack and Sherrill had been close somewhere along the way.

Renee Vallon had told me good night one sultry evening in Savannah and turned up with a banker in Jacksonville two weeks later. She wrote me a really sweet letter explaining it all, and I called her up and told her to eat shit and die. Maybe Jack was right about my sense of compassion.

I drank a cup of coffee and finished my list. Tony had an office in Marshall Center downtown, but it was only him and a secretary. Maybe it was a place to start, up there on the thirty-sixth floor. I figured that Tony was probably up in the mountains with a girlfriend, his wild departure a ruse, but I had cut back on the drinking, my room was clean and I had $2,000. I might as well work before the angry God of Dissipation came tap-tap-tapping on my windowpane again.

I drove the Buick to the Marshall Center, a mass of glass and steel that looms over downtown. Driving my car always gave me a sense of power. It also had a 350-turbo transmission and aluminum valve covers, and sometimes on the interstate I'd eat up some hot dog. Anthony did not like my car, said I was a redneck for driving such a piece of trash. Henry Prince, Redneck Detective. Has a nice ring.

I parked the car and went up an elevator with a man who looked like the cover boy for *Preparation-H Illustrated*. He got off at twenty-eight, sighing heavily and carrying his briefcase like the Cross.

I slid out of the elevator on thirty-six and looked both ways. Nothing. Tony's office was around the corner. I went inside and his secretary, Ginny Calvert, was sitting at her desk reading *Light in August* by William Faulkner. I liked "The Bear," but I had never been able to make much of his novels. I know all those italics mean something. Nothing much seemed to be happening. She knew me, of course. I'd come by a few times with Tony.

"Mr. Prince," she said, holding her finger in place, as if the delay might be momentary. "This is unexpected." She was lovely, long curly auburn hair and green eyes. She wore a white blouse with ruffles down the button line and dangly turquoise earrings.

"I never have been able to understand Faulkner's novels," I said.

"I would think you'd have trouble understanding a Road Runner cartoon," she said sweetly.

"Faulkner is so . . . *je ne sais quois* . . . dense, *n'est pas?*"

"Maybe." She smiled and slid a bookmark into the pages and put it down. She stood and came around the desk, wearing a nice plaid skirt. It did not hide the fact that her waist was slim, her hips were broad, and I had not been with a woman since Mr. Encyclopedia came through town. "What can I do for you?"

"Is Tony in?"

"No," she said. She folded her arms under her breasts, lifting and pointing them at me as it were. She was maybe twenty-three, a graduate student at Georgia State University in downtown Atlanta. "He never comes in here much."

"Then what do you do?"

"I read Faulkner," she said. "Is there something you want?"

"Other than you?" She smiled wickedly and shook her head from side to side and said the word no without making a sound. "Well, actually, I'm trying to find your boss. He's been gone for a few days and his wife is worried about him." She let her breasts drop and I watched them.

"You have a case?" she asked. Maybe I'd been coming around here too much. "Trying to find Mr. Browning?" She threw her head back and laughed.

"What's wrong with that?" I asked. I wanted to take her into Tony's office and try out some of the moves I'd seen through my spyglass in divorce cases.

"Mr. Browning is a man of varied business contacts," she said. "He only comes in here about twice a month, and the phone has only rung twice since I started here." I remembered when she started, six months before.

"When was the last time you saw him?" She slid up on the desk and looked at the ceiling, pondering the weighty question.

"Oh God, let's see, it was last Monday . . . . no, uh, Tuesday," she said. "Yeah, Tuesday. He came in and got a package and left. Wasn't here ten minutes."

"Anything unusual?"

"Who is your employer again?" she asked. "Why should I be talking to you?"

"I left my Eagle Scout badge in my other uniform," I said.

"Okay, okay," she said. "He looked like he was worried about something. But I don't think his business has been going too good, you know? I had to drive out to his house last month to get him to sign my check."

"Something's been bothering him, then?"

"I don't know," she shrugged. "Is this going to take long? I have a test in Faulkner tomorrow." I looked at her and thought of Wanda. She looked nothing like Wanda.

"Let me buy you lunch," I said. She refolded her arms under her breasts and looked demure.

"Where?"

"McDonald's?" I offered. She gave the idea thumbs down.

"How about Randolph's?" It was one of the most expensive places in town, at least forty bucks apiece for lunch, but I had two Gs in my pocket, and she was not off somewhere licking envelopes for encyclopedia invoices.

"You got a deal, cowboy," she said. She got her purse, turned out the light and locked the door. She left *Light in August*. As we pulled out of the building in my car and headed toward Randolph's, I felt that I was doing something important for a change. Fat chance.

If you carried yourself with the dignity of an Oxford don, head high and mind above the dreary mass of ordinary men, no one would notice you in Randolph's. I think they noticed me. But that's the price you pay for having cash, and I knew how rough it would be when I took the job. I ordered Beef Wellington. Ginny decided on filet of sole *à la sauce Bercy*.

Randolph's main dining room was heavy with Victorian splendor. Round tables were scattered around a massive fireplace that was not yet burning because the weather was still warm. Thick crimson curtains hung on the four windows, and I felt like reciting "The Raven," but I restrained myself. The food came and it was as rich as the trappings. I was wondering if the Emory Clinic had an outpatient facility for high cholesterol when Ginny spoke.

"You don't seem like a detective," she said, spearing me with her green eyes.

"That's funny," I said, "most of my clients say that, too." Her eyes smiled, but she tried not to let it spread any farther.

"I mean, aren't you supposed to be out frantically looking for clues?" she asked. I shrugged. "Didn't I hear Mr. Browning say you were once a baseball player?"

"Yeah," I said. "Did he also tell you about the international incident with the harem in Algiers?" This time, she did smile.

"Why'd you quit?" she asked.

"I tore up my hamstring," I said. She stopped eating and looked at me with something like pity.

"Oh." She chewed on a croissant. "That's awful." We didn't say anything for a while. Our waiter had been working at Randolph's since Sherman came through, and every time he tottered back over I had the feeling he would fall face down in Ginny's sole. He looked like an escapee from the old bloodhound rest home, dewlaps drooping sadly, eyes rheumy, huge ears. He came over and asked if we were okay.

"Compared to what?" I said. He smiled blandly. Maybe he thought Beef Wellington had a bone and he was waiting for it. He went away. "You said that Tony came in and got a package?" She was through with the filet of sole and was fiddling with her salad. Her face was not round, but it gave that effect, slightly cherubic, cheeks full of color, hair over her shoulders. Her nose was just this side of too short, but the effect was of classic beauty.

"Yeah, wrapped up in brown paper, like a grocery bag, I think," she said.

"How big was it?" She thought about it for a second, trying to see Tony walking out past her desk.

"Small," she said. "Like this." She made a gesture to indicate it was about the size of a book. "Except it wasn't a book because it was shaped funny, sort of loose looking, wrapped funny. That's all I can remember." A package of pure heroin? That would be worth making somebody disappear for. The waiter came and brought our check and then swayed off.

"I wonder if he's registered with the American Kennel Club?" I whispered. Ginny laughed out loud. Still had the old touch. I paid the bill with some of Sherrill's money, and we went back into the October air. It was getting cloudy and cooler. We got into my car and drove into the light traffic.

"What would you do if you didn't do this?" Ginny asked.

"If I didn't take beautiful women to lunch at ritzy restaurants?" She blushed. God help me, she blushed, and I felt something inside that I had not felt in a long time, not lust or any of the carnal sins with which I was a willing intimate, but more, affection.

"I'm not beautiful," she mumbled. "I need to get back to work."

"Today could be the day the phone will ring," I said. "I don't blame you. I'd want to be there for that, too."

"It's the Faulkner," she said. She was quiet for a time. I eased up on the Buick. I didn't want to get back too fast. Maybe if I juggled for her and acted like I knew what the italics meant in *The Sound and the Fury* she'd come home with me. My car requires the use of both hands, unless you want to travel as the crow flies, so I did not try to juggle. "Do you really think Mr. Browning's in trouble?"

"I don't have any idea," I said.

"What does he do, really?" She turned in the seat and looked at me, and I wanted to die before I lied to her.

"He is a man of varied business interests," I said. She smiled again and punched me lightly on the shoulder. I turned on the radio to a station that plays only older pop hits. Vaughn Monroe was singing.

"Do you like that stuff?" she asked.

"Some of it," I said. "Do you like Andy Williams?" She laughed out loud again. Not a good sign. She reached up and turned the dial until it landed on a classical station that was playing something baroque. I thought I would display my erudition. "But then again, there's a lot to be said for Handel."

"It's Telemann," she said. "Where did you learn about classical music?"

"I'm a man of varied interests, too," I said. "And you're wrong, just for the record. You are beautiful." She shook her head. She did not want to hear it. I pulled up in front of the Marshall Center, and she opened the door.

"You're really nice," she said softly. "I've gotten to where I don't expect that." I smiled. "Do you have an office downtown?"

"I used to have one in this building," I said. "But I let it go. I work out of my house now."

"You have a whole house?"

"I have a whole room." She got out of the car and leaned in.

"If I hear from Mr. Browning, how will I get in touch with you?" she asked.

"All you have to do is whistle," I said. Then I told her the number at Mrs. Gunnerson's and gave her the address. I watched her walk through the revolving door, not really hearing until the third blast the horn of the car behind me.

I drove under the leaden sky south past Atlanta Stadium, which was now silent as the Kremlin, just one more mausoleum this time of year. I often thought I would be playing there, at least for some team coming through town, rubbing elbows with the boys of summer, waiting for the sounds of popping leather and the World Series. But now, the season was over again, with nothing to show but a rain-streaked circle of steel and concrete and the wait through the week for the Falcons on Sunday.

Angel Jiminez was a pimp who lived off Georgia Avenue not far from the Atlanta Zoo, and I'd once gotten him off a narcotics rap in a trade. I parked in front of the house where he lived or, at least, worked; it was hard to tell which. The house was a two-story frame affair that looked as if it were a terminally ill patient waiting for a disinterested doctor to pull the plug. If you leaned on it in the right place, it might fall apart like a dusty skeleton in a medical school.

The air was full of mist. The house had a wide front porch that sagged in places. It was jammed cheek by jowl with other rotting structures, and the smell of dissolution, of moral dry rot, hung in the air like an overripe gardenia. I knocked on the door. Presently, it opened a crack, and a woman who looked like the mummy of a crow thrust her head out and squinted unhappily at the thin light.

"What time is it?" she asked.

"Late enough for you to be up and getting ready for work," I said.

"You're a comedian?"

"I'm the ice cream man," I said. "I want to see Angel."

"Never heard of no Angel." She tried to close the door, but I stuck my foot in it, and she stood there glaring at me, breathing through her nose like a winded animal. She should have been in the zoo. "Give me a cigarette." I gave her a Camel and lit it. There was a noise from inside and a man's voice asking who it was. "He says he's the ice cream man." I heard a soft, unmodulated curse and the door swung on back, and Angel was standing there in a pair of paisley pleated walking shorts and a sleeveless undershirt. He was about forty, I guess, about five-eight, but with a belly and skin the color of lard. His eyes were sunken and watery.

"Angel," I said, "have you turned this joint into a spa? You're the picture of health. You absolutely glow." I had obviously ruined his day, but he owed me. He motioned for me to come in. I came inside where it was so dark all I needed was a cowl to pretend I was heading for my ablutions in the monastery.

"You don't look all that swift yourself," he said. He lit a cigarette. The woman, who was wearing a skimpy gown, moved off, her bones moving as if washed by ocean waves. I expected her to fall into a clump of tibias and fibulas, but she was gone before it happened. I followed Angel into the back of the house, where a hidden stereo was playing something slow and funky. I didn't like it.

"You'd get a better class of client if you played Andy Williams once in a while," I said. He didn't invite me to sit, and after looking at the sofa, on which God knows what depredations had taken place the night before, I decided to stand.

"Is that what you come to tell me?"

"No, I came to tell you that your home has been selected by *House Beautiful* as designer structure for the month of October. It's for their special Halloween issue." He almost smiled. He waited. "I'm trying to find a guy."

"Go ask missing persons at APD," he said, his face clouded in smoke. "I'm not a damned clearinghouse for some jerk who's missing." I came up close to him, closer than I wanted to be. I towered over him, and he looked up at me sourly, but I could see the fear dancing along his eyelids.

"Actually, I haven't killed anybody in a couple of weeks and I'm getting edgy," I said. "I could forget you being a wise ass, or I could do the public a favor and take you for a swim."

"I don't know how to swim," he said, the spit gone completely. "What do you want to know, pal?"

"Pal?" I said, stepping back. "Angel, I didn't know you had grown a heart in my absence. I'm looking for a guy named Tony Browning." I'm not sure what it was, but something went wrong when I mentioned Tony's name. Angel's face twitched, he started to smile, but that was wrong, and he went blank as the end wall in an alley. "I never heard of him." I didn't wait. I jumped up to him, grabbed his shirt straps and pulled it tight. He dropped his cigarette, and I ground it out on the carpet. His lips went purple, and he did smile this time, like a hyena on the plains of Africa trapped by a lion and howling for escape.

"You're not thinking clearly," I said. "He's a small-potatoes man in the dope business. I know you heard of him. Remember how cosmopolitan you are, Angel?" He was struggling to agree with me, nodding. His teeth were showing, and they were dirty and nearly rotten, and I wanted to flatten him.

"You killing me for Chrissakes," he choked. I let him go, and he tried to compose himself, but he still looked like a cheap pimp. "I mighta heard something about him." He looked up at me again deceitfully.

"Angel, I will find out if you are lying to me," I said. "And if you lie, I will come back here and ruin your house's chance of getting on the National Register of Historic Sleaze Parlors."

"Nobody's talking about him," he said. "I heard somebody say he's been skimming, that's all. That

Shuler's after him. I don't know. I don't know from shit about the dope trade. He's not got hookers, I don't know shit. I picked it up he's got heat bad for skimming. That's all I heard, and you didn't hear it from me.''

"Angel, you are a model for the youth of our country," I said. "I'll call you again." He lit another cigarette and receded into the shadows like a roach. I didn't ask to be shown out. I felt like I needed a shower when I got back into the Buick and headed back toward Tony and Sherrill's house on Eaglewatch Drive, thinking about Wanda and watching the clouding skies.

I'd fallen hard for Wanda. I'll admit it. I had first met her a year ago when I was wandering through the Rich's at Market Square Mall, where she worked in men's underwear. That was a joke she told. She was tall and pretty and a little vacuous, but endearingly so, with a small gap between her front teeth like the Wife of Bath. I asked her out, and it was raining that night, too. We went dancing, then to dinner and wound up back at my house, the one I no longer have, sitting in front of a crackling fireplace sipping brandy from the crystal snifters I'd bought when I was in London the year before that.

We spent almost the entire next day in bed, a drizzly day with a cool breeze prodding leaves to flutter past my window, golden leaves, crimson and burnt orange. We drank champagne, and she called in sick, and we told stories about ourselves. She didn't know a thing about baseball, so I became her tutor, and she tried to understand everything but figuring ERA, which made no sense to her at all.

How could she do this to me? Every time it rained, I thought of Wanda Mankowicz, the bitch. Well, even now, driving across Atlanta more slowly than my car liked, I thought of her, not of Angel or even of Tony Browning. What Angel had told me was ominous: if he had heard that Tony had been skimming, was in trouble, then it must be news of wide knowledge. I had hoped Angel would give me a lead, say something wrong, which fools often do. I did not think he would know more than which room in his palace was occupied.

I drove by a park and a pond. Out on the pond, two swans were gliding regally. I wanted to go talk to them, see if either had been in my dream, but I had made promises, and I needed to talk to Sherrill. I pulled into her driveway on Eaglewatch Drive, and a small dog came yapping past me, into the street. It disappeared suddenly, as if it fell down a manhole. I wondered if swans ever fell in manholes, and I could almost see them in an endless line, moving silently under the streets of the city.

An elderly fat man next door was looking fearfully at his grass, no doubt suspecting an invasion of chickweed during the night. I walked up the flagstones to the front door and rang the bell. There was a shuffling behind the door, and it opened a crack and Sherrill was looking out, but she was looking her age this afternoon and had apparently been drinking. I could hear the rain beginning behind me. I didn't want to tell her what I thought, that Tony was probably swimming with Jimmy Hoffa somewhere. If Angel was right, Tony was hiding at best, terrified, and someone was likely watching his house. And me.

"God, what are you doing here?" Sherrill said in her early morning voice. "I'm a mess."

"I promise I won't peek at you," I said. "I need to look through some of Tony's things in his study. Have you heard anything from him?"

"No," she said weakly, still peering at me through the nightlatch. "Have you?"

"Nothing," I said, "but I've been working and I need to look through his things. I'm sorry. Can I come in?" She opened the door, and I went into the dark hall and up the stairs. She held on to the rail. The house was without form and void. I couldn't even hear a clock ticking. I was not sure there was life here, even with Tony around. We got to the top into another hallway. I had been here many times, but now it looked different, like a museum, and I almost expected velvet ropes across the sewing room, Tony's study and the storage room.

"It's locked," she said. "He always keeps it locked. I haven't been in it more than a couple of times. It's like his boy's club." I tried the door. She was right, but the lock was cheap, one of those designed to open through a hole with a bobby pin. I opened the Swiss Army knife Wanda had given me and inserted the longest prod into the handle and pushed gently, and it popped. "I don't want to go in there. Do whatever you want. You want a drink, Hank?"

"No," I said. "But thanks." She wandered away like one of Lear's daughters, tragic and weak, and I felt for her. I opened the door and went inside. The room was small, with a huge cherry desk in the middle and an antique lamp on one corner. A broad window looked out over the front lawn, but the curtains had been drawn. Behind the desk and to one side was a filing cabinet. The carcass of a blue marlin was on one wall, and on the opposite a reproduction of something by

N.C. Wyeth. I had been in the room once before, and it looked the same except for a frantic pile of papers that spilled from the desk top onto the floor behind it. I walked around the desk and sat in the deep wing chair, which was so plush I expected Princess Diana to come up the stairs bringing me coffee any minute. I scooped the papers up off the floor and tried to make some order of them.

They seemed to be order forms for Tony's office. He had been out of the retail business for a year or two, now selling wicker and dope by mail, I supposed. I looked through about a dozen of the forms. Nothing looked strange about them, but I had no idea what I was looking for. I opened the drawer in the middle of the desk and rummaged through pens, pencils and paper clips that were jumbled with baroque splendor. This was pointless. I saw a stack of sheets from his phone bill, and I crammed them inside my coat pocket. I'd look at them later. Maybe by that time, he would have come home, but after what Angel told me, I doubted it.

For somebody with a license from the State of Georgia to be a private detective, I often wondered what I should do next. If you waited long enough, things worked out, and you could take the credit or the blame by default. At least your chances were even.

I left the room and went downstairs. I might come back and try to rifle the filing cabinet, but I wanted to talk to a guy I knew with the cops before I did anything else. I was the only PI they knew who was an ex-jock, instead of an ex-cop, and sometimes they treated me like a human being instead of like a low-life shamus. Lately, I should have been treated like the latter, but there's no accounting for taste. Sherrill was in the living room sitting on the couch, a drink in her hand. She seemed vague and lost, like a fog that had temporarily encamped on the divan. I stood in the doorway and looked at her.

"Find anything?" she asked. Her voice was slurred.

"Not yet," I said. "I'm not sure what I'm looking for. I've got to find a loose thread somewhere and start pulling, but I haven't found it yet." She laughed once and then went silent, and stared into the unburning fireplace.

"Anything I can do for you before I leave?" I asked. She did not look at me.

"Yeah," she said. "Tell me why in the hell life is worth living." I'm always quick with a homily, but after the past few months, I didn't feel up to facing Sherrill's soul.

"I'll call you when I find out something," I said. And I went out the door. A cold rain was now falling all over Atlanta, all over the South for all I knew, and I knew what my night would be like at Mrs. Gunnerson's house.

3

I READ ABOUT MRS. GUNNERSON'S HOUSE in the want ads the day before the bank took my house with the fireplace away. I thought the ad was quaint: "Room will rent for in house which nice." Anyone with syntax like that deserved a vote of confidence from down-at-heels private eyes. So I moved in after they sold off most of my furniture, not minding so much the four other boarders who seemed Stranger than Science.

Mr. Oshman was originally from Wisconsin and had moved south to work in the Lakewood GM plant before retiring. He was over six feet tall and weighed about one-twenty, had no teeth and was always humming "Danke Schoen," for which I found it hard to be charitable. Mrs. Carreker was in her fifties and would have opened everyone else's mail if she had a few less scruples. She considered herself the nominal "lead tenant," a term she must have picked up from working in social agencies for years. She looked startlingly like Jane Darwell in *The Grapes of Wrath*.

Dicky Thacker was about thirty and worked in a garage and thought himself the Swain of Our Time. He looked like a tubercular Ben Casey and drove a 1955 Chevy with appalling orange flames painted down the sides. I never knew why Mrs. Gunnerson rented to him since he fit in with the rest like a hubcap on a tractor. Mildred Ruth was the other tenant, a shy, thin woman who had worked as a secretary at a meat-packing house for sixteen years. I liked Mildred. You could talk to her for hours, and all she would do was make a noise in her throat and look at you through her rimless glasses, which were thick as a cutting board. Sometimes I called her Babe, and she smiled wanly and chewed on her lower lip.

I fit in perfectly.

I pulled up in front of the house. It was almost dark and rain was falling steadily now. I'd done damn little my first day on the job, but I was rusty, and I'd been told more than once my techniques were hopeless. When I first started my agency, I'd practiced shadowing people and gotten good at it. All that stuff about jumping in and out of doorways is malarkey; most people never know they're being followed, and the only virtue required is patience. I read up on the tricks of the trade and all about guns. I studied how people act, how they react, pondered human nature and how most of us are as predictable as sunfall. Sometimes I was very good at it.

I dashed on to the porch and shook the water off. I knew everyone had eaten, because Mrs. Gunnerson served at 5 p.m. You walked in through the parlor and then up the stairs. I looked through the windowed door and could see Mildred, Mr. Oshman, Mrs. Carreker and Mrs. Gunnerson sitting around a table playing Trivial Pursuit. Dicky Thacker was leaning on the mantel smoking a cigarette and looking at them with disdain. I came on inside.

"Meithsor Prance," said Mrs. Gunnerson. "Youva mees fawd." I smiled. She smiled. Mildred Ruth didn't say anything.

"Did you know," said Mr. Oshman, "that yak's milk is pink?" Dicky Thacker said something under his breath and snorted out smoke like an emaciated dragon.

"I knew it," said Mrs. Carreker.

"That's interesting," I said. I felt tired. Maybe I was still hung over. The room was large with a high ceiling and furniture that had been elegant thirty years before. The floors were wooden and dark. I always felt as if someone had just died here and mourners were gathering. Each chair had doilies on the arms, but the fabric had long since yellowed.

"Do you know what Cool Hand Luke went to jail for?" asked Mr. Oshman. "Go on, guess."

"For cutting the heads off parking meters," said Mrs. Carreker.

"I asked him, not you," said Mr. Oshman unhappily. "You heard it in the game. You cheat."

"I do not!" she said. Mrs. Gunnerson put her hand on her chest and looked weak. Babe Ruth was smiling, and Dicky Thacker was smug and above it all. I bowed slightly and climbed the stairs and went into my room.

It still looked nice, that is to say, unreal, and I poured myself a drink, lay across the bed and lit a

Camel. I spread the sheets of Tony Browning's phone bill out in front of me, and immediately saw he had made twelve calls in August to a number in New York City: 212-554-1545. Maybe it was a wicker import house. The other calls were to Savannah, where I thought he and Sherrill still had friends, and to Mississippi where she had family. I heard someone shout from downstairs. I sipped the bourbon and got up and walked to the window. Dicky Thacker came out of the house and climbed in his Chevy and roared off, a few vagrant sparks flying from the tailpipe. Then he was gone, and all I could hear was the rain.

I couldn't think straight, and the liquor made me sleepy, so I stripped down, stubbed out the cigarette and went to bed. As I lay in darkness, I tried to think about what might have happened to Tony, but all I could see was Ginny Calvert's face.

The Atlanta Police station is a cream-colored brick building on the corner of Decatur and Butler in downtown Atlanta. Narcotics and Homicide, however, were no longer there. For a few years, Narcotics was over the old Municipal Auditorium, where they used to have symphonies, ballet and professional wrestling. Now, it was down the street from the State Capitol on Martin Luther King, Jr. Drive. Homicide had been moved out of the headquarters to a building over on West Peachtree during the Missing and Murdered Children investigation.

I parked near the Capitol building with its gleaming gold dome. Not many people knew the first gold rush in the U.S. was in north Georgia, up near Dahlonega, where this gold came from. I had been up since dawn and had eaten breakfast at the Primate Haus. Treena looked the same as she always did.

The streets were wet, but the rain had quit, and I was headed to the Narcotics office to talk with Paul Tenhoor, a guy I had known for a few years. I worked with the police enough to know the world is a rotten place, at times, on either side of the law, but I trusted most of them and they put up with me. Paul was a sergeant, a short but sturdy Dutchman with bright orange hair, a tough face and a love for ice hockey that had not died after he moved south from the Detroit PD half a decade earlier.

I walked up the broad stone steps and into the lobby and told the receptionist I wanted to see Sgt. Tenhoor. She made a phone call and then told me to go through a set of locking doors upstairs. I went on up. Paul's office is a small cubbyhole just large enough for a desk and a filing cabinet. I knocked on the door and he grunted and I went in. The heat clanked somewhere below us and the office was far too warm, but there were no windows. He sat behind the desk with his coat off.

"What the hell do you want?" Tenhoor said. But he said it with mild approval at my appearance. It had been a while since I'd been around. "I heard you been juicing."

"A most pleasant good day to you, too, officer," I said. "May I be seated?"

"What kind of shit is this?" he asked. I sat down in the metal folding chair across from his desk. "You want some coffee or something?"

"No thanks," I said. "It's business."

"You got something you want to tell me because you're a good citizen?" I smiled and lit a cigarette and stared at him. "I didn't think so. So what's up? How's Wanda?"

"She's gone away," I said. He nodded and waited. I liked that about Tenhoor. He wasn't the sort to ask more than you wanted to tell about personal things. "I'm trying to find somebody. Don't tell me to check Missing Persons. There's no report on him, and his wife thinks you people are out to get him, so this has to be confidential."

"Sure, sure," said Tenhoor, leaning forward on the desk and staring at me. "And can I get you some brandy or a cigar?"

"Tony Browning," I said. When I said it, I heard a noise in the hall, and Adam Steed stepped into the room. Steed was a lieutenant, a hotshot in Narcotics, tall, good-looking and often on television. He looked down at me.

"What about Browning?" he asked. I never had liked Steed, but his arrest record when he was on the streets was outstanding. Anybody above the rank of sergeant is a supervisor, but Steed still went on major busts for recreation.

"I was talking about Robert Browning," I said. "The poet. You might have never heard of him. Sgt. Tenhoor and I were just discussing the point of view in 'Sordello.' Would you care to join us?"

"You got a smart mouth for a drunk," he said.

"My reputation has certainly preceded me," I said pleasantly. He looked at Tenhoor, who shrugged. I thought Steed might say something else, but he only breathed hard one time through his nose, looked me over unblinkingly and left, his leather heels squeaking on the carpet in the hall.

"You're a class A-1 screwup," said Tenhoor. "You're going to get us both in trouble. What in the hell is it with you?"

"Tony Browning's missing," I said. "You know who he is?" Tenhoor laughed and leaned back and put his hands behind his head.

"He's nobody," Tenhoor said. "He's a weasel. If he's missing, so much the better. Maybe he's decided to do missionary work in the Belgian Congo."

"Zaire," I said.

"You do have a smart mouth for a drunk," said Tenhoor.

"Have you heard he's missing?" I asked.

"I haven't heard shit," said Tenhoor. I believed him. One of the tricks of the trade, knowing when to believe someone. He seemed slightly uneasy about Steed popping in, but no more so than I was. I had the suspicion that Tony might be in the middle of a coming bust or, worse, had become an informant. If that was so, his lifespan was negligible.

"Well, thanks for a pleasant visit," I said as I stood.

"Yeah," said Tenhoor. I turned to leave. "Sorry about Wanda." I turned and looked at him, and there was no emotion on his face, not pity or interest, and I nodded and walked back downstairs and out on the street.

Low clouds huddled over the city. I drove east to an office building in Decatur where Jack Railsback worked. I was avoiding many of the places I'd put on my list, such as where I'd see Manny Fargo, who was Jake Shuler's press liaison, Jake being one of the top drug dealers in the city. Shuler lived in a heavily guarded mansion on the northwest side with grounds enclosed by a fifteen-foot fence and filled with slathering dobermans plus a couple of stooges eager to enforce their idea of the trespassing statutes. Jake was the only drug kingpin I knew who had a press liaison.

Manny Fargo was a worm. I'd gone up there to Shuler's place with a friend of mine who was trying to save a client's ass a couple of years ago. Manny looked like he'd just come in from doing the 100-freestyle in a greasepit. Things didn't work out, and my friend found his client floating in a swimming pool, shot twice in the back of the head.

Decatur was once a small town, but it has been swallowed by the amorphous monster that is Atlanta, and now you can ride a MARTA train west from Decatur and arrive downtown underground at the Omni. Modern science hath no shame. I parked across from the rain-smeared building where Jack Railsback had his insurance agency. The rain had stopped, probably preferring to haunt downtown. An MG crossed the street in front of me, driven by a beautiful young woman in a beige trenchcoat. Her blonde hair was loose on her shoulders. I smiled at her and winked, and she grinned absently and fiddled with the radio as she puttered past.

Jack's office is on the third floor, and I went up in the elevator with a man who looked like he was on his way up to be a defendant in the Nuremburg trials. This town seems sometimes to have a patent on quiet desperation. Thoreau shouldn't be here at this hour. I got off, and the other guy went up to the courtroom to confess. I walked down a long hallway with carpet padded so thickly that you had to look down at your feet to see if you were there. The last door on the left had "Railsback and Patton" stenciled on the door in gold. I went in and stood in front of the secretary. I'd only been here once, when Jack had opened the agency two years before. I came with Tony and Sherrill and Maria Lopez, the girl I was going with then. I understand she's back in Juarez, where her husband is making terra cotta chihuahuas on the second floor of a flophouse. Love is just a four-letter word.

"May I help you, sir?" she asked. She was about thirty, small breasted, plain, but with a look of efficiency. Her desk was almost bare and an abstract painting in silver and gold hung on the wall behind her in a gleaming chrome frame. The room was small, with one window looking north. Her dress was covered in orchids and her makeup was pale.

"I'd like to see Mr. Railsback," I said politely. I smiled at her. She didn't smile back. "My name's Prince."

She picked up the phone and pushed one button and announced me to Jack, then she set the phone back down as if she were afraid it would break. "He will see you now." I smiled again, and she looked at me with the sincerity of the terminally distracted. Jack's door opened off a small hallway, and he called my name, and I went back. His office was roomy, with a squat mahogany desk and an imitation Albert Bierstadt painting of the West hanging on one wall and a fake Audubon print on another. Wild out here in the suburbs. He didn't have a window. I think Mr. Patton had a window, but he probably never looked out.

"Found him yet?" asked Jack. He looked as if he'd fallen out of an ad for elegant men's clothes, handsome and in a $1000 tailored suit. He looked disgusted when I lit a cigarette, but he didn't phone the Cancer Society. A regular guy.

"I think he's in big trouble this time," I said. I stared at Jack through the cigarette smoke.

"What makes you think that?"

"What do you think?" I asked.

"What the hell is this, *Jeopardy*?" he asked. He clawed at his collar. I once owned a tie. I used it to keep a door on my old jeep from flying open when I made a right-hand turn. "What are you talking about?"

"Have you heard anything about Tony skimming from Shuler?" I asked, leaning forward. Jack leaned back in his heavy chair and nodded slightly.

"I don't go in those circles anymore," he said in a strangled voice. "You know I'm not in business with Tony anymore." One of the first rules you learn before you take the oath of the private detective is to watch how people move their heads when you ask a question. Some people nod when they say no or shake their heads when they say yes. People lie. That's the second rule you learn.

"Then you don't know that Tony might be running because he's going to be hit," I said.

"I would have told you that when I came if I'd known it," he said angrily. "I haven't seen Tony in months."

"What about Sherrill?"

"That's a cheap shot," he said, pointing his finger at me for emphasis. He was in shape, and I wasn't, but I had a gun and I'd have bet he didn't. Nature makes everything equal out.

"It wasn't meant to be," I said calmly. I let him claw at his collar for a while as he looked at me. His head bobbed back and forth like a fighter's.

"Yeah. Look, I know you're doing your job. Maybe he did just run off. I haven't heard anything, but if I do, I'll call you. Sherrill called me and told me about Tony and wanted me to see if you would help. That's all I know." He was shaking his head from side to side.

"Well, it looks bad to me," I said as I stood. "Tony's been involved with some pretty rough characters. If he's been skimming and Shuler found out about it, then his life's shit."

"God, I hope not," Jack said. I went into the hall, and he followed me and patted me on the shoulder. When I passed the secretary, I smiled at her again, and she looked at me with the passion of a freshly plastered wall. I wondered if her boyfriend worked for the World View Encyclopedia Company. "Call me."

"You bet," I said. When I went back into the hall, it was not yet lunchtime but I felt I'd worked enough for the day. Maybe if I wore a tie I'd feel more responsible. I saw myself reflected in the glass wall of an office and noticed I was shaking my head.

I looked for Jack's Mercedes as I walked across the wet parking lot and saw it, finally, thumbing its hood ornament at all the other riff-raff parked nearby. I casually looked inside at the dash, then walked on toward my Buick, which was in the public lot across the street, looking like Camelot next to the Chevettes and other assorted crackerboxes. When I got in, I took the notebook out of my pocket and made a note and then drove back toward Mrs. Gunnerson's.

When I came into the house, Mrs. Carreker was watching something on TV and ignored me as I passed up the stairs. There was a phone at the end of the hall, and I went straight to it, taking Tony's phone bill out of my pocket, and dialed the number in New York. The first two times, there was a sequence of buzzes and relays that clacked open indifferently, and then the line went dead. The third time, the disembodied voice of some Northern person told me the line had been disconnected. Maybe it was a clue. Maybe the wicker business had just gone sour. Who the hell knew?

I went into my room and made a cup of coffee and tried to think about things. I needed somebody to talk to. Tony was a small time dope dealer who was skimming and being chased by Shuler's goons. Sherrill was a poor drunk. Jack Railsback was acting oddly. Steed seemed too ready to pillory me for mentioning Tony's name. Even Angel had heard that Tony was in trouble, so somebody was spreading the word on the street. I can add. Learned it when I was trying to impress a girl in second grade. There was only one sane thing to do: take a nap.

This time, I did not dream at all, and when I awoke, it was nearly 4 p.m. and I felt stupid and weak. I wasn't helping Tony and I didn't know if I could. I could, on the other hand, help myself, and I didn't do that by sleeping in the middle of the day. Next thing you knew, I'd be arguing with Mrs. Carreker about Cool Hand Luke. I took a shower and changed into some khaki slacks, a blue knit shirt and a cream-colored sweater. "Failure," I said to my face in the mirror, "thy name is Henry."

I drove to Tony's office. This time, nobody went up the elevator with me. It was almost the end of the day; they would all be going down in the endless procession of the damned. I got off on thirty-six and walked into Tony's office, and Ginny Calvert was sitting behind the desk reading *Sanctuary*, which is the story of a deranged man raping a girl with a corn cob.

"I'm from the Clean Books League, and the volume you are reading has been deemed unfit for the youth of America," I said. She lowered the book and smiled at me. She wore a plain white blouse and dangly earrings.

"I'm not a youth," she said. "I'm a grown woman."

"I noticed that right off," I said. "I used to be a detective." She laughed brightly. "If you insist on reading such filth, how about reading it out loud to me over a glass of Chateau Lafite?" She turned the idea over in her head and stared at me. "How'd you do on your test?"

"Fine," she said. She looked at her watch. "Have you found Mr. Browning yet?" I leaned against the wall and didn't try to be smart for once.

"I think he's in a lot of trouble," I said. "But I still don't know where the hell he is."

"So you don't just want to interrogate me?" she asked.

"What would the other members of the Clean Books League think of me doing such a thing?" I asked. "Come on, it's quitting time. I'll buy you dinner, and then we can talk of cabbages and kings. And while you're not looking, I'll mark out the offensive passages in your book." She stood. She was wearing faded, but neatly pressed jeans that clung to her as if they were afraid they'd fall. I felt a knot in my throat. This was like going to the prom. Maybe I should stop and buy her a three-pound mum before we ate.

"Okay," she said tentatively. "But I can't stay out too late."

"Neither can I," I said. "I've got to get up early tomorrow to work on my merit badges, and then after school I work in the soda shop." She closed *Sanctuary* and put it under her arm and turned out the light and locked the door.

We got in my car and drove right into the middle of rush hour traffic. I put in a Frankie Laine tape and he was in the middle of "Mule Train," when she speared me with a look of disgust.

"What in the name of God is that?" she said.

"Wait until he sings 'Wild Goose Cry'," I said. "I know you'll like it." She reached down and popped the tape out and put it back on the floor, where I carefully stored all my tapes. "On the other hand, I could be wrong." She turned on the radio to WRMM, which is a soft-rock station. Somebody was singing something about holding his girl until they both broke down and cried. Frankie Laine would never descend to such.

"You've got weird taste," she said. She pushed her long hair over her shoulders. Her body was thin and graceful.

"Not in everything," I said, looking at her. She blushed, the color spreading up her neck and into her face, and I wanted to stop the car in the middle of traffic and ask her to marry me.

"Where are you taking me?" she asked. She looked down and I did not try to stare at her, though I wanted to.

"To the Clean Books League Club and Pub," I said. "We'll dine in the Louisa May Alcott Room. But first I want to run by Tony Browning's house. I need to get something. Won't take a minute." Actually, it might have taken more: I wanted to see if there was another phone bill anywhere in his study. Then on to the Sierra Grill, a fine Southwestern cuisine restaurant on the east side.

"Are we eating at McDonald's?" she asked.

"I prefer to call it Casa Del Ronaldi," I said. "You'd be amazed at what a little chili powder does for a Big Mac." She stared at me. "It's the Sierra Grill. Big time. A sensation to the palate. Trust me."

"Sure," she said.

We finally broke free from the traffic, and I made it across town to Tony's house. The houses on Eaglewatch Drive were quiet, and lights were coming on. I envied that middle-class regularity sometimes. I had never known it, having gone into baseball right out of college. I wondered what it would be like to come home from work to a loving wife and children and an easy chair and a dog. But that kind of life was probably something I'd never have to worry about.

"You want to come in?" I asked.

"Yeah, I should say something to Mrs. Browning," she said. "I don't know what."

"Just tell her you're sorry," I said. "You get a merit badge when you share somebody's pain." She came around beside me and looked up at me, and we walked close to each other to the door. I rang the bell and waited. Somewhere, a dog barked. Evening lay against the sky like a patient etherized upon a table. No one came. I looked back past the edge of the house and Sherrill's Le Mans was in the driveway. I knocked on the door with the brass knocker and waited.

"She's not home," Ginny said.

"Her car's here," I said. "I don't think she was in shape to be going out. And they never socialized much." I tried the knob, and the door swung open effortlessly. She looked at me. I called Sherrill's name, but there was no sound. We went into the hall. The house was dim, and I stood for a moment and then called Sherrill's name again.

"Nobody's home," she said. "Let's get out of here."

"Go look upstairs," I said. "I'll go back through here."

"For what?"

"Just see what's up there." She did not want to be afraid. I could see it, but I needed her to help me search the house. Probably, Sherrill was asleep in her bedroom, which was downstairs at the rear of the house. Ginny crept up the stairs after turning on the light. I moved back into the back of the house, walking through the den. Tony's deer looked silently into the room. I went into their bedroom, and the bed was messed up, but Sherrill was not there. I was walking out into the hall when I heard it from upstairs: a scream, the kind a woman cannot fake. I pulled my gun off my hip and came around the stairs and almost ran headlong into Ginny, who was flying down the stairs. She screamed again when she saw me, then grabbed me hard around the chest. I looked up the stairs.

"What is it?" I asked. She was shaking.

"Somebody dead," she said. She gagged slightly and then held on to me tighter and tried to compose herself. "In the study. A woman." I felt sick and wanted to run. The hair stood out on the nape of my neck.

I walked slowly up the stairs, and she held on to me. We got to the top of the stairs. The light was on in the hallway, but there was no light in the study, though the door was open. We got to the door, and I pried Ginny from me and told her to lean against the door frame. I reached inside and turned on the light. Ginny did not look inside. I could hear her sobbing.

Sherrill Browning lay on the floor in front of Tony's desk, her head in a pool of blood that had snaked out several feet across the carpet. The blood was drying, and Sherrill's eyes were open and staring straight into mine. My tongue felt thick and my stomach churned. I stepped carefully into the room. She was dead. I'd seen it too many times. And she'd been dead for several hours, because the blood was dark against the thick rug. I walked slowly around her and looked down. Her hands were tied behind her back with nylon cord that looked like a window sash. I leaned over her and could see that part of her head was gone. I stood back up, feeling hot and angry, and looked around her. There was brain tissue and bits of hair three or four feet away on the carpet. She had been shot here.

I went back into the hallway, and Ginny grabbed me again. We struggled back down the stairs.

"Don't touch anything," I said. "We've got to talk to the police. This is going to be pretty rough. Don't worry. I won't let them bother you too much." It didn't sound right. I hardly knew what I was saying.

I didn't tell her about the cord. I didn't tell her it was an execution.

4

WITHIN THIRTY MINUTES, REPORTERS from two newspapers, three television crews and a clot of Atlanta's finest were swarming all over Sherrill's house. I was sitting on the front steps talking to a homicide sergeant named Wilson when the medical examiner came wheeling the gurney out the door. I lit a cigarette. My hands were shaking. I tried not to think of the time I'd gone to Savannah with Sherrill. The forensic department was already there.

They loaded her into the ambulance. There was no flashing light, no siren. The dead are in no race. I was prepared for the interminable questions, for the gawking neighbors, for the pain I felt when they wheeled her out. I was not prepared for Adam Steed.

They had been questioning Ginny and me for better than an hour when two cars pulled up out front. Paul

Tenhoor and another man were in the first car, and in the second, a driver and Adam Steed, who hopped out of the car adjusting his tie like something from an episode of *Perry Mason*. Paul came slowly over toward me and stood with one foot on the steps. Ginny was beside me. They were still taking pictures upstairs, and each flash was like a distant thunderstorm about to break. Ginny was holding her chest and leaning on me.

"Your client got wasted," Tenhoor said. He lit a cigarette and looked at me once and then at Steed, who was being surrounded by TV people. He was telling them to wait. He walked with long, graceful strides toward Wilson, the Homicide cop, who was listening to one of the uniformed officers talk to a neighbor. They were talking now.

"Elegantly put," I said. "Nice you people are letting Steed out without a leash."

"Hah," Tenhoor said. There seemed to be lights everywhere. "You know why he's here?"

"I'd like to know why you're here," I said. He looked up at the sky. It was long past dark, and a cold drizzle had started again.

"Because this thing is drug-related, jackass," he said. "At least His Nibs assures me it is. Unlike him, I don't work twenty-two hours a day. I like to go home and see my dog and my wife."

"In that order, no doubt," I said.

"Hah," said Paul Tenhoor. "Anyway, Browning's on the lam from his employers. Word is he's bought the farm already, so I guess you're out of a job, hotshot. So Steed hears on the horn that all the media between headquarters and East Jesus is out here, and so he calls me up and we come flying out here to talk to homicide." Ginny sniffed a little and looked small and forlorn.

"You okay?" I asked. She nodded.

"Anyway, he'll want to talk to you and the lady," Tenhoor continued. "Probably for hours." I could almost hear him grinning. The homicide boys knew where I stayed, and they had finished with me for now. I had no intention of hanging around for Steed to bully while preening in front of the cameras. I got up and motioned for Ginny Calvert to follow. "Where you going, Hank?"

"I haven't eaten and neither has she," I said. "You tell Steed I'll see him in your office at 10 tomorrow and she'll come with me."

"He won't like it," Tenhoor said happily.

"Then hold his hand until he gets over it," I said. I heard Tenhoor laugh. I only looked back once, up to Tony's study where strobe flashes were still going off. I opened the car door for Ginny. I walked around the Buick, got in, and we drove off. I could almost hear Steed swearing when he'd found we were gone, but he could wait. Everything could wait.

"You hungry?" I asked.

"I want to go home," she said.

"Okay," I said. She gave me the address, on St. Charles Place, an older neighborhood off Ponce de Leon. I drove through the wet streets. Everyone was inside and you could see the plumes of smoke drifting from chimneys. We turned off Ponce de Leon and drove halfway down the street, under a shower of falling leaves from the canopied oaks.

"Here," she said. "Park here. It's there." She pointed to a huge house across the street. No lights were on. It was brick and stucco, with an open porch on the second floor and a staircase leading up to it.

"You have a whole house?" I asked.

"I have a whole apartment," she said wearily. "Come on."

I turned in the seat and looked at her. A street light was just outside the car, and I could see her eyes. They were wet and she seemed to have shrunk in the seat.

"You want me to go get some food?" I asked.

"I'll cook," she said. "Spaghetti? I think I have a bottle of Chianti, too."

"You sure you want me to come up?" I said. Fool. Always have to be gallant. She opened the door, and so did I, and we walked across the street, up a cold flight of stairs and into her apartment. She turned on the light by the door and I could see into the room, small and cozy, full of knickknacks, an overstuffed wing chair draped with an India print spread, and dozens of house plants, trailing tendrils all over the bookcases, the small table. I could see a bedroom straight ahead and to the right a tiny kitchen. A Siamese cat was sitting in the middle of the table, which was in the living room close to the kitchen.

"He looks like a burglar," I said. Ginny took off her coat and scooped the cat up. It hung limp in her arms.

"You hungry?" she asked the cat. She set it down and went into the bedroom, then into the bathroom. I decided to snoop around in the kitchen. I walked in and turned on the light. It was so small it seemed designed for a gnome, but it was cheerfully sloppy, with cans of spices all over the counter top. I opened the refrigerator, and she was right: there was a full bottle of Chianti. I took it out and rummaged through a drawer until I found a corkscrew. I preferred a long sip of bourbon, but this would do. Christ, anything would do.

I tried to think why they would have killed Sherrill. But that made me think of the way she looked, so I stopped. I heard Ginny coming out of the bedroom and turned as I was opening the Chianti. She had put on an oversized velour shirt, olive drab with darker green horizontal stripes. She had washed her face and the smell of soap came with her into the kitchen. It was barely wide enough for both of us. She reached up high and took down two wine glasses. I opened the wine, and we went back into the other room.

I poured for both of us and we drank silently. She sat beside me and stared at the wall. The cat tiptoed across the room and jumped into her lap and glared at me.

"Who killed her?" Ginny said finally. I was afraid she'd ask the question. "When you came and said you were trying to find Mr. Browning, I thought this was all just a joke. But that. . ." She shuddered and drank half her glass, which seemed like a good idea, so I joined her. I felt warmer.

"The cops obviously think it was drug-related," I said. "I'm sorry. Tony was involved in a lot of things. One of them was drugs. He'd been into it for a long time. I knew him before he was, and he was a kind, thoughtful guy, the sort you'd want along on a long trip. Money killed Sherrill as much as anything."

"You don't approve of money?" she asked. She turned and looked at me. The cat jumped down and disappeared somewhere.

"I've had it, and I haven't had it," I said. "I wasn't any happier then than now."

"You're poor now?" she asked. "Is that why you took me to Randolph's?"

"That was money Sherrill gave me to find Tony," I said. "I did a fine job of that." I finished the rest of my wine and poured another glass. "As to who killed her, I don't know. Tony worked for a guy named Jake Shuler, but the cops know that. Pinning it down will be damned near impossible. These people aren't messy. My guess is Tony'll never be found and Sherrill will be buried. She didn't have much family, a sister, I think. But it all makes me sick. Somehow, it doesn't go down right."

"What do you mean?"

"Well, the only reason to kill Sherrill is because she knew something, right?"

"You tell me."

"But hell, she didn't even know what Tony did. He worshipped her. He wouldn't let her do a thing but sit in the Jacuzzi and read magazines. She never worked after they got married. When she hired me, she was rattled. I suppose she could have been involved somehow, but I don't think so. And if she wasn't, why was she killed?"

"A robbery?" Ginny asked.

"Nothing seemed to be missing. There was no forced entry. She was killed up there in the study and nobody heard a gunshot. She was shot standing up. It was quick and cold." She finished her wine and poured another glass.

"So there's not anything to be done about it all but quit?" she asked. She was asking me if I could find out what Steed could not, if I could do what I was hired to do since I still had Sherrill's money. I wanted to say hell, no — that such a thing was improbable at best. Also, I was just getting over a major league drunk.

"I'm going to keep looking," I said, with more than a hint of false bravado. "I just want to be satisfied about what happened to her. We were good friends at one time." I thought about her at the beach, about introducing her to Tony, and my shoulders fell and I stared into my glass. My God. The bastards blew her brains out. Ginny reached out and touched the back of my hand and got up and went into the kitchen. She made spaghetti, and we ate it at her tiny table. She sneaked a few strands of pasta to the cat, whose name was Benjy, after a character in *The Sound and the Fury*. We finished, and I washed the dishes while she cleaned up around the table.

We sat back down on the couch in the living room. I was feeling sorry for myself, for having to leave, for everything. If misery loves company, I had made it my wife, and just sitting and looking at Ginny Calvert made up for a lot of things.

"You going to be okay?" I asked. She sipped her wine and nodded. Her face had taken on that look of exhaustion, ready to sleep but lingering a while to savor the world of dulled pain. "I could sleep out in the car if. . ." I stopped.

"Do you always try to be a knight in shining armor?" she asked. It was hard for her to say "shining" through the wine haze.

"Lately, my armor has been in need of a can of spray paint." She laughed.

"I just can't believe I got mixed up in something like this," she said. "I'm a small-town girl from Branton, Georgia. It's just a clean place, with a town square, a few drunks, churches and clean streets. This is creepy."

"I don't say I'm that fond of it all," I said. "But it's gotten to be what I know." She nodded vaguely. "You know we've got to go downtown in the morning." She nodded again with her eyes closed. "I'll be here for you at about nine." I stood and slipped on my coat. She came wobbling over to me, and when I was half-way out the door, she reached out and squeezed my hand. If it hadn't been for Sherrill, I might have been happy. Neither of us said anything else, and I walked down the slick steps into the rain.

It took driving around under the street lights for nearly an hour before I got mad. Why had she been killed? What could Tony have done to involve that beautiful, brainless creature? It was unfair in the way you say the world is unfair, and I could not dismiss her sightless eyes staring at me, accusing in a way, saying, you were hired to find my husband and I have come to this. I didn't believe much in religion anymore, but I hoped that if there was a hereafter, Sherrill would be there, working on her tan and having her nails done.

I got back to Mrs. Gunnerson's after midnight. Dicky Thacker's car was gone as usual, and the lights were out inside. I slid my key into the lock and went up the stairs. There was a note taped to my door. I pulled it off, went inside, and threw it on the table. I poured myself a drink and lit a Camel before I opened it. I heard a sneeze through the wall. Mr. Oshman's room connected to mine, and he had hay fever badly at this time of year. The note was in Mrs. Gunnerson's handwriting, which consists of a series of dots and squiggles, more like Cyrillic perhaps than Anglo-Roman.

It said: "Mr. Prince, man call and said he meet you Friday night west sode of the Stained Mount at dirk." I was becoming expert in translating for Mrs. Gunnerson. If she was ever named to the United Nations, I could sit with those little headphones on and tell everybody else what she was saying. I translated it like this: a man called and wanted me to meet him just at dark Friday on the west side of Stone Mountain. What the hell?

I slept on it. When I woke up, it was Thursday, and I still didn't know exactly what it meant. I dressed and went to the Primate Haus and ate a doughnut and drank a glass of orange juice and a cup of black coffee. When I got to Ginny's house, she was standing on the second-floor porch waiting for me. The rain had stopped during the night and the day was windy and sunny. She came down the stairs, wearing tall boots, a long gingham dress and beauty that made me weak. I needed to study up on Faulkner to impress her. Or maybe she considered me a surrogate father. I was only old enough to be her brother. She walked across the street under a drift of oak leaves and got in the Buick.

"I always feel like I'm getting into a Nazi bunker when I get into this thing," she said, and then she tried to smile, but her face was pinched and nervous.

"Ve haf our methods of optaining beautiful vomen," I said. She didn't smile. Okay, drop the Nazi from the routine. "You sleep last night?" I slipped the car into low and we eased off toward the Narcotics office.

"I had this terrible dream," she said. She looked down and shook her head as if trying to make the spectre fly away home. "I was in Mr. Browning's office and I looked behind his desk and there was blood everywhere, spilling out of something, and I opened the filing cabinet and it was pouring out like Niagara Falls, and I was screaming but nobody came and the blood wouldn't stop."

"You ever dream about swans?" I asked. I didn't want to talk about her dream. She turned and looked at me.

"No," she said. "You?"

"Once," I said. "I was a swan in this dream. It was great. Swans never have to do laundry or wash the toilet or fix a flat tire." She was preoccupied, but she tried to be pleasant. "You're worried about this, aren't you?"

"You're not?"

"Not really," I said. "Just tell the truth. They're not going to beat you with a rubber hose under a floodlight. They only do that to private detectives. Just tell the truth. It's me they want, but I don't know much more than you do. Now, they might talk a little nasty, but that's just their endearing way of trying to make the American Way survive."

I parked in a "Police Only" spot, daring them, as it were, to do anything with my chariot. I'd make them bring it back if it was hauled. They don't call me Dirty Hank for nothing. We went inside, after announcing our presence to the stone-faced woman at the desk. I was just about to ask her if she knew Buster Keaton when she told us to go on up. Tenhoor picked us up in the hall and asked Ginny to sit in his tiny office while he took me with him down to Adam Steed's office, which looked more like a drawing room for the Duke of Marlborough. His desk was heavy dark wood, and there were dark wood panels over the plaster walls and on them hung several antique paintings. They looked real.

"Did A&P have another sale on great reproductions?" I asked, looking at the impressive paintings. Steed was sitting behind his desk trying to intimidate me with his authority. I could almost feel Tenhoor groan beside me. He seemed to shrink when he was in the same room with Steed.

"You're a real wiseass, for somebody in deep trouble," Steed said. "Sit down." I shrugged and sat in one of the two chairs across from his desk. Tenhoor sat gently in the other as if he would muss it.

"Oh God, you found out about where I parked the car," I said. "My attorney will have me out in twenty-four hours." Steed bit his upper lip and tried not to show his full head of steam.

"Shut up," said Tenhoor.

"Now tell me what you were doing over there," Steed said coldly. He seemed jumpy.

"Hasn't Homicide's report come down?" I asked. "I told them everything."

"They said Mrs. Browning hired you to find her husband," Steed said.

"That's a big 10-4," I said. "And I didn't find him and that's about all I know."

"Where did you look?" asked Steed. He leaned forward.

"Oh God, nearly everywhere," I said. Tenhoor picked at his tie. The room was silent. I gave Steed time to get really mad and then I told him about my visits with Sherrill. He didn't seem satisfied.

"I want it all," he said.

"This sounds like a scene from *Miami Vice*," I said. "I told you everything." Except about the package

Tony had gotten. You have to keep one card in your hand, about the only good advice my father ever gave me.

"What about the broad?" Steed said. I looked at Tenhoor in disbelief, and I thought he would laugh.

"Miss Calvert, as I'm sure you know, was Mr. Browning's secretary," I said. "She only saw him ten or fifteen times in the last six months, and the phone almost never rang."

"Then what'd she do?" Steed asked sensibly.

"She read *The Sound and the Fury*," I said. "Ever heard of that?"

"Hey, I went to college, you creep," said Steed, leaning over his desk, "and I don't need some cheap drunk like you being smart with me." He seemed to be going through the motions. He looked at Tenhoor as if to make sure Paul knew he'd tried to question me.

"Cheap?" I said. "You know how much Evan Williams costs these days?" He fell back in his chair.

"Get him out of my sight," said Steed. "And the girl, too. Bud, you better stay where I can see you." I shrugged. Tenhoor took me out and closed the door. By the time we were halfway down to his office, he was silently grinning.

When the door opened, Ginny jumped up clutching her purse as if I were the priest summoning her to walk the last mile. I stepped inside, and Tenhoor squeezed past me and plopped down in his chair and leaned back, looked at me and shook his head.

"Prince, you give me a big pain in the ass," he said.

"What a coincidence," I said. "I'm studying to be a proctologist in night school. Would you like to be my first patient?" His upper lip curled, and I thought he might spit at me. Ginny looked bewildered, a look I've noticed often among people who meet me.

"Get the hell out of here," he said. I took Ginny by the arm and we went out into the elevator. She looked up at me, but couldn't ask anything.

"They're not going to ask you anything," I said. "I guess Steed got a little put out with me. I wasn't exactly reverent."

"Then we can go?" she asked almost like a plea.

"Sure," I said. We went on down to the ground floor, got out and walked into the bright autumn of Atlanta. We got in my car. Nobody had bothered it, though a plainclothes officer was staring at us without much humor. I reached down and rubbed my foot.

"What's wrong?" she asked.

"Old war wound," I lied. She didn't have to know about my foot. I had been shot, after all. We moved into traffic and I said, "You want me to drop you by the office, or what?" She turned in the seat as if to hurl a thunderbolt, like Zeus.

"You think I'm going back to that place? Are you crazy? That guy's involved in drugs, his wife got her head half blown off, I'm at the police station, and you think I'm going back up there?"

"Why not? The estate will keep paying you. That's the law. Nobody will call, and it's easy money. Besides, I promised Sherrill I'd find Tony, and you could help if anybody calls."

She laughed, hard and cold. "Bull . . . shit," she said, stretching it out into two long syllables. "Take me home. I was awake half the night scared half out of my mind, and you just act like ho hum, it's just part of everyday life for something like this to happen."

"It's not," I said, "but they were my friends at one time in my life. I owe it to try and find Tony."

"What if somebody tries to kill you?" she said.

"Then I'll try to kill them back," I said. "I have an advanced degree in Law of the Jungle." She shook her head and looked at me with bitter anger.

"Just take me home," she said. I tried to think of something witty that would change her mind. God, I wanted to change her mind. But after I'd gone through four lights and hadn't said anything, I figured it was useless. Just like finding Tony Browning was useless. Just like trying to understand Mrs. Gunnerson was useless. Tell me, where is fancy bred? In the heart or in the head?

We came through two gates into St. Charles Place under a waterfall of leaves, beauty so painful it made your teeth hurt. I stopped in front of her house and tried to remember the way it looked, since I probably wouldn't ever be coming there again. She opened the door.

"See you," she said.

"You know how to get me if you need me," I said. She only nodded, got out and walked briskly across the street, up the stairs and into her rooms. I drove off and tried not to recognize the ache in the pit of my stomach. It felt something like this when Wanda had run off with Mr. Encyclopedia, but this was worse, because now Sherrill was dead and I felt no urge to work.

I came back to Ponce de Leon, turned left and drove to Decatur. I parked not far from Jack Railsback's office and walked to his reserved parking space. His car was there, like always, and I wondered why he wasn't home grieving. But there was nothing anybody could do, and I didn't want to see him again. I looked through the driver's side window and wrote down his odometer reading on the same card I'd written it the night before. I was back in my car before I compared the two figures and found that during the night Jack had driven more than two hundred miles. It bothered me, but I didn't know what to make of it.

By the time I got to the Primate Haus, it was after lunch and fair time to have a drink. I sat in a booth and got a whiskey sour on the rocks and then went to the jukebox. I put some money in and listened to "I'm Old Fashioned" by Andy Williams, "New York, New York," by Sinatra, and "I Remember It Well," by Maurice Chevalier. Nobody has a jukebox like the Primate Haus. I finished four drinks and was feeling sorry for myself when Bull Feeney came in and plopped down in the booth across from me.

Bull is a construction foreman and looks like the offspring of a gorilla and a Rambler: big, square and ugly. He is short, about five-six, with no neck, but he has other good qualities, such as an uncanny ability to know what's best for you. I didn't want to see him, but I didn't want to get up, either.

"Little early in the day, ain't it?" he said. "I heard you were hitting the bottle pretty good."

"So whose corners are you cutting today, Bull?" I asked. "Is it the welds? Are they cracked? Maybe you're using Korean sheetrock."

"Smartass," he said, "a real smartass. You're just like the fight game, Hank. It's nothing anymore. Where's the Archie Moores, the Joe Louises, the Billy Conns?" Treena brought him a beer and a plate of red sausages.

"The Leon Spinkses," I said.

"That's funny," he said. I finished my drink and left him sitting there muttering about Jersey Joe Walcott. I staggered out into the sunlight, which was altogether too cheerful. I didn't know where to go. I got in my car and sat there a while trying to think of what to do. I did not want to see Jake Shuler or his stooge, Manny Fargo, but I knew I might have to. I took out Sherrill's money and counted it. I'd already blown close to five hundred bucks. It was all I had at the moment. I decided to go home. To hell with it.

I got to the house just as Dicky Thacker, off early from work, was revving up his car, preparing for ignition and liftoff. I parked the Buick and walked over to him. He was sitting in the driver's seat looking smug as he gunned it, white clouds of smoke drifting down the street. I looked up at the house and Mildred Ruth was staring out at us silently.

"You ever heard anything like that?" Dicky asked happily.

"Once at a hog auction," I said. He did not look amused. "Slide over and let me have a drive." He grinned knowingly, as if I did not know what I was in for. I climbed in and put it in low and left a trail of rubber forty yards long. I wondered if Mildred had applauded. I stomped the son of a bitch, and we went flying down the street. I looked over at Dicky, who appeared to be having a seizure. I came around a corner and ran over two metal trash cans and then went as fast as I could the wrong way up a one-way street on a hill. When I got to the top, I hung a right and came over the curb and three wheels left the earth. I grazed a utility pole and skidded sideways across the street. I then gunned it back around the block and slid for the last hundred feet or so, stopping right in front of Mrs. Gunnerson's house. I bet Ty Cobb never slid that well.

Dicky Thacker was cursing me, but his breath was so ragged and trembling that I could make nothing of it. I always enjoy a quiet ride around the neighborhood.

"It's okay," I said as I got out, "but I think the carburetor needs adjusting." Then I went upstairs and lay on my bed and tried not to think about Ginny Calvert.

5

BLEW THURSDAY BY TAKING A NAP THEN
going to the art cinema not far from Mrs. Gunnerson's and watching *The African Queen*. I watched it
twice, to be honest. Then I went home and sat
around in my room feeling sorry for myself until I got
drunk and fell asleep.

Friday morning I got up and poured the rest of my
bottle down the sink and looked at myself in the
mirror for a long time. I tried to remember how I
looked during the baseball season, how I'd run for
miles, feeling strong and lean. I took my pack of
Camels and crumbled them one by one and flushed
the tobacco island down the john. Then I put on the
pair of sneakers I still owned and went downstairs and
out into the street to run.

It was maybe 6:30. The lungs ached as I started
down the hill toward the small shopping center that

was strung along the street like old Christmas tree lights. The city was stretching, trying to awaken. Others were out jogging, lovely girls with hair tied back, old men, a few yuppies working on their muscle tone.

It hurt. I had not run regularly in years, and although I was not fat, my muscles sloshed with liquor and my lungs felt like balloons about to pop from the rapid inflation. What would I do? I would try to find Tony Browning. There was nothing else to do. I could start taking new clients, open my office again, advertise. I would. But first, I had a debt to pay, and I wanted to be in shape for it.

I got back an hour later, weak-kneed, covered in sweat but feeling better about things than I had in a while. I took a shower, shaved and dressed. I went to a McDonald's and got an Egg McMuffin. Then I drove over to Sherrill and Tony's. I had a key, one she'd given to me months before when I was coming over while they were out of town. No one was around. I parked four houses down and went straight inside.

I knew that both Steed and the Homicide boys had been over the place thoroughly, but there was no reason I couldn't look again. It was like walking through a crypt. I had called Tenhoor that morning and found out that Sherrill's sister had come and taken her body away for burial. Then I had called Jack, and he seemed broken up, but his voice was poorly modulated, as if he were confused about how to approach his grief. Now I walked slowly up the stairs. The place had many shadows.

There were three bedrooms and Jack's study upstairs. One bedroom had been made into a sewing room for Sherrill, but she never sewed on more than a button. The other two were empty. I went into Jack's study. The stain was still on the floor where Sherrill had been shot. I walked around and sat in the chair behind the desk and tried not to think of her terror just before she left this life so suddenly. Ginny Calvert said Tony had come into his office and picked up a package about the size of a book. What could it have been?

The study had two closets, one behind the desk and to its left, the other in front and to the right. I opened the door behind the desk. The closet was empty, and I presumed the other would be also. I turned on the closet light and looked around. It was large enough to walk in. I tapped on the walls, but they were smooth, without a visible break. I looked up and nothing seemed unusual. In his house in Savannah, Tony had several hidden safes to keep up with all his money; he didn't want it flooding into his bank accounts so he trickled it in. I didn't know if he had any here; he'd never told me. The cops knew about Sherrill's safe downstairs.

I couldn't tell anything about the other closet, either. It seemed sturdy. I spent an hour going over the study, but there was nothing of interest, and I could not keep my eyes off the stain on the rug so I turned out the light and went downstairs to their bedroom. The bed was not made. How long since there was love here?

The police had not taken everything. The closet was a walk-in nearly the size of my room at Mrs. Gunnerson's. It was full of expensive clothes, mostly Sherrill's. The sister would come back, I guess, and look over the place, presuming Tony was never found or turned up dead. For now, it was nobody's. I tapped along the walls. There was a shelf along the top of the closet, and

I stretched and looked at it. Nothing much was there, a few hats and, in the middle, a large cardboard box. The closet fixture lit things brilliantly. I stared at the shelf for a while, realizing something was not right. Then it hit me. The shelf was coated with dust, and there was a long smear in the dust where the box had been slid to one side and then back. It probably didn't mean anything. Maybe the cops had done it. But if they had moved it to one side, why had they moved it back?

I reached out and slid the box to the right. It was heavy. The only sound in the closet was my breathing and the scraping of the box against the shelf. I stared at the panel for a long time before I took my knife out. The panel was nearly square and there was no visible clasp. I stuck the blade in the edge and popped it and the door squeaked back on its hinges. Inside, there was a wall safe looking as secure as Fort Knox. I felt suddenly as if getting into it were the most important thing in my life, but I was terrible with safes. I'd spent two days one time with Willie Arklow, using a stethoscope, trying to learn about sequential tumblers, about listening for clicks, but in practice, it had rarely worked. I didn't even remember what I'd done with my stethoscope. I reached out and turned the handle, just for the hell of it, and it came down, and I pulled the safe door open.

I knew when it opened there must be nothing inside. Tony had gotten something out of it earlier in the week. I stood on tiptoes and took out my key ring, which also held a penlight that I'd used often. I pointed it into the safe and looked around. It was large, maybe two feet square. And lying on the bottom was a small package. I reached in and took it out, closed the safe and the outer door panel, pushed the box back, then closed the closet.

I sat on the bed and looked at the package. There was a noise in the rear of the house. I took out my gun, wedged the package inside the waistband of my pants and crept back through the darkened hall toward the den. If Queen Elizabeth had suddenly come into the hall in her royal robes at that moment, I would have shot her in the chest. My heart was beating as fast as it had when I'd run along the streets that morning.

I went into the den. The deer head seemed to be breathing. The whole room seemed to be breathing. I whirled around. Nothing was there. I muttered an oath and walked as soundlessly as I could to the front door and came out like I had business there, cut across the lawn to the curb and went up the street to my car. Nobody seemed to be around. I got in, drove off and waited until I was two miles away at a K-Mart parking lot before I stopped. I laid the gun on the seat beside me and took the package out of my pants. I suddenly felt like I'd lost ten pounds.

It was covered in newspaper and tied with rough packing string. I looked at the newspaper; it was an *Atlanta Journal.* I recognized one story about new construction at the zoo. It was recent. The package weighed maybe two pounds, pretty heavy for something that small. I took my Swiss Army knife out of my coat pocket and cut the strings. The newspaper hung loosely, and I pulled it off, and there was a black box. I looked around me. An old woman and her husband were arguing about something she'd bought at K-Mart. He didn't think they needed it.

I took a breath and opened the box. At first, I felt a

compulsion to laugh when I saw it. A joke, surely, one of Tony's ideas of splendor, something worth not much more than the paste of which it was made. It was a cross. It lay uncomfortably crowded in the box, which was obviously designed for something else, maybe an electric razor. It was about five inches long and encrusted with jewels. But there was something slightly crude about it. I took it out and held it up, and the morning sun came through my windshield, through the cross, and the light was broken down, and colors sparkled all over my face, all over my shirt and jacket. I felt the hair go up on my arms. It was gold, with what appeared to be diamonds and sapphires down the front, with row after row of tiny rubies and opals along the sides.

"God in heaven," I said out loud. I put it back in the box and slid it under my seat with my Frankie Laine tapes. I put the car in gear and drove out on the Stone Mountain Freeway, then turned back toward Atlanta after trying to figure out what it might be.

It seemed obvious. Tony had been skimming from Shuler and had bought this cross with the money, hoping to change it back into Swiss currency or something as exotic. It was like Tony. He loved things that shine. Like Sherrill. When Shuler found out what was going on, he ordered Tony killed. Maybe they came looking for Tony, couldn't find him and decided to kill Sherrill. No. Damn. Nothing made sense.

I went back to Mrs. Gunnerson's and put the cross under my mattress and then went back out and goofed around until the sun started to go down. I drove out to Stone Mountain. It is the largest mass of exposed granite in the world, rising to eight hundred and twenty-five feet. When I was young, it was undeveloped, and you could go out there anytime you wanted to. Now it is an amusement park, and in the summer they project a laser show on the side of the mountain where there is a huge carving depicting the heroes of the Confederacy.

The western slope of the mountain is the easiest to walk to the summit, where there is a flag plaza, an antenna for a public broadcasting TV station and an office of the National Weather Service. Anything for science. I parked near a Confederate museum and started walking up. You could see lovers bundled against the cold in a couple of places low on the mountain, as the sun eased west. I didn't know who I was looking for or what. Mrs. Gunnerson could have misunderstood. I adjusted my jacket so I could feel the weight of my gun on my hip, and I kept thinking about how long it would take to get it out.

The mountain is covered with pines nearly to the top, on which is mostly clean stone. I came up higher, and to the west I could see Atlanta whole, looking like a fairy city in the slowly fading light. I kept hearing strange noises, and I had the sick feeling I was being followed, though I saw nothing. A cold wind was coming out of the northwest. It took about fifteen minutes to walk to a spot just below the summit not far past a picnic shelter. I had seen dozens of names carved into the stone on the walk up, and now I stood, reading the names "W.W. Roark" and "J.W. Mehaffy" and the date they had been there, 1879. I stopped and listened. I edged around to the south, not ready to go higher because I didn't think anyone would meet me on top. I was full into the shadows of a few thin pines now, and I took my gun out and held it down so it would look like part of my hand to any casual observer.

There was a sound about fifty yards behind me like a limb breaking, then somebody running. I bent down, turned, moved slowly toward the sound. I felt weak and afraid, but there was no use in going the other way. I followed the sound and came near it and stood for a moment, hearing only the wind in the pines. I stopped, breathing hard, and thought then that the noise was behind me, then to my left. There seemed to be sounds everywhere. I leaned against a tree, and then there was only silence.

"Hank?" a voice whispered hoarsely.

"I'm here," I said. "Who is it?" I came forward a couple of steps, and I could see him in the fading light not fifty yards ahead, looking worn and tired.

"Who is it?" I said. He said nothing but motioned for me to come: like the Angel of Death, he motioned for me to come. I had moved about twenty yards forward when I heard movement suddenly from two sides of me, and I didn't know which way to turn.

"Police!" a voice shouted. "Don't move!" I stopped and looked forward to the man ahead of me. He moved slightly to his left, raised his gun hand, and when he did, there was a deafening explosion to my left and the leap of flame from a gun barrel. The man in front of me crumpled to the ground and lay there, convulsive. You bastards, I thought. I started walking toward the man, and I could see men coming out of the shadows. Someone was talking to me, but I ignored him and kept on coming. The man was lying on the ground now, his legs shaking. I knew what it was, the final jerk of the neuromuscular system. I leaned down to the man. Someone was grabbing my arm, but I turned and pushed him hard and he fell. I lifted the shot man's head and in the crazy light his face looked like a skull, skin drawn back tightly over the bone. It was Tony Browning. He looked at me and tried to lick his lips.

"It's okay, Tony," I said. He coughed and choked and grabbed his throat. Blood was coming out of his mouth.

"Hank. . ." he said. Then he coughed again and died. His body shuddered once, and then he was looking up into the autumn sky. I let him down, and someone came up behind me and grabbed me and jerked me to my feet. He spun me around and I found myself looking into the grim face of Lt. Adam Steed.

"What the hell are you doing here?" he asked bitterly. "About to make a pickup or something? I should've known you were involved." I swung at him. Maybe it was the fatigue, but I missed him wildly; he shoved me, and I tumbled down a small ledge and landed hard on my shoulder. I got up and came back toward him. He leveled his gun at me. There must have been ten other men on the side of the mountain, some of them cops from the small nearby town also called Stone Mountain.

"How did you know about this?" I asked. He held his palms up and then turned and walked away. I stood there looking down at Tony when Paul Tenhoor took my arm and pulled me to one side.

"Come on," he said softly. "You got a lot of explaining to do." I looked at him and shook my head and felt my eyes filling with tears.

"How did you find him?" I asked. I felt empty and stupid. Had I led them to him?

"Just a tip, Hank," he said. "Just a goddamn tip."

I had the feeling they had not been there long; I caught snatches of conversation, about securing the area, about seeing if others were around, questioning people. I felt numb. Tenhoor put me in the back seat of his car. We drove down to the parking lot. He let me get the Buick, and I followed them downtown. I kept shaking my head. I looked at myself in the mirror. I needed to get on with my life. Sherrill was dead. Tony was blasted into eternity with her, and his blood still stained the wind-rushed granite of Stone Mountain. I tried to feel sadness, but it would not come. I was angry. If Steed had not been there, I might have been able to save Tony. But Tony had been set up. And I had the odd feeling that I had been set up, too.

We parked out back and went inside. It was hot. I felt like I was walking on stilts; my knees did not seem to be working right. We got upstairs, and by then I was sweating with a dark fury. I sat in Steed's office until he came in, Tenhoor staying with me but saying nothing. So the Homicide boys had given me to Steed, first. Well, well, well.

"Okay, let's have it," Steed said abruptly as he sat down royally behind his dark desk.

"Have what?" I asked. I glanced at Tenhoor, and he was chewing on his gum as if it were poison.

"I'm appealing to you, Prince," Steed said with all the magnanimity of Machiavelli.

"You're not at all appealing to me," I said. "I like you, but you're just not my type." He looked down at his hands. He closed and unclosed his fists. I had the impression he wanted to beat the shit out of me. I was almost hoping he would try it. Steed is a big man, but not as big as I am.

"I want to know what in the hell you were doing out there with Tony Browning," Steed said. His lip trembled. He kept fiddling with a paper clip.

"I was studying geology," I said. Tenhoor spit out his gum in a metal trashcan and shook his head.

"You're involved with it, aren't you?" said Steed. He squinted so tightly I didn't know how he could see. He bounced nervously in his seat, and I imagined him as a bus driver.

"Come on, Lieutenant," I said with mock exasperation. "Tony was my client, and you blew him away. I didn't even know who I was meeting. I got a call and my landlady took the message. It could've been Slim Whitman for all I knew."

"You see him at the Civic Center last year?" asked Tenhoor.

"I'm holding out for Frankie Laine," I said. Steed made a strangled sound.

"Then I guess you don't know who ransacked the Browning home today?" he asked. I stared at him not quite knowing what to say. I tried.

"Ransacked his house?"

"Damn near tore it to fucking smithereens," said Tenhoor. "Like somebody was trying to turn over everything in the house." When I left, it had been neat; somebody had come in after me and looked for something. I thought I knew what it might have been. I was wrong; I was going to have to see Manny Fargo after all. This was getting crazy.

"Maybe it was a committee from *Better Homes and Gardens*," I said. Steed was trying to restrain himself but not doing very well. We chatted for about another half-hour, and I tried not to be smart, but it was hard. Still, I wanted to get the hell out of there, so I told him my life story, reeled off My Favorite Things and let him know that I was going to walk the straight and narrow. I didn't tell him I still believed in the Tooth Fairy, but I might as well have.

It was nearly midnight when I got through with the guys over on West Peachtree in Homicide who were nicer than Steed. The Stone Mountain cops were there, too, having cooperated on the case. I think I understand how people became obsessed with violence. I still did not understand what Tony was up to, but it involved money. I still liked money, and my supply of it was adequate.

When I got home, Babe Ruth was sitting in the parlor reading *Gone with the Wind*. She was wearing a long, ugly house dress that looked as if it were made from a purple camel. I sat down across from her in one of Mrs. Gunnerson's chairs.

"Hi, Mildred," I said. She looked up at me. "Cap'n Butler done anything despicable this evening?"

She smiled blandly. "You stay out late," she said.

"Yeah," I said. "I do that." I went upstairs, locked my door and took the package out from beneath my mattress. It might be a matter of time before someone came and tore up my apartment looking for this thing. I had to move it somewhere the next morning. I opened the box and took the cross out and held it under the lamp on the table. Then I hid it again and went to bed.

I woke up crying sometime in the middle of the night. I think I was dreaming about Sherrill, but it might have been about being a swan and leaving my lady swan. I sat there in bed a long time. In the glow from the street light, I could see Wanda's face where she still hung over the bureau with a knife in her

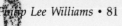

forehead. I thought about Tony. Then Ginny. I thought about a drink. A cigarette. A loaf of bread, a jug of wine and thou. I had never been so stinking miserable in my life.

I got up and dressed and drove over to Shelleen's, a piano bar that went on all night long. I didn't go in there much, but enough to know I could find a friend if I needed her. I bought a pack of Camels, in the hope they would help purge my lungs of the unpleasant fresh air I had inhaled that morning. Then I bought a double Evan Williams on the rocks. I went to the piano player and leaned on the piano and drank the bourbon in two gulps. He smiled at me like he knew I had money.

"Play 'Someone to Watch Over Me,'" I said. I put a Lincoln in the jar. He broke into a transition.

"Gershwin fan?" he asked. I stared at his fat fingers and wondered whom he would go home to. He looked to be over fifty, and if this was a bad life, you couldn't prove it by him.

"Yeah," I said. I walked over and sat at the bar. After a stiff drink, small dark bars turn into caves, and I held on to the bar while I drank a second. I was beginning to remember why I had become a teetotaler the day before. The hurt didn't go away; it just hid until you quit drinking. I was staring at a painting of a moose that was advertising beer when I felt someone sit next to me. I looked, uncaring, to my left. It was a woman about my age who had been drinking for a while. She looked at me like I was the Maharajah of Ranshipoor. The piano player had told her about my fabulous wealth.

"Hi," she said. "Mind if I join you?"

"If you were a mother moose and you found out your kid was advertising beer, what would you do?" I asked. She smiled at me brilliantly, but it didn't do much good. By morning, she would look much older than thirty-five. Hanging out in bars did that to you.

"I'd tell him to bring me a case home," she said. She extended her hand and told me her name, but I wasn't listening and I didn't catch it. Her hand felt like a halibut that had been on the dock too long. I bought her a drink. "So what do you do for a living?"

"I'm a professional baseball player," I said. I could almost hear her admire my salary.

"You don't mean it!" she squealed. "Your team must not have made it to the Super Bowl."

"You want to go home with me?" I asked. I didn't want to talk sports anymore. Probably hopeless to try and explain ERA to her.

"Okay," she said, trying to act excited. But I didn't get up. I just sat there and kept drinking, and she kept talking about her ex-husband and what an animal he was, how he'd expected her to cook, for Christ's sake, and were these hands meant for a hot stove, were they, huh?

I remember not really caring anymore, throwing a twenty down on the bar and starting to walk off, with her yelling at me about treating her like an animal. Nobody in Shelleen's seemed to care. I walked out and got in my car and managed to drive home without killing anyone. I got out and lay in the cool, damp grass in front of Mrs. Gunnerson's and looked up at the sky. I wanted an answer. But the only thing I saw were the constellations turning over the city.

I went upstairs, checked on the cross and went to bed. When I awoke, the sun was up, had been for sometime, it seemed, and Mrs. Gunnerson was shaking me. I wondered if Jack Railsback would come in and tell me Tony Browning was missing. I looked up at her and gave her my blank look.

"Meithsor Prance!" she said urgently. "Iss a women in ve phune." I nodded and sat up. A phone call. I reached down to take the covers off and found I was sleeping on top of them in my clothes. Mrs. Gunnerson looked at me with great pity. I came out into the hall and coughed a few times and tried to clear my throat. A phone call. I knew what she had said this time. I tried to say it over, to think sequentially. I still felt drunk. I picked up the receiver.

"Yeah," I croaked.

"Please help me," the voice said. She was frightened; no, more. Terrified.

"Who is this?"

"It's Ginny," she said. She started crying. I ran my hand through my hair and pulled the curtain back and looked out the hall window. It was either early morning or late afternoon.

"What's wrong?" I asked. She groaned and made a windy, moaning sound.

"They want to hurt me," she said. I felt the blood pump.

"Where are you?"

"My house. Can you come over please? Now?"

"Lock your door and put a chair from the table under the handle," I said. "I'll be there as fast as I can. Are you in danger now?"

"I don't know," she said miserably. "Should I call the police?"

"No. Just wait."

"Okay."

And I cleaned up and broke the speed limit several times on my way over to Ginny Calvert's house.

TOOK THE CROSS WITH ME. IT WAS NOT
nearly morning, as I had feared, but late afternoon,
and it was becoming cloudy, and a cold wind
droned over the car as I pulled up in front of Ginny
Calvert's house. I thought I knew why they were after
her, why they'd be after me. Or maybe their pressure
on her was intended to frighten me into giving the
cross to Manny Fargo as a Halloween present.

I went up the steps two at a time. I rapped smartly
on the door, and I heard her voice asking who it was. I
told her, and then she looked out the window to make
sure and moved the chair away from the door and
opened it and let me in. I had not been inside a second
when she grabbed me and held me tightly around the
chest. She was shaking.

"It's okay," I said. "I'm here." I still felt like hell, but I
couldn't let her know it. That was part of the Prince

Code, never to let anyone know when you suffer. We walked to her sofa, and I sat down and took the cross box out of my waist band and set it on the table. She sniffed.

"What's that?" she asked. The room was comfortable and warm. Benjy the cat stared at me for a moment and then undulated back into the bedroom.

"Probably the thing they want," I said. "I found it over at Tony's." I opened the box and took it out and she stared at it for a long time.

"Is it real?"

"I think so. It looks too crude to be a factory-made thing. If it's real, it must be worth Monte Carlo. Now, what happened?"

"I had finished my classes, and I was going to an employment agency, and when I got in my car, this man came up to the window. It scared me so bad I didn't know what to do. He just stood there and stared at me, and I wanted to scream, but it hung in my throat and I couldn't do anything. He just said, 'Don't be a fool. You don't want to get hurt. We'll find it.'" She got up and put on a pot of water for tea, and I followed her to the edge of the kitchen. "Well, why not just give it to them," she said. She folded her arms across her chest. I noticed for the first time what she was wearing: faded blue jeans and an old white blouse with some kind of embroidery around the neck.

"Not yet," I said. "Did you hear about Tony Browning?" She had not, and as I told her, we drank our tea and she cried.

"Then there's nothing to do but give them the cross," she said. I shrugged. "You don't think so?"

"I don't know what I think," I said. "Somebody came by Tony's house and ransacked it yesterday after

I left. It doesn't make sense that Shuler's people did it. They just wouldn't have done it during the middle of the day. Whoever wanted to get this back was desperate. I can't think of a man like Shuler being desperate about anything. It must have been done by somebody no one would notice. This is probably worth a lot of money, but it's not worth getting caught there in the middle of the day. Since I was hired by them and their friend, I could get away with it, and maybe Shuler's people were following me. I don't know. The only things I know for sure are that Tony and Sherrill are both dead, and I have a piece of jewelry."

"So what are you going to do?" The tea tasted just right, and I felt the caffeine helping my head. I wondered if the lonely ladies were already at Shelleen's. It was a sad way to live.

"Go see Shuler," I said.

"Isn't that dangerous?" she asked. Her eyes were large and fearful. I wanted to tell her I was the Maharajah of Ranshipoor.

"I spit in the face of danger," I said. "I'm going tomorrow. Don't worry. I'll clear you. They won't bother you anymore." That was a palpable lie; if they wanted it bad enough they might kill her or me or anybody. They already knew she was the right one to pressure. Maybe it was a lucky guess, but I didn't think so. Someone had been watching over me. She visibly relaxed. She made us ham and cheese sandwiches, and we ate them as what was left of the sun went down. By dark, it was raining, a slow, pleasant rain. I loved the odor of wet autumn lawns and the feel of leather on slick streets as I walked. It was my time of the year.

"I don't understand you," she said. "Chuck said private detectives are all alike, policemen who couldn't make it, but you were never a cop, were you?"

"Who's Chuck?" I asked. "Your boyfriend?"

"My ex-husband," she said. I felt like I were a kid's helium balloon, and I'd been poked with an ice pick and all the surface had gone.

"Oh," I said.

"Don't look so glum," she said. "We were only married for eight months. I still see him sometimes at school. He's an assistant professor of statistics."

"Oh," I said. More of this, and I'd get an invitation to address the Toastmasters.

"Anyway, I told him about you and he said you were probably just another loser," she said. "I told him you weren't." I started to say "oh" again, but I didn't want her to think I'd come with a prepared speech. "You like to think you're so tough and mean and you carry a gun, but I think you're not so mean."

"Promise you won't tell," I said. We talked for probably three hours, and she got out the jug of Chianti that we had not finished earlier. Once I had a little alcohol in me I felt better, but that fact didn't exactly cheer me. She told me about herself, and I told her about baseball, about Nellie Fox and Hank Greenberg and Mantle and Maris and the Gas House Gang and other things I loved. By 10, we were both a little drunk, and she was sitting beside me on the sofa with her feet in my lap. She was talking about her high school boyfriend when a look of confusion clouded her pretty face. She stopped in the middle of a sentence and leaned out and picked up the cross and stared at it.

"What's wrong?" I asked.

"Didn't I read somewhere about a jeweled cross being stolen?" she asked. I frowned. That didn't make any sense at all.

"Oh, it probably happens all the time," I said. She shook it off and stared at the cross, her brows knit so much she looked like a Neanderthal for a moment.

"I could have sworn . . ." She shrugged and set the cross back down. "Maybe not. Who knows. Tell me about growing up." She shifted and her foot rested on the inside of my thigh. I needed to suffer mortifications of the flesh.

"It's not much."

"Where are you from?"

"Second turning to the right and straight on toward morning." She sat up and crossed her legs and looked at me, and her eyes watered.

"Oh my God, I don't believe it," she whispered hoarsely. "That's from *Peter Pan*. My father used to read that to me when I was a little girl." She looked away from me dreamily. "I had forgotten all about it. What is it Peter says at the end when Captain Hook can't beat him?"

"I'm youth. I'm a little bird that . . ." She said the rest with me: " . . . has broken out of the egg. I'm youth. I'm joy." She turned to me again.

"This is the first time I've felt this good in such a long time," she said. For once, I kept my mouth shut, and she came over to me and we leaned into each other and she kissed me gently. We kissed for a long time. On the way to the bedroom, she turned out each light as if it were a ritual, and the cat stared at us without making a sound.

We lay down in darkness, and later I lay on my back listening to the wind rake the branches across her window. Her head cradled on my shoulder, and she breathed lightly like a little girl as she slept. You pay a price for living alone and living intensely. It had been too long since I had loved a woman who loved me, not the love of the ages but of the moment, one perfect moment when there is nothing base about it, only affection and union. I kissed her on the top of the head and fell asleep listening to the wind and thinking about a small boy who could fly.

I got up at dawn the next morning and showered. I hated climbing back into the same clothes, but one sacrifices for the good times. I was dressed, gun on, standing in the kitchen waiting for the water to boil when she came walking out in a long orange robe, stretching and yawning. She stood in the doorway of the kitchen and smiled at me.

"You brute," she said.

"Heck, I thought I'd been able to subdue the beast within me," I said. The water came to a boil and the kettle whistled merrily as I took it off. I poured us each a cup of coffee. It was not Sanka. I never like Sanka. We sat at her small table and sipped.

"What are you going to do?" She asked it as if she were afraid I'd give the same answer.

"I've got to find out about Tony," I said. "I don't know if he's got family who wants to deal with it. I don't know if he left a will. Sherrill didn't have one. Then I've got to see if I can get rid of that cross." I gestured to it where it was lying on the coffee table. "At this point, I only know to see Shuler."

I got up and took the cross into the bathroom and hid it in the back of her closet in a box of some of those female things that always litter the area. I came out and got my jacket, and she stood and hugged me. I kissed her, and I wanted to spend the day in bed with her, but I had work to do. Maybe the morning before had not been a failure. I did still have a code.

"Are you coming back today?" she asked. "Should I go outside?"

"Just go on to school," I said.

"It's Saturday," she said.

"Time flies when you're having fun," I said lamely, but she laughed anyway. "I'll be back late this afternoon. Just take it easy, and if anything happens, call Tenhoor at APD. He's the guy with the red hair. Remember him?"

"Tenhoor," she said. I kissed her again and went out into the cool morning, down the stairs and was ten feet from my car when Manny Fargo stepped smartly out from behind a huge water oak and stuck a gun in my ear. I knew it was him immediately because his face is pointed like a ferret's. He is about five-nine, weighs one-sixty, and the gun was cold and real.

"Get in," he said, escorting me to the passenger side. "Slide over and drive." I looked around and could see, not far down the street, another car, exhaust idly puffing from the tailpipe. I had been careless. It was the kind of thing that got people killed.

"Where to, mister?" I asked. "I get double fare on weekends." He laughed like a ferret and nodded at the car ahead of us. It left, and I followed it. He kept the gun pointed at my ribs. It looked like a Mauser, and I knew from this range it could leave a hole the size of a volleyball in my chest. "I was coming to see your boss today. How is the old boy?" He took my gun.

"Shut the fuck up," he said.

"Well, it's a lovely day in the old town," I said. "Doesn't it make you feel perky?"

"The hell should I know?" He shrugged. We drove back onto Ponce de Leon, past where the old Atlanta Crackers' baseball stadium once was. I had come there with a Little League group when I was a boy. We kept driving until we got to I-85, then we went north out of Atlanta, heading northeast.

"Mr. Big move?" I said. "I thought he lived in northwest Atlanta with two dobermans and twelve weasels."

Manny Fargo shook his head and clucked sadly. Dealing with me wasn't going to make his Saturday. I wondered why he hadn't searched me for the cross. Maybe he was saving that pleasure for his boss. I hoped they wouldn't bother Ginny. They'd never think to look in a box of Kotex.

"Someday, somebody's gonna stuff a gun up your nose," Manny said unpleasantly. He was still pointing his gun at me, but his finger was on the outside of the guard. He didn't want to shoot me and he knew I wasn't Dirty Harry. I drove nearly to the South Carolina line. He told me to get off at the Carnesville exit, and then we drove about five miles north and came to a dirt road with a chain across it. He handed me the key, and we got out and I unlocked it while he thought about shoving his gun up my nose. We climbed back in and drove past it, then he covered me while I restrung the chain and snapped the padlock again.

"We've got to stop meeting like this," I said. I didn't know why I was so cocky, except that I had the cross and Jake Shuler didn't. He would be crazy to hurt me. Then again, he could use a cattle prod to convince me and have one of his weasels take me down in the woods and shoot me. I wished I hadn't thought of that.

The road wound for nearly a mile through the woods. Finally we came to an enormously expensive log cabin built on a bluff overlooking a creek. It was two stories, with a chimney at either end, rough-hewn logs and a broad front porch on which there were several chairs. Three men with Uzis sat on the front porch. I counted four cars, all large and dark and ominous as the crows in a Van Gogh painting. A plume of smoke was coming from the chimney on the left. There were no construction scars; this house had been here for a couple of years and looked like a hunting lodge, a getaway for someone who had plenty of money.

"Park it here," Manny Fargo said. I stopped the Buick, and we got out and slowly walked toward the house. The Three Musketeers on the porch did not stir, and Manny Fargo kept his gun on me. The car that had been following us, the one in which Manny had come to Ginny's house, had kept going when we turned into the dirt road. I felt humiliated that a worm like Fargo had brought me in, and they knew it.

"Morning, boys," I said as we passed. One of them said "Shit," and we went inside. The house was warm but not uncomfortably so. Directly in front was a stairway and to either side was a door opening into a great room. The one on the right was dark and empty, though I could see a massive deer head over the fireplace. The door to the left opened into a large, vaulted room. I could see a fire burning in the broad fieldstone fireplace, and there, too, was a deer head staring dolefully out over the room; I knew how it felt. Fargo prodded me and we went inside. I could smell something that made me think of *The African Queen*, and then I knew: it was popcorn. It was so out of place that it momentarily disoriented me. Two men were sitting on the sofa, men of the weasel persuasion. Across from them in a large chair staring into the fire was Jake Shuler. When we came over near the fire, Manny Fargo cleared his throat.

Shuler looked up. He was a massive man, hard fat, with thick gray hair that flowed over his flushed scalp like sea waves. Once, he had been good looking, but now he looked tired and unhappy. I knew how he felt, too.

"Get out," said Shuler to Manny. "You all get out and leave us alone." He gestured to the men on the couch and they got up.

"You sure?" asked Fargo.

"For God's sake, Manny," said Shuler. While they were leaving I looked around the room. You could tell a woman had never been here. There were none of the embellishments that make a house a home. This was no one's home. It was a place to come to. The door closed. I sat on the couch across from Jake Shuler and we stared at each other. He had a large bowl of popcorn in his lap. He nibbled at it desultorily.

"Popcorn?" he asked politely. I started to ask if he had any Milk Duds but decided it would be rude.

"No thanks," I said.

"We need to talk, Prince," he said slowly. I had the impression he had trouble breathing. He wheezed between words. The fire crackled. I could hear the men on the porch talking softly. I didn't feel threatened, but I was looking at all the angles. They hadn't taken my keys away. I could go through the window on the back of the room. Then I could get so many holes in me I'd make pencil marks when I sat down.

"Okay," I said.

"Tony Browning," he began, but he had to search for the word as he turned from me to the fire, "was once a good man for us. He worked hard and did what he was told. But then something went wrong with him. I don't know. I talked to him myself. I don't like trouble. When I was a younger man, I liked trouble all right, liked a rumble now and then to keep the juices flowing, right? But now I just have a business to run, and I don't need trouble."

"I think you have it now, though," I said carefully.

"I know," he said wearily. "You know it's probably the price I have to pay. You can't decide you don't want to keep things in line in this business. You just do it. That's why we built this place, so we wouldn't have to worry about the problems. But sometimes you can't help it." I thought of Sherrill, and my face felt hot, but I didn't want to get shot so I held my counsel.

"So?"

"So we have kept this place a secret," he wheezed. "A tight secret. But somebody has set out to cross us. We don't know who. The fact is, Mr. Prince, that we had nothing to do with killing either Tony Browning or his wife." I leaned forward and stared at him. He was telling the truth. I felt even hotter and more confused.

"Sure, Jake. I'm a nice guy and believe you, but who else will?" I asked. He smiled ruefully.

"That's the trick, now," he said, "making yourself innocent again. Tell me, Mr. Prince, can one ever be innocent again? Sure, we had reason to be worried about Browning. In fact, we had talked about what to do with him. But we did not kill him. And I do not kill women."

"Why should I believe you?" I asked.

"Because we want you to find out who did kill him," he said. "We are having to lay low now. Half the civilized world is looking for me." He ate a piece of popcorn and stared at me. His eyes were watery and colorless, so pale they looked like smoke. "We checked everybody we know, and nobody seems to know what is going on."

"What do I get out of this?"

"We won't harm you."

"You didn't mind threatening Miss Calvert," I said with as much bitterness as I could summon.

"Who?"

"The woman I was with last night, where Manny picked me up," I said. He shrugged.

"We didn't even know who lived there," he said. "Manny and the boys didn't start following you until yesterday. We didn't know you had been working on this." If it wasn't Shuler who had threatened her, then she might still be in danger.

"You're saying you've had nothing to do with any of this?" I asked.

"I'm saying it," he said.

Through the window I could see leaves, gold and crimson and vermilion, blowing down the hill. I wished I had a cold bottle of Perrier-Jouet brut, a roaring fire and Ginny Calvert on the rug. I tried to think of something to tell Shuler. He ate the popcorn and stared at me.

"I thought you knew everything that goes on in Atlanta," I said. He licked the salt off his lips.

"Years ago, Mr. Prince, I did," he said slowly, "but I am getting old, and money can't help me much anymore. We still do well enough, but we can do nothing at all, even find out what is happening, when the fire has been stoked so hot. Earlier this week, someone shot at me."

"In Atlanta?"

"Here," he said with wonder. "Here. Oh, the boys went after him, but it was dark, and there are dirt roads that cross all through these woods."

"Maybe it was a poor, lost deerhunter," I said, looking at the baleful head over the mantel. He looked at me with such scorn I didn't press it. "So why did you bring me up here?"

"You thought it was me, did you?"

"Yeah," I admitted. "And so do the badges." He nodded as if he had heard it all before.

"All men are bad men," said Jake Shuler. "Some have the misfortune to be caught, and others only are bad up here." He tapped his thick head. "I want you to clear me."

"What do I get?"

"I'll think of something," said Shuler. He called for Manny Fargo. With a deal like that, I'd be a fool to turn it down. Fargo came into the room. "Give him his gun back." Manny reached in his coat and handed me the .38 back without showing any emotion. I slid it back into my shoulder holster, which I alternated with the hip clip.

"I'll be in touch," said Shuler. I nodded and walked back outside, winked at the weasels on the porch and got in my car and drove off, looking occasionally at the road but more often at the rear-view mirror where I expected a car to swerve in behind me and come gunning. Nobody moved. I got to the chain, and a man was there, had taken it down and when I passed I watched in the mirror as he put the chain up and locked it again.

On the way back, I tried to think about who might have killed Tony. Shuler obviously did not know about the cross, but whoever had threatened Ginny did. I needed to find out more about the friends of Tony Browning. I needed to find out who had that phone number in New York. And I needed to make sure nobody got near Ginny Calvert. The last woman I had tried to save had wound up dead.

I got back to Atlanta about two and drove to Ginny's on St. Charles. She had given me a key and I found a note inside on the table that said she had gone shopping and would be back by four. When it was six and getting dark, I felt my hands sweating and checked to make sure my gun was loaded.

7

THE PHONE RANG AT TEN PAST SEVEN. I jumped fifty-seven feet into the air and came down with my heart clattering like a Christmas train. I let it ring again to make sure I hadn't had a stroke or something. I picked it up.

"Hank?" a voice asked.

"Jesus Christ," I said. "I've been sitting here with my brow knit in anguish. Where are you?"

"I'm at the grocery store," she said. "What do you look like with your brow knit in anguish?"

"Jack Palance," I said. She laughed brightly, and I thought the night before had been more than drunken lust after all. "Why aren't you here?"

"I went down to the library today," she said. "I found out about a cross that was stolen." I could hear someone in the store talking about the price of bananas.

"Come on home," I said, not trying to sound as confused as I was. "You don't need to be out."

"Okay," she said. She paused for a moment. "Are you all right? Did you talk to that man?" I didn't want to tell her I'd been kidnapped and hauled off nearly to South Carolina by a pack of ferrets.

"Yeah," I said. "How far are you?"

"At the Quick Stop on Ponce de Leon," she said. "I'll be there in ten minutes. What do you want to eat?"

"That's a dangerous question to ask a man who's been with the foreign legion for five years," I said. She ignored me.

"I'll get some beer, too," she said. She hung up and I sat around thinking about crosses and Stone Mountain and Jack Railsback. Plenty of pieces, no puzzle. I went into the bathroom and reached into the box of Kotex and felt for the cross. For a moment, I thought it was missing, but then it was there, and I left it and went and looked out the window over the damp porch, waiting for her to drive up. A few minutes later, as if nothing were wrong, she pulled up out front and parked her Colt behind my Buick. It was like a gnat getting ready to bite a water buffalo. I came out on to the porch.

"You need help?" I yelled.

"Nope," she said. She was wearing a yellow slicker and high leather boots with a pair of corduroys. When she came up the stairs, I took the beer from her and she kissed me lightly on the lips.

"Was that supper?" I asked. We went inside and closed the door.

"That wasn't even a light snack," she said. She had bought a six-pack of Olympia Light. I wanted to comment about its qualities, but I never could tell one beer from another. Most people judge beer by its can. Olympia has a pretty can, so I like it; Budweiser's can is ugly, so I don't.

"Be still, my heart," I said. I took a beer for each of us and put the rest in the refrigerator. She had bought a pound of hamburger, some buns and a large yellow onion. "Stroganoff?" "You really can't cook?" she asked as she took off the slicker. She wore a blue work shirt. It was carelessly tucked into her pants.

"I can make coffee," I said thoughtfully. "You cook and tell me about what you found out."

"Then you tell me what you found out," she said.

"Then I'll tell you what I think of what you found out," I said.

She started preparing cheeseburgers and then read from a notebook and told me about spending the afternoon at the Georgia State Library. Georgia State is an urban school, a stone's throw from the State Capitol and the police department, a place where someone could hurt her and be lost in the city in moments.

"I found the longest article in *The London Times*," she said. "The cross was thought to have been made by monks for a monastery in France, but it seems there's no direct evidence. It was in the Musée des Beaux Arts in Paris but was stolen about eight weeks ago. The *Times* article said that someone had disconnected the alarm system, someone who knew about electronics. It was the only thing missing. The Sûreté went absolutely bonkers about it for a couple of weeks — and then, nothing. I don't read French too well, but I checked a couple of Paris papers, and they seemed to think it was not such a professional job." She flipped the burgers, laid on two slices of cheese and wiped her hands on a towel. "What we have here must not be that cross. No way it could wind up in Atlanta, right?"

"No pictures in any of the papers?" I asked.

"There was some stipulation in its bequest to the museum that no photos ever be made of it," she continued, peeling the onion while the cheese melted. "Some eccentric Belgian widow gave it to them in the thirties." How could it have wound up in a wall safe owned by Tony Browning? "Did you talk to this guy? Did you tell him that I had nothing to do with all this?"

"Yeah," I said. "Except he doesn't, either." I finished my beer and opened another. She stood there and stared at me.

"He doesn't either what?"

"Have anything to do with it," I said. I opened her second beer, and she sliced the onion and put the cheeseburgers on the buns. We went out to the small table and sat down. She looked pale and tired.

"Then who does?" she asked.

"I don't know yet," I said. We ate in silence for a time. "It had to be somebody Tony knew, because it wasn't like him to deal with strangers. So what I need to do now is find out more about him, who he worked with lately. Anything you can remember from the office?" She chewed disinterestedly on her bun and tried to think.

"Have you been back down to his office?" she asked.

"No," I said, "but Steed and his boys have probably been all over it. Why?"

"He's got a wall safe there," she said. I stopped eating and took a gulp of beer and nodded as if she'd just told me to pick up the laundry on the way home. "I came into his office one day and it was funny." She pushed her hair out of her eyes. "There's a picture of the seashore on the wall and behind it there's a panel, and he was noodling around inside it. He looked mad so I backed out. Surely they went through it."

"I'll be damned," I said. "Maybe not. Real people don't always think about wall safes. That's something you don't see many places outside the movies. Besides, maybe there's something else they missed. Want to take a ride?"

"Now?" she said.

"It won't take long," I said. "Besides, I need to go by my place and get a few things. These clothes are starting to get a mite rumpled." She looked at me pleasantly.

"You are staying here to protect me," she said.

"My professional duty," I said. We stood and I kissed her, and we both tasted like onions, but neither of us cared. I got the rest of the beer and the cross, and we set out for Mrs. Gunnerson's.

We took my car. When I gunned it a little coming out of a light, she looked at me with disdain.

"This car is like something out of *Smokey and the Bandit*," she said. "Why do you drive this thing?"

"It's a way of reaffirming my belief in America," I said blithely. "It's a big gesture in a world of small, toad-sized cars. Besides, it makes me feel young to get out on the interstate and drive so fast my teeth hurt." She looked disgusted. I figured it wasn't time to put on the Frankie Laine tape.

They were playing Trivial Pursuit again when we got to Mrs. Gunnerson's. Babe Ruth was staring at the game board, Mrs. Carreker was preening and Mr. Oshman was rolling the dice like a Las Vegas lounge lizard playing with his last quarter. Dicky Thacker was sitting on the sofa, not playing, letting the smoke from his cigarette curl around his head like a caliph in an opium den.

"Meithsor Prance," said Mrs. Gunnerson, coming into the room with a tray of cookies. She looked at Ginny, half bowed and smiled. "Whoth yar freend?"

"This is Ginny Calvert," I said. Mrs. Gunnerson put the tray down and shook hands with Ginny. I introduced Ginny to the rest of them.

"What's the largest satellite orbiting earth?" asked Mr. Oshman, rubbing his hands together.

"The moon," said Mrs. Carreker. "I told you that was a trick question. It's not fair." Mr. Oshman looked like he wanted to swat her one.

"I was asking her," he said petulantly, pointing to Ginny, "and you only think it's a trick question because you missed it."

"Hah," said the caliph.

"Thith bad mannerth," said Mrs. Gunnerson. "Yourda be beeter to mannerth."

"You can say that again," I said. We went on upstairs and I got a stack of clothes. Ginny stared at the picture Wanda Mankowicz had given me back when I thought she loved me, the bitch.

"Do you fish?" she asked as she looked at the Rapala knife.

"This could be the start of a beautiful friendship, Louie," I said. "Aren't you going to ask who she is?"

"No," she said. She put her hands in her hip pockets. I got a stack of clothes and turned out the light, and we went down. When they saw us, me carrying the clothes, they started mumbling under their breaths, the women and Mr. Oshman did. Dicky Thacker smiled.

"Get that carburetor fixed?" I asked him.

"You wish," he said inscrutably. I told Mrs. Gunnerson I would be in and out for a few days, and she smiled and offered me a cookie, which I declined. When we got outside, I noticed that Ginny was looking warily all around, so I tried to put her at ease as we drove downtown to Tony's office.

Marshall Center was surprisingly busy for 9 p.m., but then the city never sleeps. Some people up North still don't think of Atlanta as a city, but they haven't been here in a while. We took the express elevator up to Tony's floor, and Ginny opened the door with her key. Sometimes, the cops will change locks in a case like this, but they hadn't bothered.

"I feel cold," Ginny said. We went through the outer office into Tony's private office. That's all there was to it, that and a tiny bathroom. I saw the painting on the wall and I swung it back. The safe was there, and this one was locked. I twiddled with it a while, but nothing happened.

"I'm not very good at these things," I said. "Sometimes you get lucky, but I guess not with this." I sat down at Tony's desk. Ginny sat in the overstuffed chair next to it. The room was small and cheerless except for a picture of Sherrill in a small gilt frame just by the phone. I picked it up and looked at her and shook my head. I set it back and slammed my open palm down hard on the desk, so hard Ginny jumped a foot.

"Why in the hell'd you do that?" she asked. I shrugged.

"I'm just tired of being passed around like a day-old newspaper," I said. I opened the middle desk drawer and it was empty except for a small black address book that was lying in the middle. I got up and pulled the drawer completely out and held it up to the light. I set the address book on the desk and crawled under the desk and could see, dangling from the surface, a piece of duct tape where the book had been secured. I pulled it off and showed it to her.

"I'll be damned," she said. She glanced at the door. I knew how she felt; I expected Steed and Tenhoor to come breaking into the place any second. I sat back down in the chair and opened the book and flipped through it. It was blank except for the first page. This is what it said:

SANDY MARCELLO
COPENHAGEN---HARTSFIELD
ANDER. S.C./EDVARD
CHEESE

"You ever remember hearing him mention that name?" I asked.

"I don't think so," she said. I studied the inscription for another minute. "Ander. S.C." could be Anderson, South Carolina, a small town not far from the Georgia border, not far from Jake Shuler's spacious retreat. But what in the hell did "cheese" mean? Hartsfield is the name of Atlanta's airport. I lightly touched the inside pocket in my coat and felt the cross there. Jewels could be popping off all over the place. I put the book in my pocket, the one opposite the cross. I felt like a card in a "Clue" game.

"Let's get out of here," I said. She didn't need any prodding, and soon we were back in the Buick rumbling over the streets of Atlanta. I opened one of the beers. It had stayed cool in the autumn air, and Ginny took one, too.

"Why shouldn't we be giving all this to the police and getting the hell out of it?" she asked.

"I don't know," I said. "I've just got a feeling they don't really care about what happened. They think Shuler's men killed Tony and Sherrill, and Shuler says his men didn't do it. It just boils down to the fact that there are people in this world who should not be trusted, and just because they wear a badge doesn't mean a thing. I want to figure things out before I tell Steed."

"Would you keep the cross?" she asked.

"I'm not that curious," I said. "At worst, I'll finally turn it over. I like money, but not that bad."

"But if somebody thinks I have the cross, they've been following you and . . ." she stopped and looked at me as if it were coming clear for the first time. "Goddamnit."

"Yeah," I said. "I've got one more trip to make before we go home. You game?" She didn't look game, but she shrugged and nodded disconsolately. We were in that proverbial corner now, and getting out was going to be hard. Somebody was after this cross, and nobody seemed to know who. I drove south past the Capitol building with its shining gold roof and then crossed I-20, passed the Stadium and drove to Angel's place. Several cars were parked out front. I didn't want Ginny staying alone, so I told her to come with me.

I walked up to the front door with the firm purpose of someone who had mislaid his brain.

"Who's place is this?"

"This?" I asked innocently, pointing at the sagging structure. "Oh, this is just a whorehouse." I thought I heard her say "great" in a sarcastic voice but I wasn't sure. I banged on the door, and a black woman about 25 who looked like 50 peered out of the gloomy interior and stared at us. We didn't look like customers.

"I'm from *People* magazine, and we're here to do a profile on Mr. Jiminez for his work with the under-privileged slime of Atlanta," I said. "Would you tell the gentleman that William Randolph Hearst is here?"

"Mr. Hearse?" she asked.

"Hearst," I said. She stared at me. I smiled and tried to act like a reporter, but it wasn't easy; most reporters I knew acted a little weird. She left the door open a crack and disappeared. From somewhere in the catacombs I heard bitter laughter — as if anything here were funny.

"I feel clammy," Ginny said. I put my arm around her and held her against me for a moment.

"I'm the number-one enemy of clammy in the big city," I said. "We won't be here too long."

I could hear his heavy soft footsteps coming to the door, and I stepped back into the shadows so he couldn't see me. There was no porch light on, and it was dark on the street. He poked his head out the door, and I pushed Ginny gently away and grabbed Angel by the collar and jerked him out the door as if he were a Cabbage Patch Doll.

"Angel, how pleasant to see you," I said. The ciga-rette fell out of his mouth and rolled off the porch and under a nondescript bush. "I won't take up your valu-able time. How much is your time worth, anyway? Fifteen minutes for twenty bucks?"

"You got a smart mouth," Angel said. I set him against the wall. "You're making me mad, asshole."

"What are you going to do?" I asked. "Stomp your foot and run away from home? I want to know who told you Tony Browning was skimming from Shuler." He coughed and took out another cigarette. I backed off and lit one myself and gave him time to think what I'd do to him if I found out he lied.

"I heard about him and his old lady," he said. His face was only half in the light, and he looked more vulnerable than sinister. My life had been no one's prize lately, but it had been a damn sight better than this poor mess. "God, it makes you sick. I seen that press conference on the TV tonight."

"What press conference?" I asked. I hated to be getting information from Angel. But what the hell, you do what you can.

"That Narc lieutenant," he said. "He comes on and says that Tony and his old lady were offed by people in a drug deal, and that there's other suspects they're looking into now. Everybody's rattled."

"Son of a bitch," I said. "Now that you've gone through your soliloquy, how about answering my question." I could see his cigarette ash glow.

"I heard it from our man down here," he said. "I don't want you touching me again."

"From a cop?" I asked. He nodded silently.

"Said everybody knew it," he said. "I think he was trying to impress me with the law or some such shit." I nodded.

"When was this?" I asked.

"Week ago, maybe," he said. "Funny, you coming down here and asking just after that. Sort of spooks a guy, you know?" We were friends now, comrades, buddies from the war. Hell.

"You've done a great service for your country," I said. "I'm going to see that you are promoted to full private for this heroic action."

"Smart mouth," he said. I took Ginny's arm, and we went back to the car and drove off. I expected somebody to follow us, but there were only the stars, the city lights, and the weight of another person on the front

seat with me. We got back to her house without incident and went up the slick stairs and into her warm
apartment. I hid the cross and the book in the closet in
the bathroom. We sat on the couch. I tried to think of
something to do to get us both out of the mess and find
out who had killed Tony. I had a sudden inspiration,
the kind that oftimes sneaks up on you and bites you on
the knee like a crazed dwarf. I got up and went to her
phone and dialed information for New York City.

"What are you doing?" Ginny asked.

"Being a detective," I said. There was a sputtering
ring, and an operator finally asked me what in the hell
I wanted. Say what you want to about antitrust, the
breakup of the Bell Corporation just left a bunch of
surly operators.

"New York City information?" I asked.

"Yes?"

"Do you have a number for a Sandy Marcello? I
asked. "Or maybe Alessandro Marcello." I heard her
muttering something, hitting computer keys. She
cleared her throat. I wanted to ask if she'd been eating
pâté de foie gras and drinking Zinfandel when I
interrupted.

"That number has been disconnected," she said.

I frantically took my billfold out and looked in the
dim light at some numbers I had written earlier.

"Oh, that was the 554-1545 number, I remember
now," I said.

"Yes, sir," she said. Laurence Olivier, eat your heart
out. I hung up and cackled like a maniac and rubbed
my hands together. Ginny smiled at me, and I calmed
down somewhat. It was easy to lose sight of the Big
Picture when you got so excited by a minor victory.

"Are you going to tell me, or do we play charades?" she asked.

"I got Tony's recent phone bills from his desk before Sherrill got killed, and the one call that seemed wrong, lots of calls, was this number in New York. I just happened to guess that it might be the number of the man in the little black book here. I got lucky."

"So what does that mean?"

"I don't have a clue," I admitted.

"Then why were you crowing like a rooster?" she asked.

"Don't ever ask a question like that," I said. "We sleuths are devious people and will do anything to find out information. It means that a guy named Sandy Marcello lives in New York and might be connected with the theft of the cross."

"Maybe he's with the Mafia," said Ginny. She stared straight away from me vacantly, and I could see she did not think much of the idea.

"Let's not think about it now," I said. I wasn't, in fact, thinking much about it. I was thinking about going to bed and holding her against me. And I was thinking of sleep. It felt good to be working, but I was still out of shape. I didn't know if I'd live long enough ever to get back in shape.

"It's all awful," she said, but she seemed to snap out of her reverie. "All day today, I had the feeling they were watching me but wouldn't hurt me because they didn't know where the cross was."

"You should be the sleuth," I said. "With Tony out of the way, their best bet is to follow us for a while, figure out what we're doing and then do something."

"Like what?"

"They'll ask us to give it back," I said. I turned out the light and we sat there in the darkness.

"Oh great," she said. We were both silent for a long time, neither in a hurry for what we both knew would happen next. "Hank, I keep asking myself what in the world I'm doing here with you."

"Has your self answered yet?" I asked.

"I do like the way you look and all," she said. "Maybe I've always been attracted to older men."

"Older men?" I cried. "Wait till you see my collection of trusses. That'll dazzle you." She giggled in the darkness.

"That's not what I mean," she whispered. "And even though I'm supposedly aiming for the life of a scholar, there's something about jocks. I don't know. You used to be a jock and all. In some ways, you're still a jock."

"I've been invited to the Bean Bag Internationale in Paris next summer, too," I said. "I'm a physical kind of guy."

"That's it," she said. "I've known lots of guys who were either smart or physical. You're the first I've ever met who was both."

"Like for me to quote one Leaf of Grass?" I asked.

"I'm ready for bed," she said.

"That's what the dark is for, sweetheart," I said.

"I can't see," she said. Her voice was smiling. A small light oozed through the window and into the room, and after a moment I could see her standing and starting to take off her blouse.

"Lust isn't a pretty sight, ma'am," I said in my deepest voice. She said something like "Jeez," and I followed her through the door and into the bedroom.

S UNDAY MORNING IS THE PERFECT TIME to
bother people because they believe you will
have the common courtesy to leave them alone
on their day of rest. I didn't.

I left Ginny's house early and drove to the Decatur
Greyhound bus station and rented a locker and put the
cross in it, something I learned from watching old
movies on TV.

I came cruising into a Waffle House, where the food
is so-so, but the coffee is always terrific. I read the
Sunday *Journal-Constitution* as I munched on some
whole-wheat toast and sipped my black coffee. A dour
man and his wife were eating in the booth behind me;
she kept correcting his behavior and he kept snorting
like a hog.

The story was on page ten, about twelve column
inches worth. I read it a couple of times. It said that

there would be a coroner's inquest into Tony's shooting, but that no such action was contemplated for his late wife, who had already been buried in her hometown. There was a picture of Steed looking steely-eyed at the camera. The writer said that the APD suspected a drug connection in the slaying and went on to mention that Tony Browning was a known drug seller. It was all wrapped up neatly. But it wasn't so neat. I knew it, and someone knew I knew it.

I finished the toast and coffee and paid a waitress who came from the same factory as Treena at the Primate Haus.

"My compliments to the chef," I said as I was leaving. "The texture of the toast was a marvel." She looked at me the way Treena does. It was partly cloudy and too warm for October. I still had to wear a jacket to conceal the gun, but that's the price you pay to stay alive sometimes in this wretched world.

I decided to drive over to Jack Railsback's house. He lived on the northeast side, not far from Tony's place, and when I got there, a heavy fog had settled in over the suburbs. My car sounded like a jungle cat in the stillness of the neighborhood. I turned it off and got out. Jack's house was an embarrassment to anyone with a sense of restraint: three stories, Scandinavian, with blond wood everywhere, angles and glass, and a huge weeping willow out front.

"Willow, weep for me," I said. My voice was lost within the warm shroud of the fog. I went to the door and was staring at the lighted doorbell and thinking of how it looked like Tinker Bell when the door opened, and Jack was standing there in a stylish robe.

"What are you doing here?" he asked, yawning. "I was coming out for the paper." He didn't seem happy to see me.

"I just wanted to talk for a while," I said. He nodded and yawned again.

"Let me get the paper," he said. He went down the driveway and plucked the paper from his mailbox. It's illegal to stuff a paper in a mailbox, but sometimes delivery people like to live life on the edge. I waited at the door as Jack walked back and then followed him inside. We walked down a long corridor that ended at the kitchen where a pot of coffee was brewing. His kitchen was larger than I remembered. I had only been over here two or three times, and not in the past year. At one time, he was living with the most beautiful woman I had ever seen. I forget her name, but she had a tiny body that bulged in all the right places and just seeing her walk across the room made my palms sweat.

"The world's a sick place," he said with more emotion than I suspected. "I just can't figure them out."

"But you were once in that game," I said softly. His jaws were set and he looked grim.

"Coffee?"

"Is it decaf?"

"Hell, no," he said.

"Okay," I said. "Black." I waited for him to say something as he poured me a cup. I sat on a barstool and sipped my coffee while he leaned against a counter. Through double glass doors you could see his back yard, which had been beautifully landscaped with rocks and cacti and pathways.

"I wish you would stop bringing that up," he said unhappily. "I sold a few bales of marijuana for Tony.

That's it. When I found out what it was like, I got out."
Jack was a smart man. Maybe the most clever man I
had ever met. It could be the truth.

"Had you seen Tony and Sherrill much lately?" I
asked. He sighed and walked to the glass doors and
looked out.

"No," he said. "They were like children, both of
them." He looked down into his coffee, and I could
guess he was checking his reflection. He chewed on
his lip absently. "I hadn't seen either of them for
weeks until Sherrill asked me to go get you to find
Tony."

"So you didn't have any idea of the kinds of things
Tony had been doing lately," I said. Jack nodded
slightly.

"I told you at the office I didn't," he said. He nodded a few more times. "I'm sorry I lost my temper
with you, but I was upset about Sherrill." I started to
say something, but I was unrolling the chronology in
my mind. It took a few seconds, but then I put it in
order: I talked to him *before* I went over to Sherrill's and
found her body. Maybe he just wasn't thinking clearly.
Maybe he had said exactly what he meant.

"That's understandable," I said. He cradled his coffee and leaned aganst the glass, trying to look like an
ad from *Gentleman's Quarterly*. His studied pose broke
for a moment, for one of those transparent flashes of
honesty that cannot be calculated or contrived. His
cheek twitched and then became still. He looked at me
and narrowed his eyes.

He walked around me and sat on a barstool next to
me. If we'd had a Ouija board, we could have asked
the spirits about Sandy Marcello. "Is this something
about Tony?"

"Might be," I said. I lit a cigarette, as much for effect as pleasure.

"All I know is that those people he was dealing with are real bad," he said. "I asked around, few people I know, and they said Jake Shuler is not somebody to fool with. I think the police have it well under control. If I were you, I'd get rid of the case, turn over any evidence you have to the guys who are looking into it and look for some other business."

"What makes you think I've found any evidence?" I said. He sighed heavily.

"I just think it's bad news," he said. "I'd hate to see you get hurt."

I remembered the first time I'd met Jack, one night at a bar when he'd tagged along with Tony and Sherrill. I did not dislike him, but even then he was vague to me, like oil on a puddle, all surface. Jack was friendly to me, but I could never see behind his words as I could with Tony. There was no guile in Tony and he was almost incapable of sham, which is why he never really got rich in the drug business. Jack seemed capable of great salesmanship even in those days. He could make you believe things. It was an art I did not possess.

We saw a lot of each other then, but it was always as if through a screen. There was a distance that never dissolved.

Jack never talked about his past. He always wore clothes just this side of flashy, and the effect of seeing Jack was like seeing a zircon so marvelous you hoped it might really be a diamond. He was good-looking in the way all inexpensive things are.

"I'd hate to see me get hurt worse than you would," I said. "Thanks for the coffee." I got up and started for the door. He followed me, and when we got to the door, he said "Sure" very softly and closed the door as I went out. It was still foggy, but the sun was burning it off, and soon it would be another fine Sunday in the Land of Cotton.

I thought about the list of people I had first made up when Sherrill had given me the money. There was Jake Shuler and Jack and a few people I associated with Jake, like Sugar Barvano, an ex-fighter who liked to hang out, acting tough. And there was Carlyle Fallows, who, like Jack, had once worked with Tony Browning, but had long since given it up to enter legitimate business. And there was a woman. Christ, it seemed there was always a woman.

Her name was Rebecca Sanderson, and Tony had brought her around to show her off to me a year before. I am genetically old-fashioned, and the idea of him cheating on Sherrill as if it were nothing but an adolescent lark made me feel surly and uncomfortable. She was pretty in the way that ex-sorority girls are pretty, her face a fine lattice of makeup and guile, and she ran a boutique in Lenox Square, the oldest major league mall in town, which had lately undergone the facelift that one day she would need. It was open on Sunday, but it was early yet, so I decided to drive to Sugar's gym, which was in a defunct warehouse on the west side, just off I-20, which bisects the city east to west. I would go bother Carlyle Fallows later. He would just now be starting to read the financial news in the *New York Times*, and I hated to interrupt his reverie. Business is such a wonderful thing, and it has more addicts than heroin.

As I said, I don't like gyms very much. I don't understand abstractly pumping iron until your muscles strain the seams of your polyester leisure suit. But I understood staying in shape, since I once had been in shape myself, back when I played ball and the world was young.

The sun was out full, and the fog was wisping away when I pulled up in front of a warehouse on Casey Street that had only one word over the front door in letters six feet high: FISH. I knew Sugar would be there; he was always there. When I had first come to Atlanta and started my agency, I would come down and run around inside the old main warehouse to stay in shape. Tony had introduced me to Sugar. He had a small workout area with some weights, a ring and speed and heavy bags. It was warm or cool there, depending on the season, because of the forty-foot-high ceilings. It attracted mostly inner-city kids who thought they were Sugar Ray Leonard because they'd punched out the punk who had made a pass at their sister. It was a sad place, but all places are sad if you look at them long enough — stores in malls, insurance agencies, even Tunnels of Love.

The door was open. I went inside and saw three black kids working out, covered with a fine layer of sweat, two in the ring without headgear, banging on each other, the third lying on a bench and trying to keep a York barbell loaded with fat black plates from crushing his sternum.

I was staring at the light filtering from the skylight and thinking about nothing at all when I felt someone behind me. When you are tall as I am, you can gauge the size of someone coming up on you, and this man was much shorter, about the size of Sugar Barvano.

"I don't have the big room no more," he said. I turned and it was Sugar, of course. He looked a little to me like Carmen Basilio, the brow beetled from beatings over the years, the left ear pounded into an amorphous pulp. His hair was short and oily, and he wore a gray workout suit. He was sweating. I knew he stayed in shape, but it had been months since I had been here. I didn't know what he did with Shuler, but it was small stuff, probably nighttime enforcing. Tony and Sugar were great friends for a time, since Tony loved to talk boxing.

"How's it going, Sugar?" I asked. I lit a cigarette and waited for him to say something, but he sighed and folded his arms over his chest and looked up. His arms were huge, probably bigger than when he fought. I didn't understand someone wanting to make their muscles so big they were barely contained by flesh and sinew. I understood the kids grunting and sweating in the ring. The guy with the barbell got it off his sternum and put it back on the bench.

"It's shit," he said bitterly. "I don't understand nobody doing something like they done."

"Me neither," I said. He motioned for me to follow him into the tiny cubicle he called his office. I didn't know what it had been when this was a fish market. The only sound was the swish of gloves in the air, the sound of leather smacking on glossy flesh.

We went inside, and he closed the door behind us. He had a desk that was so high with old sports pages and bodybuilding magazines I felt like I should be wearing a hard hat. He sat in a beat-up old chair behind the desk and I eased down in a spindly ladder-back. On the wall were two posters, one from some fight with Archie Moore and the other for the Thrilla in Manila, with the much younger Muhammad Ali staring out ferociously.

"I was working for Sherrill, trying to find Tony," I said.

"You done a hell of a job of that," he said. "I read in the papers you was out there on Stone Mountain meeting the man when he got shot. I got me the idea they wanted to of shot you, if you'd a give a reason."

"Don't give me a hard time," I said wearily. "It's been rougher on me. I just want to know what you hear. I'm trying to find out why it all happened."

"I don't work for Jake no more, Hank," he said. I stubbed out my Camel in an ashtray surmounted by an indifferent-looking hula girl. I thought for a moment she had winked at me, but it was probably just an illusion when smoke gets in your eyes.

"Everybody tells me that, Sugar," I said. "To hear his protégés talk, the man's sitting alone up there with his ferrets, out of business. I just want to know what you heard." He shrugged, and the massive shoulders and neck pulsed. You could set a quarter in the cleft of his deltoids and it wouldn't fall out.

"I heard Tony'd been screwing around with Jake's money," he said. "You do something like that, you wind up with extra lead in your body."

"Who told you that?"

"I heard it around."

"Around where?" He stared at me as if he wanted me to put on the gloves so he could beat me until I looked like Poppin' Fresh. I stared back as hard as I could, but he knew he could kill me with his hands, and that gives you the advantage every time.

"This is a damn thing," he said finally, looking away from me. Maybe staring was the career I'd been looking for. "Just on the street. I heard it from a guy I know.

A guy used to fight. Ain't nobody you'd never heard of."

"Do I get three guesses?"

"Name's Silvio, never heard no last name," he said. "He's a fink."

"You mean a paid informant?" I wanted to make sure my criminal slang was right. I grew up reading about shivs, but you never hear about them anymore.

"That's what they tell me," he said. I didn't ask Sugar what he was doing talking to a stool pigeon, but maybe I should have.

"Have you heard anything from Tony in the past two or three weeks?" I asked. He stared at the hula girl.

"Not for about a month, I reckon," he said. "Last time I seen him, he come by and tried to work out, but his heart wasn't in it. You can tell. He looked like something was bothering him." I could hear, outside in the gym, the grunts of the fighters hitting each other harder than they needed to. Sad.

"You hear anything on the streets about Tony being involved with a heist?"

He stared at me again, so I went to work and stared back as if it were my profession. He blinked first again and merely shook his head slowly from side to side. I got up and went back out of the smoky office and into the gym. Not much was happening. The black kid doing bench presses was now working on the speed bag, hammering away with an angry rhythm. I took out my Parker ballpoint, the one Wanda had given me, and wrote my phone number on a piece of paper.

"Call me you hear anything," I said as I gave it to him. He folded it without looking at it and I went back outside. I felt better going out, as you feel better going out of a doctor's office when you find out your brain tumor was only a headache. I stood there for a minute, trying to decide who to see next. By now, Carlyle Fallows would be doing his situps, breaking into a sweat and then smiling like Buddha at his own good health. I needed to see him. More, I needed to see Ginny Calvert. When I had left her, she had been curled up against me, breathing deeply, her hair spilling off the pillow and onto my shoulder. In only a few days, we had come to care for each other. Such things only seem improbable to those who have never really been alone. But I knew that such loves were often thin as the fog that was now dissolving high over the city.

I was standing there thinking poetic thoughts when two men grabbed me from the side. I turned and raised my hands, but it was too late. Both were large and meaty, one a black man with thick features and a body like a garage door. The other was white, about three inches taller than me, weighing maybe 280. They jerked me back around the side of the old warehouse like I was a Ken doll, and they were going to break my arms off for the sheer boredom of it all.

"Excuse me, gentlemen, but I think you're mugging the wrong person," I said. I was glad I'd left part of the money at Mrs. Gunnerson's and part of it at Ginny's. But I knew these men were not after cash, though they'd take it for a lark if I had any.

"Shut the hell up," the tall one said.

"I'm just in town for the Elks Club convention and I was looking for a newsstand to buy a copy of *Punks Illustrated*," I choked. They took me into the shadows. One of them reached behind me and lifted my .38 with practiced skill.

"What's this, a damned toothpick?" the black man asked. I was about to make another snappy comeback when the white guy hit me in the stomach so hard my knees buckled, and I went down to the greasy pavement. The whole placed smelled of garbage. I felt sick to my stomach, queasy. It had been a while since I'd been hit that hard, and most people have no idea how much a swift smack in the solar plexus can hurt.

"Get up, asshole," said the white guy. I groaned and jumped up with all the power I had, which wasn't as much as it once was. You lose some of your timing when you drink as much I had lately. I came up under his shoulder and knocked him down, and my gun, which he was holding, went skittering across the dark pavement. I turned to the black man and he hit me in the mouth so hard I went down faster than any law Newton ever formulated.

They were both on me then, kicking me, hitting me. I covered my face as best I could, but when I did that, they were breaking my ribs. I thought about screaming for help, but that was another part of the Prince Code, so I was dumbly getting the shit beat out of me when I heard a voice from the front of the building and felt the fists and shoes suddenly leave. The leather smacked as they ran to a car somewhere and drove off. I was lying there with my face on the pavement, wondering if they'd broken anything important, when Sugar Barvano leaned down and looked at me.

"Jesus H. Christ," he said. He helped me up, but it hurt so bad I could barely walk back inside. The boxers stared at me as I came in, but they did not offer to help, and I didn't blame them. For most of these in-town kids, pain was more like a brother than a fiend in the dark.

"Did you see them?" I finally asked, propped up back in the chair in his small airless office.

"Never seen 'em before," he said. "Looked like hired help. Bat men. Think they wanted you to think things over."

"Yeah," I managed to say. He took a cigarette from the pack and slid it between my lips and lit it, a gesture of friendship that spoke more than we ever would. My right eye was swollen completely shut, and there was pain all over my skull and from the top of my rib cage to my pelvis on both sides. I was getting pretty damned easy to follow, too. It was the perfect place to get the shit stomped out of you.

I sat there for maybe half an hour with a wet towel over my face before I creaked up and went back out the door. This time, I was wary, but they were long gone. I should have gone to a hospital, but I walked back into the alley and found my gun where they'd left it in their rush. No telling what they would have done if Sugar hadn't come out for a breath of air.

Maybe one of the guys was Sandy Marcello. Whoever they were, they might soon make another push on Ginny, and the thought hurt almost as much as my ribs. I got in the Buick and, looking in the mirror so much I nearly wrecked a couple of times, drove back downtown to Peachtree.

Downtown Atlanta on a late Sunday morning moves along anyway, not caring for a day of rest. I drove up Peachtree for a while and then cut over to Piedmont before turning right on Ponce de Leon. I drove out past the Yaarab Temple with its green bronze onion dome, through small shopping centers propped against the morning light, many open for business. I came past the old Sears Building, looking like a monument to Queen Victoria, and just past it, through an underpass, traffic was being routed to the left lanes while a gang of workmen with long metal poles punched the glass windows out of an old building. I stopped at a light and the sound of glass on the pavement was like a waterfall, bright and inviting.

I turned off on North Highland near the old Plaza Drug Store Building. It was now a renovated pharmacy, and the rest of the building was divided into several smaller shops. Once, Plaza Drugs was the only all-night pharmacy in the area, with a lunch counter and the most unintentionally funny ads on TV.

I turned left on North Highland, then right on St. Charles and rolled to a stop in front of Ginny's house. It was not yet noon.

Walking up the steps was painful, and just before I got to the door, Ginny opened it and stared at me with her mouth open and managed to say "My God," before she took me by the arm and helped me to the couch.

"What did they do to you?" she cried. Her voice was shaking. I took off my shirt. I glanced down and could see the bruises already starting to wander down my chest. I felt my ribs for a moment and none seemed broken, though they hurt. I'd broken a rib in spring training once when I fell over an outfield fence, and I knew the difference.

"They urged me to use the power of positive thinking," I said. I lay down, and she went into the bathroom and got a damp washcloth and came back and bathed my wounds. It was almost worth getting mugged for. She had showered not long before and smelled freshly of soap, and as she touched my face gently I pulled her down and kissed her.

"What did they say?" she asked, her face not more than an inch from mine.

"I was at the gym run by a guy I know named Sugar Barvano, who used to work for Jake Shuler," I said. "When I came out after talking to him, two escaped gorillas from the Atlanta Zoo pummeled me until Sugar happened to come out." I winced and tried to get comfortable, but it wasn't much use. "They didn't say much of anything. They just took me in an alley and tried to perform some freelance chiropractic."

"My God," said Ginny Calvert.

I lay there most of the day, dallying in Ginny's cool splendor. The football season had begun and the Falcons were playing the Giants, and I had been a Giants fan back when Robustelli, Katkavage, Tittle, Gifford and other great men played. I didn't know any of the Giants now, but I pulled for them anyway. But beating the Falcons is like tripping a dwarf, so I went to sleep long before New York had put in its third string.

When I awoke, I hurt so bad I could barely move, but I struggled up anyway and took a shower. I stayed under the hot water for a long time and when I came out, there was a note on the table from Ginny saying she had gone out for a pizza. I did not like it. I didn't want her out at all. In fact, I was thinking of asking her to come with me to Florida where we could spend the thousand I had left lying in the sun drinking rum and living the good life.

An hour later, Ginny had not come home, and I began to think that my worst fears might be realized. I clipped on my gun, and wondered when I should start searching for her.

WAITING AROUND HER APARTMENT WAS unbearable, so I drove out looking for her. There was a food store on Ponce de Leon that she used, so I went in there first, and they knew her, but she hadn't been in that evening. I had rummaged through her dresser until I had found an old photo, hoping someone could recognize her.

Choked with panic, I drove. By then my face was a throbbing mask and my chest hurt so bad it felt like I'd been backed into a wall by an elephant. But all pain is relative, and the pain I felt was from stupid impotence; I should have taken her away or offered to give the hoods the cross right off. What was I doing getting her more deeply involved every minute?

I drove down Ponce de Leon to Peachtree and turned right, past the Fox Theater with its domes and turrets, passing men and women in evening finery gathering there for a concert. I felt like a leper among them, and when I stopped at a light, I half expected them to come running up to the Buick yelling, "Unclean! Unclean!"

I didn't know where to go. I drove past Ginny's house after making a big loop out to I-85 where they had been rerouting everything in an anarchic fit for a couple of years. Her car was still gone. I drove over past Mrs. Gunnerson's, but I didn't stop.

After a time, it occurred to me that if she were in trouble, she would call me at her apartment or maybe they would, whoever "they" were, so I drove back over there. When I got out, a wind had come up, blowing the leaves idly down the street. The stars had gone. A cold rain would soon settle in. It reminded me of the last scene in *On The Beach*.

I sat on the couch for a long time sipping a beer and being miserable, looking at the icons of her life scattered around me: fuzzy house slippers, a copy of *The Portable Faulkner*, her tall boots standing there waiting for her smooth legs. I stared at the phone until I thought it would rise and drift around the room.

After a while, I was too sleepy to think sequentially, and I went to sleep on the couch. I dreamed of William Faulkner, seeing him walking lazily under the umbrage of live oaks. He smiled at me, and we drank together, and then he was dressing out with me for a game. He looked really natty in uniform, white hair and dapper mustache. I was throwing around with him in the outfield when a bell rang for the start of the game. He looked puzzled and then said, "They don't ring for the start of baseball games; that's horse racing."

It was the telephone. I jumped up and stared at it and let it ring twice more before I left Faulkner and moved back toward Ginny Calvert. I stood, feeling the familiar drunk's equilibrium problem, and picked it up.

"Yeah? I said groggily. I took out a cigarette and lit it. The person on the other end wasn't in too much of a hurry.

"You ready to talk?" a man's voice said. I tried to hear more than he said: it was uneducated, rough as a blister.

"Yeah," I said. The room seemed very small and I realized my hands were shaking.

"We won't hurt her," he said. "Unless you screw up."

"I want her back," I said.

"You smart," he said. He put his hand over the mouthpiece and said something to someone else in the room. It was a local call, no feedback on the lines or interference. "You know what we want."

"Tell me."

"You want her to get hurt?"

"No."

"Then bring it." He turned away and said something else to a man. The caller did not have his hand completely over the mouthpiece, and I could hear the other man, and there was something oddly familiar about the timbre and cadence of his voice.

"Where?"

"Wait a minute." They talked some more.

"Yeah?"

"Down across from the old Sears on Ponce de Leon, where the Crackers used to play," he said. "It's a parking lot now."

"I know where it is," I said.

"In the back," he said. "You bring it."

"You'll bring the girl?" I asked.

"Yeah," he said. "Then you forget about it, and we forget about you. Or we'll hurt you again and her, too."

"Nobody hurt me," I lied. He laughed, a short, cruel laugh.

"Be there at four on the dot," he said. I looked at my watch. It was 3 a.m. They probably weren't far away or they would have left themselves more time.

"Okay," I said. He hung up and I slowly eased the phone back into its cradle. At least something was happening. I washed my face and went back outside. It was not raining yet. I drove to the Waffle House and got a large black coffee and drank most of it in four gulps on my way to the Decatur bus station.

I was feeling better, blood throbbing with adrenalin, a substance that makes you win baseball games, possess unaccountable bravery or have heart attacks. The bus station was quiet, and no one was around but an old wino leaning against one wall, snoring merrily. There but for fortune, I thought. I retrieved the cross from the locker and walked crisply back to the Buick. I laid my gun out on the seat beside me, turned on the light for a moment and stared at the cross. I threw it casually on the seat and rumbled off into the pre-dawn darkness.

I came out of Decatur and turned left onto Scott Boulevard and headed back toward Atlanta. Scott Boulevard turns into Ponce de Leon not far from the Fernbank Science Center. They have a planetarium, and once I had taken Wanda Mankowicz there to watch the stars revolve over our dreamy heads.

I lit a cigarette. I was scared. They could take the cross and shoot both of us on the spot. I had seen honor among thieves in practice before, and I knew that pulling a trigger requires more anger than courage, and most people have more anger than anything except maybe fear. Love is way down the line.

Atlanta is quiet at 4 a.m. I slowed down as I came toward the old Sears Building. No one was breaking glass anymore, but the traffic was rerouted away from the building next to Sears where urban renewal was in full bloom by day. I came through the underpass and tried to remember what it looked like when old Ponce de Leon Stadium was there, how my old man had brought me up here to see the Crackers play so many years ago. I could almost say my love of baseball started here.

I pulled slowly into the parking lot. The lot is long and deep and all kinds of chic stores and offices are scattered along the third base sides. Many of the stores had lights on to ward off the night, the way Pennsylvania Dutch farmhouses have hex signs painted on them.

I drove slowly toward the back of the lot, past a crippled children's clinic, toward a dark area bordered by kudzu. My hands felt wet on the steering wheel. There are times when you have to be prepared to die for something, and you know, almost genetically when they are. For country, for family, for flight. For what you think may be love.

A dark green Volare station wagon was parked up against a corner, pointed out. Whatever happened to sleek back limousines? When they saw my car coming toward them, the two front doors sprang open like an albatross flapping its wings once before flight. I stopped about fifty yards from them and put the car in park, opened my front doors, grabbed my gun and stood up in a crouch, my head and shoulders just over the door. Two men got out of the Volare. They looked around. It had to be done quickly. A cop driving past would stop, and then I would lose Ginny. One of the men walked to the back door, opened it and pulled Ginny out. Her hands were tied behind her back. It was the same two men who had beaten me.

"Get your goddamn hands off me!" she shouted. Both men tried to shush her, which would have been comical had the situation not been deadly. "I mean it."

"You got it?" the man still at his door shouted in a choked voice.

"Yeah," I said. My voice sounded like God's in the parking lot. I leaned back down and picked the cross up and came up carefully and held it up. I also held up my gun, just over the door. "Let her start walking and I'll set it down on the pavement between us." The two men talked, as if they had not planned how to make the swap. For them even to be considering my terms was odd, as if they were amateurs at all this instead of professionals. They should be dictating terms.

"Okay," the man with Ginny said.

"Help me, Hank," Ginny cried as she walked past him. There was no sense in trying to make a move to keep the cross. They would get it sooner or later. I met Ginny midway between the cars, but we said nothing as I set the cross down not far from a water-stained coupon. I held my gun up and started backing up. They stared at me. Ginny struggled into my car.

I was almost to the car when I heard the explosion. There is no other way to describe the sound. You get to know the sound guns make, the "crack" of a .22, the "bam" of a .38 and the hollow "choom" of a .45. This was an explosion, the sound of a high-powered rifle, probably a .30-.30. I went down instinctively and pointed my gun at the men ahead of me. One of them groaned and collapsed on the pavement. The other looked wildly around, pointing his handgun. I started scuttling like a crab back toward the Buick. I could almost hear the rifleman taking a bead on someone. The second thug started running across the parking lot wildly, out of control, gone with fear. There was a second explosion, and he pitched forward on to his face and did not move. I made it to the Buick, put it in gear and screeched off, leaving a trail of rubber forty yards long across the lot.

"Get on the floor!" I shouted at Ginny. She fell down awkwardly. It was hard for her, with her hands tied up, but she got down in the ample floorboards of my car. I put my head down low where I could just see over the steering wheel. She was cursing angrily. I waited for the third shot, but it never came.

"What in the hell is happening?" she asked.

"Somebody set those guys up," I said.

"Are they shot?"

"They won't have to worry about breakfast," I said.

I came out of the lot onto Ponce de Leon without looking in either direction, hung a left and got the hell out of there as fast as I could without attracting the attention of every policeman in north Georgia. I kept glancing in both rear-view mirrors, out both windows to cover my flanks, and I thought I saw a car. But the streets were nearly deserted, the only car I saw driving toward Ginny's house being an asthmatic old VW bug that couldn't catch an elephant in a bowl of milk.

I pulled to a stop in front of her place, breathing hard, trying to think of what to do next. They obviously knew where she lived. But perhaps the only ones who knew that were the men who had been shot. I did not know what was safe. We could go over to Mrs. Gunnerson's. Maybe that made the most sense.

"Where the hell are we?" Ginny asked. "My hands are killing me." I told her where we were, and after making sure no one was near us, I lifted her up off the floor and untied the heavy hemp cord with which she had been bound. I put it in the glove compartment.

"I want you to get some clothes and come back over to my place," I said. "It might be safer there for a while." She was trembling and unhappy. She rubbed her wrists as we walked up the stairs, and then she put her arm around my waist and held me to her for a moment and looked up at me.

"Thanks," she said softly.

"Yeah," I managed. My ribs and skull were hurting again from the drubbing down at Sugar Barvano's. I opened the door and lunged inside with my gun drawn but the room was quiet and Benjy the cat merely sat on the table staring at me.

"I'll have to take him," she said. She piled a couple of days' worth of clothes on the sofa and I carried them out while she took out Benjy's litter pan and a few cans of food. We locked her apartment up. She looked wistfully around.

"You okay?" I asked.

"I was thinking about 'you can't go home again,'" she said.

"Thomas Wolfe always was full of shit," I said airily, and we went down the steps and drove off, me, Ginny

Calvert and her fuzzball cat, just as the sun was yawning over the city.

No one was up yet, not even Dicky Thacker, but by the time we had everything in my room, you could hear the stirring, showers running, a radio somewhere talking in muted tones about what had happened the night before. I closed the blinds and smoked a cigarette. We undressed and got into bed. Benjy was prowling around the room trying to find a way out.

"Do we go to the police now?" she asked. We were far too tired for love, but she put her cheek in the hollow of my chest and snuggled close.

"I need to hear what happened, first," I said. "It's become a conundrum." I could feel sleep coming over both us. If I had known death was there in the room with us I would not have cared.

"I never met anybody who talks like you," she said, her voice becoming thick.

"I never met anybody who listens like you," I said. I tried to think of something else to say, but she was breathing deeply by then, and I could only see the emerald eyes of the cat watching me as I went under.

Later, we sat in a booth at the Primate Haus, eating eggs and toast and sipping our coffee, sitting side by side as we read the front-page story in the *Journal*. It would be the same story as the one in the *Constitution*. Once, the papers had separate staffs and competed to give the city a better product, but now it was the same paper with a different name. Let's hear it for individuality.

What I read hurt almost as much as my bruised body. When I had awakened at about two that Monday afternoon, I could barely move, but Ginny helped me into the shower, and now I was feeling better. It takes a while to get over a good beating. Mrs. Gunnerson had tactfully not said much about my swollen face or the way I walked, or even the fact that I had a girl in my room. I think somehow it comforted her.

But our "lead tenant," Mrs. Carreker, saw the matter in a different light. A red one, to be precise. She stared icily at me throughout the time we stood in the foyer trying to get away from Mrs. Gunnerson, then pulled me aside and said we would have to have a talk about the rules. She should know about the house rules; she wrote them and posted them on all our doors one night like a suburban Luther. I could see Mildred "Babe" Ruth sitting on the sofa watching a soap opera, smiling blandly at us. She approved of anything that irritated Mrs. Carreker.

"You didn't hear?" I said to Mrs. Carreker. "The Supreme Court has thrown our rules out. They said it violated the thirtieth amendment."

"What is that?" she asked unhappily.

"It outlawed statutory tackiness," I said. Ginny coughed to hide a laugh, and Babe Ruth licked her lips, which I took as a sign of approval. Mrs. Carreker's arrogance crumbled just a bit, and she was still standing there trying to remember the Bill of Rights when Ginny and I came outside into the October light.

The story in *The Journal* was nearly stupefying. I read it twice, all the while saying clever things like, "No!" and "What in the hell!" Like a nightmare, like a recurrent dream that kept leading me down the same corridor, Adam Steed stared out at me from the page. Drugs. It all had to do with drugs, he said. They had found half a pound of pure heroin in the car. There was no mention of a cross.

The men were Kenneth Shallowford, 36, and Renee Labatte, 46. They were apparently from out of town. They had both been shot to death by someone using a high-powered rifle. There was a picture of the back of one of the men. A dark snake of blood wandered from him across the parking lot. Steed said they were drug dealers connected with Jake Shuler and involved in the deaths of Tony and Sherrill Browning.

"I don't believe it," Ginny said testily. "I don't think they were into drugs."

"Is that a face that would lie to you?" I asked. I pointed at Adam Steed.

"They were ignorant men," she said, shuddering.

"You want to talk about it yet? Did they hurt you?" The thought made me mildly ill.

"I was parking at that store to get a frozen pizza when they jumped me," she said. It was only a block away, but I'd missed her car, which was parked to one side where the light was bad. She had told me that much the night before, and I had called and told them we'd pick up her car sometime today. "I knew what was happening as soon as they grabbed me. It was so quick I only had time to get mad. They put a cloth over my eyes. One drove, and the other held me in the back seat and tied my hands behind my back and shoved me in against the door."

"How long did they drive?"

"Must have been a couple of hours, but I think it was all around town, not out anywhere, because I could hear cars all the time, and we kept stopping for lights. They made me lie down on the seat, and after a time, the man in the back seat with me got out and sat in the front. The large one was the same man who threatened me the other day."

"Really?" I didn't know what that meant. "What did they say?"

"Not too damn much," she said. I lit a cigarette, and she fumbled in her purse and took out one, and I lit it for her. "One of them kept saying 'Now, you think?' and stuff like that. Then we drove down a gravel driveway and the car stopped. We stayed there a long time and one of them went somewhere. I thought they were going to kill me, and I had all kinds of ideas about escaping, but I was just paralyzed I was so scared. The man on the front seat turned on the radio. He listened to a country station, and that seemed so odd to me. I don't know what I expected but I didn't expect Porter Waggoner."

"Then what?"

"Then, after a while, the other guy came out, and we drove to the parking lot where you saved me," she said.

"Gee, you make it sound so dramatic," I said. She looked at me the way Treena looked at me. "Sorry. Okay. When you were stopped earlier, can you remember hearing anything, smelling anything?"

"It was just a gravel driveway," she said, trying to remember. "With bushes close on either side of the car. They scraped when we went past. A couple of potholes in the road. I had the feeling it was still close to town. I could hear the man who got out walk on a plank porch or something and the slamming of maybe a screen door. That's about all."

"Hmmm."

"But Hank, who killed them?" she asked. "When I heard that gun go off, I thought I'd been shot it scared me so bad. I thought they were shooting at us."

"Somebody hired them to get the cross and then killed them," I said. "It was easier to hire two thugs and kill them than risking rifling through your apartment or mine with people all around. I'd guess they never had anything to do with Shuler, and that they were just petty crooks who had patsy tattooed across their foreheads. They must have had about ten seconds to realize it when the firing started."

"I think we ought to tell the police," she said. She blew smoke out her nose like a dragon. "And I think I ought to be in class." She looked at her watch. "Jesus Christ. My seminar on Faulkner starts in twenty minutes."

"I don't want to talk to the police," I said. "Everything is so neat, and Steed is beginning to hate the sound of my name."

"What does that mean?"

"It means I'm going to find out who killed Sherrill and Tony," I said. The words sounded brave and mindless, but the effect was even better than I had hoped, both on Ginny and me. She started to smile, and then she did. "Smile like that, and I'll have to do something macho and sexist in front of all these good people." There was nobody there but us, Treena, the cook and the hole Bull Feeney had smashed in the wall.

"Like what?" She leaned her face on her hands and her eyes looked soft and vulnerable. I kissed her, good and long, and her lips were soft and loving. It was likely the best kiss in Atlanta since Rhett Butler had stomped off from Scarlett. "Oh," she said when we finally came apart, "that." And then I kissed her again.

10

S HE STAYED WITH ME FOR TWO DAYS
    before she decided to go home. During that
    time, I drove her to class, picked her up, took
    her out to eat — everything but put my class
ring on her finger. I pretended I was working with
what was left of Sherrill's money, but I was becoming
indolent and slothful in Ginny's company. Maybe
that's why she left.

I felt sure, by then, that whoever had set up
the recovery of the cross was gone or had no intention
of causing more trouble. He had what he wanted.
I didn't. So I didn't worry too much about
Ginny.

"Give me a few days," she said when I took her
home. "Then call me. I don't quite know what to
think." When I drove off, she was standing at the
window holding Benjy. Maybe I should stop this crap

and try to get tenure at Georgia State teaching the gestalt of private investigation.

I got up on Wednesday morning and drove out on the interstate, driving east on I-20. Sometimes I'd drive over to Madison, a small town sixty miles away, and look at the antebellum homes. Today, I just wanted to drive. I went slow. My car objected strenuously, so I went fast, about eighty, and soon I felt like Richard Petty. I put in an Andy Williams tape and stopped and bought a six pack of Olympia. King of the Road.

There was only one thing I could do: follow people around and see where they went. I couldn't afford to go to the Big Apple and search for Sandy Marcello, and I didn't know what Tony's little black book meant, though I was thinking on it when I wasn't singing along with Andy. What in the hell did "cheese" mean? I'd see about Rebecca Sanderson and Carlyle Fallows soon enough.

I decided to turn around and head back when I was halfway to Augusta. When I got back, I did what any experienced investigator would do. I went home and went to bed and slept until dark.

I decided to follow Jack Railsback first. I drove over to his office in Decatur. I knew his car would still be in the lot because he made a great show of Working After Hours to impress the employees. I didn't know what he did in his office, but I was reasonably sure it didn't involve insurance.

His Mercedes was parked in the same place I'd last seen it, arrogantly staring at a VW Rabbit not far away. I backed up in a spot right in front of Jack's car and gunned the Buick a couple of times to see if I could layer his hood ornament with high-octane exhaust.

Then I pulled away and parked in a spot where I could see the lights on in Jack's secretary's office, in the waiting room. Sure, it was a vapid gesture to try and deface his car, but character is only an unbroken series of successful gestures. Tell me I'm not literate.

About eight, the lights went out and, in a few minutes, Jack came walking across the parking lot carrying a briefcase. I watched him, unmoving, thinking about what he might know and how I might find it out. Unless I was off the mark, he knew about Sandy Marcello, and it was a presumption on my part, perhaps an incorrect one, that Sandy Marcello was involved in the theft of the cross.

I waited until Jack got in his car. I was having an idea altogether different from my first one. Sometimes I sit and think so fast that the ideas fight for a place to inhabit. Sometimes I just sit. I would break in his office. Why not? This building had next to no security and I had a way of acting official when caught in an illegal act.

Jack drove off, his car coughing and trying to dispel the heady bouquet left over from my Buick. I hoped his car didn't rat on mine, but you never can tell what a luxury car will do next. The lot was nearly deserted. I got out and slowly walked to the glass doors on the back side and went in.

Nobody seemed to be on the third floor. I always expect to see someone in Victorian dress, looking like Alistair Sim in *A Christmas Carol*, hunched over a ledger, worried and thinking about getting an extra lump of coal on Christmas Day. The Chamber of Commerce would probably never offer me a job. I stood in front of the door with "Railsback and Patton" on it for a moment, listening, making sure nobody was home.

Unlike cracking safes, I was pretty damn good at breaking and entering. Most door locks aren't interested in putting up a fight, and the one on Jack's office was screaming surrender after I'd been poking at it only a minute or so. I went inside and locked the door back behind me. I tried to remember what Jack's secretary looked like as I stared at her desk. I went on back to Jack's office, the one without the window. I closed the door and turned the light on.

The place was so bland that when I sat in his chair I expected a hygienist to come in the room any minute and tell me the doctor was ready for my root canal. I opened the middle drawer and slid it out as I backed up in the chair. It was full of paper clips and packs of Sweet 'N Low and, in the back, a copy of October's *Penthouse*. I did not have much time. You never can tell in a job like this when someone will come bopping in to ruin the party. I couldn't look at the *Penthouse* without being in danger. But what the hell, Sir Edmund Hillary didn't get to the top of Everest by being afraid.

Five minutes later, I finally folded the magazine back up and laid it to rest. I felt like breaking into a girls' locker room and falling on the floor and foaming at the mouth. I opened the top drawer on the right and found Jack's flipfile. I went straight to the Ms and there, right in front, was "Marcello, Sandy." It had the same number Tony had had on his phone bill. There was something written upside down at the bottom of the card. I picked up the entire file and turned it over. It said, "Anderson."

I was no fool. This was A Clue. I went through the rest of the file quickly. I didn't see much of interest until I got to S. When I first read the card, I went past it, the name seeming familiar but skating off my memory as a water bug skates on the patina of a swamp. I nearly didn't go back, but three names toward T something seemed odd, and I went back.

The name was Adam Steed.

I suddenly felt paranoid, sure that someone was heading for the office, maybe already inside. I felt trapped, wondering what in the hell Jack Railsback was doing with Steed's number. Maybe he just had a policy with Railsback and Patton. That was probably it, but I couldn't understand the coincidence. I scanned through to the end, put it back in the drawer. I opened the drawer under it and nothing much was in there but a bottle of Crown Royal and a $50 bill. I took a large gulp of the liquor and stole the money. Sometimes I act like pure trash, but if it's genetic, what the hell can you do about it?

I got up and pushed the chair back and turned out the light and went back out to the secretary's reception area. I listened. Nothing. I went back outside without seeing anybody, got in my car and drove toward Jack's house, not quite sure what I'd do.

There is a hill behind Jack's house that had not yet been bought up by developers because some rich people in the area have the silly idea that green space will add value to their homes. Any developer knows that trees are useless obstacles to the true reason for living: condominiums. I parked on the street a few houses away from Jack's mansion and walked through a yard where a chihuahua no bigger than a wharf rat was standing in a fenced-in back yard whining at the moon. Chihuahuas are okay, but I wonder sometimes if they should be technically classified as dogs. Bull Feeney told me one time he'd seen one mating with a frog, but Bull lies sometimes.

I found a comfortable place up on the side of the lightly wooded hill where I could look down into Jack's back yard, across the cactus garden, through the double glass doors. I got out my binoculars and looked down toward Jack's. He was not in the kitchen, but the light was on. He was home because his car was there. I waited. Patience, thy name is Prince.

About ten minutes later, I noticed that three houses down an indiscreet woman was undressing in her bedroom. She was probably my age, but so well preserved I wondered if her husband owned a formaldehyde company. Maybe they made it in the basement and bottled it, using a family crest.

A movement caught my eye back to the left. I glanced at Jack's house, and he was standing in the kitchen with another man. Having established that fact, I went back to the Formaldehyde Lady, but by then, she had slipped into a robe. Drat. I went back to Jack. I could see him and the other man clearly, and they were arguing. I had never seen the other man before. He was about thirty-five, shorter than Jack and out of shape, gut bulging out over his white shirt. His hair was longish. He looked strong in the way hard-fat men are strong. He probably couldn't run to the front door without getting winded, but he could break your head like a cantaloupe with one squeeze.

Maybe it was Sandy Marcello. Maybe it was Jack's bridge partner, and they were discussing strategy for the neighborhood tournament. I watched them for about twenty minutes, and then Jack turned the light out, and they went into another room. I checked out my other case (the woman down the street), but she was probably well into the third chapter of either *Buddenbrooks* or *Love's Flaming Passion*. I got up and came back down the hill. The chihuahua had apparently been let inside. Or maybe it had married a toad and moved into a less trendy neighborhood where the children wouldn't be teased as they grew up.

I took Jack's $50 and bought a bottle of Perrier-Jouet brut, 1964, which is so dry that if you didn't drink it you could put it in an hourglass. Then I drove toward Ginny's house.

I had called Paul Tenhoor that morning before I'd gone out driving to ask about Tony's body. They had finally completed the inquest, and a nephew in Wilmington, North Carolina, was flying down. According to Tony's will, his body had been cremated already and there would be no funeral service. Tenhoor only snorted when I asked when the results of the inquest would be made public. I figured a toast to the good times was at least in order. I tried to remember the good times, but all I could remember was Tony dying on the side of Stone Mountain. As he lay there, he kept reaching out for me, perhaps for a button on my shirt, but his hand kept falling back as he bled out. I say the cops murdered him. But he did have his gun out, and his wife had just been brutally killed. Damn.

I turned off Ponce de Leon on North Highland and then to St. Charles. I was becoming as accustomed to this neighborhood as I was to her face. I pulled to a stop in front of her house and went bounding up the stairs. I'd been working nearly all day, and I was feeling so sanctimonious I half thought someone would whisk me away to Bless the Fleet or perform a bar mitzvah. I cradled the Perrier-Jouet in my left arm and rapped smartly on the door. A man opened it.

"You must be Prince," he said without much enthusiasm. "Ginny." He called her name quietly, and she came behind him and touched him on the sleeve as she came out the door and pulled it to. We stood there. The man did not turn the porch light on and it was dim and breezy and very cool, almost cold.

"The Clean Books League has asked me to bring over this token of their appreciation for having been the last person on earth to read *Heidi*," I said, proffering the champagne. She didn't smile. "What's wrong?"

She walked to the balcony and looked down at the street.

"Who is that guy?" I felt ridiculous.

"My ex-husband," she said, turning to face me. She was not wearing a sweater, and she folded her arms tightly across her chest. "Look, I . . . I want to get away from all that. I needed somebody to talk to." She shuddered. I picked at the label of the bottle and nodded stupidly.

"Meaning me?"

"Don't put words into my mouth."

"Is that what he told you to do?"

"If he did, it's none of your business," she snapped. "Quit acting like you own me. I don't like feeling like property."

"I just thought the man who saves her life always gets the girl," I said.

"Please," she said. She was begging. She was scared, and I didn't blame her. She was scared of the kind of life I led, of what had happened to her quiet studious life since I had come to visit. For all she knew, I was involved in the crimes somehow and had her next on my list. Maybe the man inside had told her that.

"Okay," I said. "I understand. Well, it's time to be gallant and leave, I suppose." I wanted to do the final scene from *Casablanca*, but I felt too empty to be clever. "You've meant a lot to me. I just want you to know that." Her eyes were large and wet as I turned to go down the stairs, holding the bottle by its sweating neck.

"Hank?" she said as I hit the fourth step. I turned and looked at her.

"Yeah?"

"Take care of yourself," she said, voice shaky and full of pain. I only winked at her and came on down, crossed the street and sat in my Buick until I calmed down a little. Then I lit a cigarette and drove off, toward downtown Atlanta, opening the bottle of champagne on the way.

I knew what I would do. I had two pieces of information that had to mean something. In Tony's little black book, I had "Ander. S.C.","" and from Jack's flip-file, I had "Anderson." I had nothing better to do than check out that angle. Maybe I could get arrested and be made a ward of the state. That would be in the morning. Tonight, I was going to find out about the dead goons, Shallowford and Labatte.

Without Ginny to think of, my bruises were causing me some discomfort by then, so I drank most of the champagne in four or five gulps. What a waste to drink good champagne alone. I was drunk in short order, but I needed to be anesthetized to do what I was planning now. No arrests had yet been made, so I presumed somebody might be at Jake Shuler's place, maybe even the Big Cheese himself. I drove north on Peachtree Street. If you live in Atlanta, you're supposed to love Peachtree Street, but actually it's a general pain in the muffler.

I don't remember much about driving up to Shuler's house. I do remember stopping in front and staring at the tall fence around it and wondering if Steve McQueen could jump over it on a motorcycle. Except Steve McQueen was dead.

I was sitting there looking at the expanse of lawn and the house at the back of it when a man came out of nowhere and stuck a gun halfway up my nose as I leaned out the window. The man was enormously fat. He looked Samoan and had graying, curly hair and a beard. He wore a flower-print shirt that hung out over his pants and was big enough for a funeral tent. The gun was cold, and by looking directly down the barrel, I could see it was a magnum, a Dirty Harry gun that could blow my head clean off my shoulders. I was impressed by the man's sincerity.

"Bureau of Streets and Roads," I squeaked. "Is this where the pothole was reported?" He opened the door and jerked me out and pushed me up against the car and took my gun. "Or maybe it was a pothead. Sometimes I can't read my secretary's handwriting." He looked at me hard.

"You Prince," he said in wonder.

"That's funny, I am, too," I said. I extended my hand for him to shake, but he declined without much grace. I had lost my girl, just like I had lost Wanda Mankowicz. I didn't care what he did at the moment.

"Come on," he said. He took my arm and escorted me down a long driveway outside the fence on the side of the house. There was a gate, and he pushed a button and grunted something and there was the sound of a relay clicking and the gate suddenly opened.

"Whee doggies," I said. "Look at that." We went on inside and up some steps into the house. The furnishings had the look of being bought all at one time at a Norwegian clearinghouse. Everything was white or ivory: carpets, chairs, wall hangings, tables. "I thought bad guys were supposed to decorate everything in black."

"I'm gonget unhappy widju," the Samoan said. I thought about correcting his diction, but it seemed unwise for the moment so I merely smiled benignly. Maybe I'd send him a copy of *The Elements of Style* for Christmas. "Wait here."

I sat down in a white chair and took out a white cigarette and put the white match in an ivory ashtray. My head was swimming from the alcohol. The next day, champagne is something like an icepick in the cerebellum, but oh, the night!

I was sitting there admiring the decor when Manny Fargo came out, looking more like a ferret than ever. He was smoking a brown cigarette.

"Your decorator won't be happy with the brown cigarette," I said. He sat down across from me and made a face. "Is my old pal Jake here?"

"He's not here," Manny said. He looked drawn and worried. Maybe it was time to act my age.

"Well, I just want him to know that I was there when Shallowford and Labatte got escorted into the next world," I said.

"We know," said Manny Fargo.

"I beg your pardon?"

"We've been keeping a tail on you," he said. "We watched the whole thing happen, up until the shots were fired. Our man looking after you followed you and the girl instead of finding out what happened. You can't get decent fucking help these days."

"Elegantly put," I said. "Do you know who those two worms were? Steed said they worked for Jake." I had been followed again without knowing it.

"Steed," he said with much disgust. "Let me tell you something, that guy's a pain in the ass. I don't know who's talking to him, but they're full of shit. Those clowns never worked for Jake Shuler." He shook his head emphatically. A good sign. "They aren't even local, for Christ's sake. They come down here from Philadelphia, I heard. They was just punks up there, come down here looking for strongarm stuff, just amateurs, which is obvious by the way they was snuffed." He sniffed. "What I don't know was what you give them in a trade for the girl." I stared at him as clearly as I could. Maybe in all this they really didn't know about the cross. I shrugged and tried to smile winningly.

"It was what they were after," I said. "But I don't think it's going to do Jake any good any more. If I were him, I'd pack up the white cargo and leave before Steed finds something serious. Is it barely possible that a former confederate of Mr. Shuler somehow finagled this situation?"

"Fucking what the hell you're talking about?" said Manny Fargo. Maybe he could give Mrs. Gunnerson syntax lessons.

"I'm sorry," I said. "Let me rephrase it. Any ex-fucking guy work around here might have been the one to set it up on Jake, so's to make it look he's the one who done it?"

"Hell, no," said Manny Fargo. I can pick up a new language in a matter of minutes. A linguistic genius, that's what I am. "Nobody we know knew jackshit about these two clowns before they got here. Just punks."

"Would you tell Mr. Shuler that I asked after his health?" I said. I stood and wobbled toward the door. I heard Manny sigh, but he had nothing else to say. Business was bad. Maybe Adam Steed wasn't such a bad guy after all, if he put these weasels out to pasture. I made a mental picture of a cowboy placidly watching over a herd of weasels as the Giant Samoan escorted me to the fence, where he gave me back my gun.

"Thanks, pardner," I said. "It's tough riding the range, but a bit of hospitality makes the saddle sores disappear, right?" I turned and walked down the driveway, fighting off the bushes on either side. "Yup," I said out loud. I tried to walk like John Wayne, but the hips were still too sore from my beating.

I got back to Mrs. Gunnerson's a few minutes after midnight. I had stopped on the way and bought a couple of Budweisers. I felt ugly; it was the perfect beer. When I opened the front door with my key, Babe Ruth was standing in the middle of the floor in the den holding a copy of some leather-bound book. She seemed to be floating a few inches above the floor.

"You're in so late," she said.

"It's a jungle out there, sweetheart," I said. I was not in possession of the best equilibrium. I walked toward her, looking all the time like a gymnast about to fall off the balance beam. Her mouth was shaped in a small "O", and she looked so insignificant she might just dissolve. "Whatcha reading?"

"Plato's *Dialogues*," she said softly. "I'm trying to educate myself."

"By reading a book about Mickey Mouse's dog?" Okay, so I was drunk. She smiled blandly, and I walked up to her and kissed her full on the lips for about seven or eight seconds. When I broke I wanted to say something about the problems of two people not amounting to a hill of beans in this crazy, mixed-up world, but I just wheeled around and struggled up the stairs and into my room.

It looked the same. For the past week, I had been playing cards with life, and so far I had been dealt a two, a six, a nine and a jack, all in different suits. I sat on the edge of the bed. Maybe I would amount to something tomorrow. Maybe I would straighten myself out, quit drinking and smoking and hanging around with the wrong crowd. After all, tomorrow is another day. Maybe I would solve my case.

Yeah, I thought as I undressed and climbed into the cool sheets, and it don't rain in Indianapolis in the summertime.

TO SAY I FELT LIKE HELL THAT NEXT morning as I drove over to the Primate Haus is to say that Jack the Ripper had a minor scrape with the Bobbies. Champagne will do it to you every time, and though I believe man is capable of learning from his mistakes, I seemed to have some character flaw that prevented it.

When I got to the restaurant, I took five Anacins and asked Treena for some black coffee.

"Can't you get it any blacker than this?" I asked when the coffee came.

"I could pour a bottle of shoe polish in it," Treena said thoughtfully. A carpenter was there, hammering and sawing on some sheetrock, fixing the hole Bull Feeney had made in the wall back near the restroom. I declined her offer.

Before I left Mrs. Gunnerson's, I had called Patton

and Railsback and successfully convinced the secretary my name was Steed. I wanted to know if my policy was paid up. She checked while putting me on hold with *101 Strings Play Neil Diamond*. I gagged a couple of times, but I survived by sheer force of will. She came back and said the policy was paid through May. Damn. It still bothered me for some reason, but I knew it probably shouldn't.

I had done one other useful thing that morning. I got the forty-pound Atlanta phone directory and looked up the Anderson Shipping Company. It had an office on the west side of town not far from Six Flags Over Georgia. I would go out and visit the gentlemen and see what I could stir up. If my equilibrium had not improved, I could stop by Six Flags on the way back and stand by the roller coaster and pretend I was riding it.

The day was warm. The stretch of I-20 between Atlanta and Birmingham is like being stranded somewhere between Murmansk and Vladivostok with a phonetic alphabet book, no rubles and an empty bottle of vodka.

The Anderson Shipping Company's office was in one of those anonymous ten-store shopping centers that huddle fearfully on the side of the road. On one side was a lamp store and on the other an agency for State Farm. I pulled to a stop and got out, my head feeling like a basketball that had been dribbled for half a season in the NBA. Maybe a whole season.

I never plan very far ahead. That way, my life is a constant surprise both to myself and my victims. It takes a certain amount of cheek to go storming into someone's office armed only with the truth, but I had always believed the truth will set you free, so I opened the front door of the Anderson Shipping Company and went on in.

"Excuse me," I said as I strode up to a woman sitting behind a desk. She was probably sixty and her face looked like it had been baked in a kiln. Her hair was piled up in a cone, and I half expected a swarm of hornets to buzz out and harass me.

"Sir?"

"I'm Councilman Fargo from Atlanta's public works committee, and we're doing a survey for the Chamber of Commerce." She wiggled her lips and stared at me. Maybe I'd have to revoke their business license to get cooperation.

"You need to see Mr. Webster," she said. She got up and walked back to an office and whispered something. The office was tiny, a narrow corridor off of which opened two doors. The one on the left was Webster's. I presumed the one on the right was the can. She came back. "Walk this way please?" Should I do it? Naaahhh. It was an old joke. What the hell. I slunk right behind her, knee bend for knee bend, until I got to Webster's office. She moved past me and I went inside.

"Councilman Fargo," I smiled. I reached out for his hand and he shook it. His hand was rough. He was about five-ten and fat and mean looking, but I could tell he felt some awe at dealing with a servant of the people.

"Have a seat," he said, smiling like Torquemada. "Coffee?"

"Black," I said. He got up and poured me a cup from the brewer on a small table next to his desk. It didn't look like a shipping office. The walls were plain panels, no decorations. His desk was cluttered, but mostly with outdoor magazines. The coffee tasted like lightly aerated loam, but I remembered my manners. "We're doing a survey for the Chamber of Commerce on ports of entry, destinations, that sort of thing." I didn't know what in the hell I was talking about. "I'll only take a few minutes of your time, and it could come in handy next time around." I winked at him. He wore shapeless jeans and a checked shirt, the kind Roy Rogers used to wear with a neckerchief.

"Uh, yeah," he nodded. I'd envisioned a place full of nautical doo-dads, a place from where I could ship out myself, become the Wandering WASP, legend of the high seas, subject of operas and epic poetry. He did not seem pleased to be seeing me but you owe some sort of fealty to your city government.

"Well, let's see," I said. I took out my little note-book, careful not to let him see my gun. "You do business normally in imports with several foreign companies. You work mostly with air shipments to this country?"

"I don't know about this," he said. He shifted uncomfortably in his chair. "You sure you want to talk to us?"

"Maybe I looked at the wrong card before I came over," I said. "But you import. . . ."

"We have lots of places we import from," he said, "Norway, Sweden, Belgium."

"Copenhagen?"

"Yeah. Look, you need to talk to Mr. Johannsen about all this." I think he suspected I might be misrepresenting myself. Nobody trusts government anymore.

"Edvard Johannsen?" I asked.

"He's the agent," Webster said. "But he's at home. Never comes in here much."

"Johannsen," I nodded. "Y'all hear much from Mr. Marcello these days?" He looked blank.

"You sure you got the right place?" he asked.

"Perhaps not," I admitted. "My secretary has terrible handwriting." I stood and shook his hand. "I guess I'll go see Mr. Johannsen."

"Okay." I nodded, looked around the office one time like an over-zealous OSHA inspector and went out the door whistling "Heart and Soul." When I got outside, I looked around for a phone booth and did not see one, so I mounted my chariot and drove until I saw one in front of a Gulf station. I stopped and flipped the phone book to the Js. He lived on Fearney Circle, an upper-class neighborhood on the northwest side that I had once visited for a party.

Most people are improbably gullible and can be duped with the slightest effort. The bad guys know this, but the boys with the white hats can sometimes be devious to good ends.

I found 325 Fearney Circle and went past it to the next street, parked the Buick and walked back around the corner to 325 Fearney. The Johannsen house was brick with four phony antebellum columns on the front. A small porch hung over the front door. Mrs. Johannsen probably came out there in the morning and waited for our boys to come back from Vicksburg.

I politely rang the doorbell, and presently an enormously fat black woman opened the door and stared at me for a moment before saying, "What do you want?"

"Excuse me," I said. I snapped my fingers. "I hope you don't find this rude, but you bear a striking resemblance to Lena Horne."

"Yeah, and you looks like Robert Redford," she snapped. "What you want?"

"Is Mr. Johannsen in?" I asked. I wanted to ask her to sing "Stormy Weather" but she would probably get more unpleasant with me.

"Who wants to see him?" she asked.

"I do, " I said.

"What's the name?" she asked. If Jake Shuler had her, he wouldn't need his pack of ferrets.

"Tell him I'm Councilman Fargo here with the Chamber of Commerce." She lumbered off. I looked past her into the foyer. It was richly appointed, with a huge mirror hung over a Chippendale chair on the left and an ornate hat rack on the right. Straight ahead were stairs, and there was a room on either side of the stairwell. It looked a lot like Tony's house.

In a moment, she came back.

"Follow me," she said.

"You aren't going to say 'walk this way'?" I asked. I thought she laughed, but she might have been clearing her throat. We went straight back behind the stairs, through a den and out a glass door on to a patio. A man was sitting in a chaise longue, holding a beer and staring at the dull October sky. Before long, it would be too cool to sit out here.

"Sit down," the man said. I sat in a chair near him. He sipped his beer and shifted uncomfortably in his chair.

"Thanks for seeing me," I said.

"Who did you say you were?" he asked.

"I said I was working for the city council, but actually I'm trying to find out something about Tony Browning."

"Never heard of him," he said. He stared at me for a moment and then got up without saying a word and went inside. There was a wall around his back yard. He probably called it a fence, but it was a wall, eight feet high and made of some kind of expensive hardwood. I suddenly felt as if he didn't want me here.

I whistled part of "Girl from Ipanema." I stood and walked around his pool and was thinking about how successful I'd been in finding out things when a man I hadn't seen before came out the back door. He was carrying a handgun at arm's length. He started walking double-time toward me.

I began to back up and felt just under my left arm for my own gun. This was not going to be pleasant.

"Hold it," the man said. He pointed his gun at me. He was still about forty yards away, and I started backing up quickly. "I said, 'Stop!'"

I took off running.

There was a small house behind the main mansion, a tool shed of some kind, and I ran for it. I heard a soft thud, and a bullet smacked into the fence behind me. He had a silencer. That was bad; it indicated Mr. Johannsen was a serious man. But it was also good, because silencers make the path of a bullet erratic. He shot at me again and missed just as I got behind the tool shed and pulled out my gun.

The fence came in behind the tool house and joined it in a small alleyway. I ran toward it as fast as I could and grabbed the top and began pulling myself over. I felt like Shelley Winters trying to go over, and when I finally strained to the top, I fell. I landed in someone else's yard. The man behind the fence fired three times through the fence, splintering the wood just over my head. I ran off in a crouch, hidden by thick bushes and

Mr. Johannsen's wall. I ran as fast as I could through the yard, down a pretty slope with a creek at its bottom, past a trellis covered with wizened vines and back up a steep driveway, coming out not twenty feet from my car. Lewis and Clark should have had me along.

From the top of the drive I could see them across the little creek valley, coming out of Johannsen's house up the hill, three men looking wildly concerned. I got in and let the brake off and rolled a block before I started the engine with the clutch. I drove down the street, turned left, circled in an area where the houses all stuck out their porches like tongues at the effrontery of my car. Then I drove out of the neighborhood and back toward a northside bar, The Leopard.

I watched in the rearview mirror, but they were no match for me. Cheating death was invigorating, but you couldn't make a career out of it. Sooner or later, the man with the scythe and robe would take you by the hand and help you walk the last mile.

The Leopard was small and clean, a neighborhood place that sometimes had amateur strip shows. When I had been saintly for too long a time, I would come to amateur night and leer. I went in and ordered an Olympia. I might as well reward myself for being so astute. I had found out who Edvard was. I had found out that the Anderson Shipping Company imported goods from Copenhagen. It appeared Mr. Johannsen was not in legitimate business. He knew who Tony Browning was and also that I had nothing to do with him or if I did, that I needed to be shot. Either way, he looked like no friend of Tony's.

I drank three more beers after I finished the first. I felt better. Maybe I was getting somewhere. I felt like a million dollars, but maybe it was the beer. I whistled "September Song" for a while. Then I had two more beers, which made an even six, and I sang along when somebody put "Hello Darlin'" by Conway Twitty on the jukebox.

Somewhere in the Big City there was a regular rat's nest of villains. It was being run by someone with plenty of contacts and an ability to see the Big Picture, to orchestrate things. Tony Browning was just a stupid pawn. It had occurred to me that Jake Shuler was simply lying. I didn't think so when I had talked to him at his retreat, but perhaps I was just a pawn, as Tony had been. Shuler would pop up somewhere, grab me just when I had somehow gotten him off the hook, and he would smile ruefully and have a ferret blow half my head off.

The place was slowly filling up. It was not amateur night, so I went out, got in the Buick and left. Regardless of what people think, it is nearly impossible for one person to solve a complicated crime. One person can, however, stir things up enough to cause someone involved to lose his head and foul up the works. That was what I was trying to do. I had pushed over a few dominoes, and the next day I would try to see where they fell.

I drove downtown and got a room for the night at the Peachtree Plaza Hotel, the uniquely cylindrical skyscraper in downtown Atlanta. I loved the place, loved driving by it every day and wondering what was happening in there. It was the size of a small town. I had never been flush enough to stay there before, but I still had some of Sherrill's dough and I felt nice and high. Or drunk.

I sprawled across my big double bed, feeling lonely. I called room service and told them to send me a magnum of champagne and a brunette. They ignored the second part of my request. I drank half of the bottle and stood in my open doorway smiling until two stewardesses came by and went into a room four doors down from me. I waited until they had time to take off their jackets and went outside their door and started singing "Delta is ready when you are."

Apparently, they weren't fans of commercial music, because in a couple of minutes a house detective escorted me back to my room.

"It's a wonderful life," I said. He nodded and shoved me in the room. I promised to remain in my room and not bother the flight attendants again, though I did briefly consider rappelling from the roof and singing "Spanish Eyes" while dangling in front of their window. But all I did was lie down on the bed and start thinking about Ginny Calvert, goddamnit, and though I slept for the rest of the night, it was none too well.

My head hurt even worse the next morning. I wasn't a kid anymore, even though I seemed to have a talent for acting like one. I could do lots of interesting things today. I could drive to Birmingham and, on the way, connect up with a clot of camel herders, jingling in a merry caravan, looking for some sign of civilization. Lots of luck.

I spent the day drinking black coffee and taking Anacins at a few watering holes. Acetaminophen never works for me, but I have boundless faith in Anacin. It's good to have things that form your personal code.

I finally drove home to Mrs. Gunnerson's late in the day. Everyone was in the parlor but Dicky Thacker, who was still at work caressing camshafts or something. They were all sitting around sullenly.

"What's wrong?" I asked. Mr. Oshman hummed "Danke Schoen" distractedly.

"Someone has stolen our Trivial Pursuit," said Mrs. Carreker. I wondered if she had studied the Bill of Rights yet. She got up and came over to me. I heard Mrs. Gunnerson banging around back in the kitchen, starting to cook dinner for the tenants. "And since you are a detective, I charge you to discover the culprit."

Mildred Ruth looked at me and smiled shyly. I wanted to be an anchorite, travel alone in the desert and wear a hair shirt. I did not want to look for Trivial Pursuit.

"It was probably just misplaced," I said, heading for the stairs.

"Does this mean you aren't taking the case?" she asked haughtily.

"Write down everything you know and I'll think about it," I said.

"Indeed I shall," she said. I went on up.

A week passed then two. I wasn't doing very much. I watched Jack Railsback for a while, but he didn't seem too hysterical, though distracted and erratic, driving around sometimes for hours before going home. I followed Sugar Barvano. He was only pumping iron, not breaking arms. I had a nice chat with Carlyle Fallows, who threatened me if I ever came back.

The only one I had not talked to was Rebecca Sanderson, Tony's old squeeze. On a Tuesday, I went to her shop in Lenox Square, called Buttons 'n' Things. I couldn't tell what the "things" were, but they had something to do with sewing. A clerk asked me if I needed help.

"I'd like to see Ms. Sanderson," I said. The woman looked young, not over twenty-five, quite pretty, but she was unhappy when I mentioned Rebecca's name.

"She's not in today," she said.

"When will she be back?"

"Uh . . . I'm not sure."

"I'm an old friend," I lied. "Is she at home?"

"I think so," she said, "but she probably won't want any visitors. She's been ill."

"Goodness," I said. "Nothing serious, I hope." She chewed on her lip and tried to decide what to tell me.

"A dear friend of hers was murdered," she whispered, closing her eyes as she talked. "She has taken it very badly. She's been out of work for several weeks now. It's been a real strain on her."

"Goodness," I said. "Does she still live on Juniper?"

"Juniper? I think she lives on Martin Circle, over in Buckhead," she said. "At 2354 Martin Circle."

"I'll give her a call," I said.

"If she comes back, who should I say called?" she asked.

"Colavito," I said. "Rocky Colavito. We were old friends." I walked back into the mall. It was possible, I suppose, that she was still torn up about Tony's death, but that had been weeks ago and even the most sensitive are healed by time. At least I kept telling myself that.

Her house was quite modest, a white frame structure that sat about a hundred feet back from the road. I drove past it and parked beside a Unitarian church or mosque or whatever it is they call them. I'd never make it as a religious gadfly.

I decided to watch for a time. I was pretty sure she wouldn't remember me. I sat on a MARTA bench at a bus stop across the street and took from my coat a copy of that morning's paper that I had folded up. The day was cold and cloudy, and some weatherman had said excitedly that we might have some snow flurries. People all over town were walking around looking at the sky.

I read all of sports first, including the box scores, then the news section and People. I was reading an article on convertible debentures, which sounded to me like something you buy at an orthodontist's, when a car turned into the driveway that went through some overhanging bushes along the edge of Rebecca Sanderson's house. I peeked over the business page. The car stopped by her front door.

Sometimes, when you see things in the wrong place, out of context, it takes a moment to register.

The man getting out of the Mercedes and walking into Rebecca Sanderson's house was Jack Railsback. Maybe that domino had fallen after all.

WATCHED THE HOUSE FOR NEARLY AN hour before Jack came back out and got in his Mercedes and drove off. I was thinking more and more about Sherrill and Tony by that time, feeling sure I could make something happen if I stayed with it. I was certain that the cross had been smuggled out of France, into Denmark and then to Atlanta with a shipment of cheese. Jack Railsback was involved, and so were Edvard Johannsen and Rebecca Sanderson. Somebody had gone to a hell of a lot of trouble to make it appear that it was all Jake Shuler's doing.

The puzzle was coming together. But I needed several more pieces before I could go to the police and demonstrate what had happened. I knew, unless it was dumb coincidence, that Sandy Marcello was connected both to Tony and Jack. That might not mean anything, but I had a gut feeling that it did, since it had been a long time since they had been in business together. Somehow, Sandy Marcello was involved.

I followed Jack again at a safe distance. My car is not designed for repeated tailings because of its distinctive contours. He drove back to work, and I drove back to Mrs. Gunnerson's to think about it for a while. Mrs. Carreker tried to stop me at the door and interest me again in the Case of the Missing Trivial Pursuit, but I brushed past her and went on up. I felt the thrill of the chase now and could almost smell blood.

There was a note tacked to my door. It just said, "Call 786-1123." That was Ginny Calvert's number. My heart leapt up as if I beheld a rainbow in the sky. I went to the end of the hall to the phone and called her. It rang once before she picked it up.

"Hello?"

"This is the chairman of the Louisa May Alcott for President Committee, calling on behalf of the Clean Books League," I said.

"Hank, come over here," she said excitedly. "I think I found something."

"An autographed copy of the Complete Works of Edgar A. Guest?" I answered breathlessly.

"I don't know what it means, but I think it's important," she said. "Come on over." She sounded warm and friendly.

"I've missed you," I said. She was quiet for a moment.

"Not as much as I've missed you," she said. I wondered if she could hear my heart doing a half gainer down the stairwell. "Oh hell, please come over. And I do have something to show you. Have you found out anything else?"

"Of course," I said blithely. "Prince is my name, detection is my game." She laughed. I wanted to eat the phone, crawl on the roof and howl.

I got over there faster than ever before. I cut off a low-slung Jaguar trying to speed into my lane, nearly causing him to crash into a dumpster. He blew his horn and gave me the finger. I waved at him cheerily. If he pulled up behind me, I'd layer his hood ornament with exhaust. I came up the stairs three at a time. They needed a stair-climbing event in the Olympics. My friends had thought little of my other suggestion for the Winter Olympics, the 90-meter bobsled jump. I still think it would be exciting.

She opened the door, and we stood there looking at each other. Easy, boy. Don't seem too eager. Don't fall down at her feet and tell her you'll paint her living room if she'll but hold your hand.

"Hi," she said.

"Hi," I said. She came toward me and took my arm and pulled me inside and held me tightly and then looked up at me. I leaned down and kissed her gently.

"I'm sorry," she said. "I was scared."

"Don't think about it," I said. "I'm here now." We walked to the couch and sat. On the coffee table, right beside Benjy the cat, was a newspaper, folded back neatly and creased to a small photograph of a woman dressed in an evening gown, looking cheerful and elegant. The caption said Country Club Ball. She handed it to me. This is what it said:

"The annual fund-raiser at the Briarcliff Driving Club was held Thursday night, raising money in the fight against leukemia. Shown here helping host the event is Maria Marcello Steed, wife of well-known APD Lt. Adam Steed. More than $25,000 was raised."

It was like opening a lock. I could feel the tumblers turning inside my head, each new opening bringing with it the possibility of solution. I sat back on the couch and stared at the wall where she had a poster of Bogart in *The Big Sleep.*

"Marcello," she said. "Did you see that?" Her voice seemed vague, far away. I could barely think quickly enough.

"When did this come out?" I asked, opening the paper, looking for the dateline.

"Yesterday," she said. "Remember the book in Mr. Browning's office with that name on it?"

"My God," I said. "It's starting to make some sense to me."

"What?"

"I need to think about it some more," I said. "You hungry?" She smiled and put her head on my shoulder. She rubbed my chest, and I kissed her on top of the head.

"I'd like to get something to eat later," she said. My heart did two and a half somersaults with a full twist.

It was much later, two hours later. As we lay tangled on the bed, I could see a trail of our clothes from the den. You could probably track me by following the popped-off buttons.

"Boy, you sure were eager," she said, rolling toward me.

"Aw hell, did it show?" I asked. "I was striving for my usual taciturn approach to things." She propped her elbows up and put her chin in her hands.

"So what do you think it means that Steed's wife was a Marcello?" she asked. I ran the tip of my index finger down her cheek.

"Think about it," I said. "People on the street had heard that Tony Browning was running from Jake Shuler, when he really wasn't. Somebody with a reason to confuse the situation put the story out. Angel Jiminez, remember the pimp we saw, said that the beat cop down there told him about it. Sugar Barvano told me that a police informant told him. Then Steed shows up in two places, at Stone Mountain where they killed Tony and on Ponce de Leon where those two men were killed when we gave them the cross."

"Then how do you fit into this?"

"It took me a long time, but here's what I think happened," I said. She snuggled close to me. Our faces were only an inch apart. "I may have trouble concentrating on my line of detection this way." She kissed me gently.

"Go on."

"Okay. Jack Railsback, the guy who came and told me that Sherrill wanted to hire me, is somehow involved in this. He used to work for Tony. Steed may have something on Jack, could be using him like he used Tony. I've been following him around for the past few days, and he's acting strange. Here's how I see it. Tony had disappeared when the heat got too strong, okay?"

"Okay."

"I think Jack went to Sherrill and convinced her that Tony's disappearance, which he knew about, put Tony in danger because of things Jack had heard around. He suggested to her that she hire me to find Tony. The reason is that Tony is no fool, and if he found out I was working for Sherrill to find him, he would try to contact me, which he wouldn't do with anybody else. I think that's what happened. Tony was watching the house or following me or something. But Jack Railsback and his cohorts couldn't find Tony. They knew if I was involved, Tony would find me. He did, out on Stone Mountain."

"Then how did the cops show up out there?"

"Tenhoor said Steed said it was a tip."

"But no one but you and Tony would have known about it," she said, puzzled.

"I think Steed was having me followed," I said. "That's the most confusing part. It would have required some mobility, having some people out looking after me all the time. But I've seen it done before. If Steed told them it was a major drug case, he could have gotten instant cooperation from any jurisdiction. There were Stone Mountain city cops there, too. So they followed me. That's all. I had been drinking for a week, and I could have been followed by the Space Shuttle and not have noticed. I led them right to Tony Browning, just as they figured."

"Just as who figured?"

"Right now, I'd say Adam Steed."

"Why?"

"He set the whole thing up, unless I'm off the mark," I said. "Look at it this way. He has Tony on some minor drug offense and tells him the way to get off is to cooperate in setting up a major drug dealer. Only Tony doesn't know what is really happening is that Steed and Sandy Marcello and Jack Railsback have obtained the cross and need to get it back into Georgia. So Tony gets the cross, then realizes what is happening and disappears."

"Why did he disappear?"

"He knew he'd been set up as a sucker," I said. "When he got the cross he knew that it was not legit, that what would likely happen is that he would be killed when Jack got the cross. So he disappeared, but not before he left the cross in the safe in his bedroom. Maybe he was leaving it for Sherrill."

"I don't understand why they would go to all that trouble," she said. "Why wouldn't they just get the cross and bring it here?" She put her leg across mine. My heart did a backward two-and-a-half with a half twist in the pike position.

"Because a lot of people are after this cross," I said. "It's priceless. It's called crossing the trail. What you do is set up situations that confuse whoever is looking. First, you tell everybody around that Tony Browning is skimming from Jake Shuler, which he was, a little bit, I guess. So everybody thinks Shuler is trying to kill Tony. That gives you an excuse to kill Tony and blame it on the mob, right? Now, Tony doesn't know about this, only that he is supposed to be a middle man on getting this thing. But he is being set up, only when he disappears and they can't find him, they panic."

"Then they hired you because you could find him?" I sighed and shook my head.

"They got me because I'm a drunk, and they thought Tony would find me," I said. "Then they figured I'd been too stupid to do anything but go home and get drunk again." I didn't feel like Prince Charming.

"But what about poor Mrs. Browning?" she asked.

"That's the part that hurts the most," I said. "I think somebody panicked. They figured if Sherrill was killed it would shake Tony loose. So they killed her, and then he called me. It worked just as it was supposed to."

"Who killed her?" Our faces had hardened, and I realized as I chewed on the thought that we might both be in serious danger now. I think maybe she realized it, too.

"I don't know yet," I said. "I think a woman named Rebecca Sanderson who once dated Tony is involved. Jack Railsback was at her house today."

"What about that stuff in the book we found in Mr. Browning's office?"

"Okay," I said. "We know about Sandy Marcello. Edvard is Edvard Johannsen, who is the shipping agent where the cross was sent in from Denmark with a shipment of cheese, remember. The 'Ander. S.C.' is the Anderson Shipping Company. I figured that out. Mr. Johannsen tried to have my skeletal configuration rearranged."

She moved her leg farther over mine, and we stared silently into each other's eyes for a while.

"So what is left?" she said.

"We have to detain the perpetrators," I said.

She started to ask me how we were going to do that. Before I could let her ask, before I could say I had no earthly idea, I kissed her, and then we didn't talk anymore.

It was another hour before we finally showered and left the house in my car. We didn't talk much as I drove around looking for a place to get a bite to eat. I was thinking.

Jack Railsback seemed to be getting edgy and erratic. Why not assume that he felt like he might be double-crossed? And what was Rebecca Sanderson's part in this? I had found out a lot, but could I wrap it up neatly? The odds were long enough. Now that I had Ginny back, I didn't want to get shot. But I knew then that the life I led was transitory, that all things such as that perfect afternoon ended too soon, as winter swallows a perfect autumn. It was now early November, and soon the last leaf would fall. It was late in the year, late in the case and, for all I knew, late in the life of Hank Prince.

I finally found a French restaurant on Buford High-way that was a clean, well-lighted place. We went inside, and I ordered a bowl of bouillabase, and Ginny ordered crepês. We ate quietly for a time. I tried to act cheerful and full of answers, but we soon lapsed into silence.

"Look," she said finally, "are we in some kind of danger still?"

"Yeah," I said. She nodded and moved a sprig of parsley from one side of the plate to another. "I think it might be a good idea for you to move to a motel for a few days."

"For how long?" she said. "I'm scared." Then she smiled, a radiant, heart-breaking smile. "But I feel safe with you. You make me feel like nothing could ever happen to me again."

"Things are going to start happening quick," I said. "I've been pushing on things and pulling threads, and I think things are starting to fall apart. I'm going to put my shoulder into it and see what happens."

"How?"

"I have a plan," I said.

"You always have a plan," she said. "I don't think they knew you very well when they thought you wouldn't figure things out."

"I didn't know myself very well, either," I said. "And I could still be wrong. But I don't think I am." I paid the bill and left a larger tip than I should have, but the waitress kept looking at me with huge sad eyes.

We came outside and walked around to my car. Before I had time to say "Whoa," three men had grabbed both of us and hustled us around back and stuffed us into a dark blue Cadillac. One of the men stuck a gun in my ribs. I looked at Ginny and made a face of disgust and shrugged. Maybe I should spend the rest of my life as a produce clerk at Kroger. Right now my life expectancy might be four minutes, for all I knew. We were in the back seat.

"There must be some mistake," I said. "My wife and I are in town for the Arsonists' Convention at the Omni. The Thug Convention is not until January. Perhaps you gentlemen have arrived too early."

"Christ," said the man with the gun in my ribs. He took his gun away and put it in a shoulder holster. Ginny sat beside me as we roared off and held on to my arm so tight my hand started to go numb. I tried to loosen her grip, but she would have nothing of it. "We'll be there in a minute. Nothing's gonna happen to you."

"Is there anything you gentlemen would like burned down?" I asked brightly. "We have a special this month on business insurance. You name it, we flame it. Pretty good motto, huh?" He looked out the window and shook his head. They didn't try to keep us from seeing where we were going. The two men in the front seat looked like extras from *Night of the Living Dead*. We drove about three miles and stopped in the empty, silent parking lot of a Catholic church. Another long, blue car was parked around back. We stopped. The man beside me got out and told us to get out. What else could we do? He had his gun back out.

"In there," the man said, pointing to the back door of the second car. "The girl stays with me."

"Okay," I said.

"Hank!" she said. My arm needed a rest.

"It will be all right," I said. "Trust me." She let go and backed up, nodding. I got into the back seat of the car and found myself face to face with Jake Shuler. He was wearing a long overcoat and a dour face. He could have passed for Vito Corleone's accountant. He had a bowl of popcorn on his lap and nibbled at it.

"Popcorn?" he asked.

"No thanks," I said.

"This weather will be the death of me," he said. He wheezed and leaned back heavily. "I'd like to know how you've helped me so far, Prince."

"Oh boy," I said. "All my life I've wanted to help somebody like you." He raised his eyebrows and shrugged.

"Mr. Prince, you have no grounds for feeling morally superior to me," he said reasonably.

"Jeez, you've got me there, Jake," I said.

"Anyway, we would like to know what you have managed to find out so far to exonerate me," he said.

"Exonerate?" I said. "Where did you learn words like that, Jake?"

"I have an A.B. from Vanderbilt," he said. That stopped me cold. I thought at the time he had lost his mind and was becoming a doddering old fool, but sometime later, I found out he was telling the truth. They didn't have Coercion 101 where I went to school.

"So what do you want to know?" I asked. I wanted a piece of the popcorn, but I didn't want him to know that.

"Just who has been involved in setting this all up," said Jake Shuler. I nodded and leaned back against the seat and lit a cigarette. Jake lowered his window because the smoke bothered him. I should have been more thoughtful. I wasn't.

"I know," I said.

"You know?" he said.

"Is there an echo in here?"

"What do you know, Prince?" he said. He set the bowl of popcorn on the floor and turned his body, with great effort, in the seat toward me.

"I know that Tony Browning was used as a patsy, and that he found out about it too late," I said. "I know that it revolves around the theft from a museum in France of a priceless cross, which was shipped here from Copenhagen. I got it from Tony's house and tried to trade the cross for that woman out there, and the two men who made the swap were gunned down over on Ponce de Leon. I lost the cross, but it wasn't mentioned in the police report, even though the cops must have gotten it."

"A cross," he said with wonder. "A cross? Ahhh." He put his right index finger on his heavy lips and thought about it for a moment.

"I think one policeman is involved, that he set up the entire thing," I said.

"Of course," he said. "Steed." The hint of a smile crossed his face. "From the beginning, he seemed to be set on pinning these murders on me. I knew I had nothing to do with them and so did anyone else with real connections in this town. They only believe Steed because of who he is."

"That's a big 10-4," I said.

"Did you know," he said, leaning back heavily, "that Adam Steed was an expert rifleman in Korea?" Now it was my turn to stare dumbly, disbelieving.

"How do you know that?" I asked. He licked his lips and stared straight ahead. I glanced out the window and Ginny was standing there, looking frightened and impatient.

"Because," he said, "he and I once lived in the same barracks at Benning." You could have knocked me over with a Milk Dud. He laughed, a low gurgling, rumbling laugh. "We knew each other quite well in those days." I tried to think of something to say. Things were becoming clearer by the minute. "I suppose you can see the ironies in this situation."

"I'll be damned," I said.

"Did you know," he continued, "that Steed collects *objets d'art*?"

"I'll be damned," I said.

"Or that he has written regularly on antique jewelry for several national magazines?"

"I'll be damned." I could have brought a tape recorder and punched it each time I was to react. I had underestimated Adam Steed. He knew exactly what he wanted and how to get it. I only wondered how the cross had been stolen in the first place. Jake Shuler didn't say anything else. I sat beside him, trying to think of what to do. I had an idea.

"I suppose you would like to get off the hook and have the murderers get their just desserts," I said, thinking out loud.

"So?"

"So I need your help," I said.

"Anything," he wheezed. I told him what I had in mind. He thought about it for a moment.

"Can you do such a thing?" he asked.

"I think so," I said. "What do you have to lose?" He sighed. Then he nodded. I got out of the car and turned and looked back in at him. "Shall I try to call you in a few days?"

"We shall be in touch," he said. His voice sounded like a 32-foot organ pipe. He and Orson Welles would have had a great time talking things over. I walked over to Ginny and took her arm, and we got back in the back seat of the other car, and they took us back to the French restaurant.

"We surely did enjoy the tour, fellas," I said. "Let us know if we can torch something for you. And hey, it's on us. Right, babe?" Ginny got out of the car and didn't say anything. The men inside sped off to their screen test for another sequel to *Night of the Living Dead*.

"Who was that man?" Ginny asked as we got back into my car.

"That, my dear, was Jake Shuler, the man who is going to solve this miserable mess once and for all," I said.

I had changed my mind about one thing. To hell with waiting, with worrying about everything. If it were done, 'tis better it were done quickly. We drove back over to Ginny's house, and I told her what I had in mind to do. She seemed skeptical.

The next morning, I was going to put my drunken shoulder behind the problem and start breaking things instead of pushing over dominoes. There were still several things I did not know, but I knew enough to start the inevitable solution rolling. It would take three or four days to resolve, and I would need plenty of luck and even a bit of skill. And Shuler was right: the ironies were more than a bit forced. But I held allegiance with no party, no government on its own accord; I only trusted what I knew with my own hands and eyes to be just, and though most cops were the good guys and most hoods were equally evil, the world is such that one can sometimes lose the line where one crosses into the other.

But that was all for the next morning. For now, I only wanted to be with Ginny Calvert, to hold her and love her. I had never had much luck with women, but such luck was of my own making. I lost many things without anyone else's help. I think I knew that night that I would not have Ginny forever, but I lied to myself, lied and lied and lied and lied.

"I'm afraid for you," she said deep into the night, her voice thick just before sleep.

"The only thing we have to fear is fear itself," I said, but she was already gone, sleeping and safe in my loving arms.

BENJY THE CAT STARED AT ME FROM HIS perch on the stove. Ginny and I sat at the table, sipping the last of our second cup of coffee. I had finished telling her my plan to catch the men who had killed Tony and Sherrill Browning, and how she would have to help me. She nodded and took a deep breath and let it out. I looked through the window on the front of her apartment and could see it was going to be one of those cool, foggy, misty, head-cold kind of days in Atlanta.

"You can make this work?" she asked. She was looking at me now, asking me to say, *I will let no one harm you; I will always be there to hold you against me, away from danger.*

"I think I can," I said. "So much of what people do is based on their expectation. They expect a formula to be the same each day. Get up, shower, go to work, shuffle the paper and go home and get drunk with your dog. If one thing's out of place, most people become disoriented and don't know what to do next. The easiest decisions become onerous and, invariably, wrong decisions start getting made."

"That sounds more like philosophy than catching a killer," she said.

"It's not," I said. She looked down into what was left of her coffee. Then she looked up and made a face of mock disgust.

"Why am I going to say yes to this?" she asked, breaking into a smile.

"Because you have been swayed by the cogent arguments of my complex mind," I said. "Or maybe it's because I'm so cute."

"Shit," said Ginny Calvert.

Once again, it involved hauling Benjy the cat over to Mrs. Gunnerson's for a couple of days. I wasn't sure how long it would take, but if not in that time, then not at all. I went out first and looked around, my hand under my coat and on the gun. No one seemed to be there, but I'd been followed so many times lately that I felt like a duck in season. At one time, I was good at picking up tails; lately, I was so bad I wondered if I should run for mayor.

There were two reasons for taking Benjy over to Mrs. Gunnerson's. The first was to leave him where someone would feed him. The second was to get my old .22 target pistol for Ginny. The streets were wet, and the endless wayward mass of humanity was staggering to work. I did not know work had undone so many. We got to Mrs. Gunnerson's just as Dicky Thacker was coming out of the house with a toothpick in his mouth, heading off for work. He came by and leaned in my window just as we pulled to a stop.

"Ginny," I said, turning, "this is Dr. Thacker, our resident eye, ear and oil pan specialist." Dicky Thacker snorted.

"Howdy," he said.

"Or maybe he's really Gary Cooper," I said. He rolled his eyes and shook his head.

"Them women's getting on my nerves," he said, looking up toward the house. "Miz Carreker's driving everbody nuts looking for that damn game. She wants to call the po-lice, but Miz Gunnerson says she don't want no po-lice." He looked thoughtfully away. "At least I think that's what she said."

"The evil that men do lives after them," I said. I opened the door, and he stepped out of the way. Ginny got out with Benjy and his litter pan.

"What the hell's that supposed to mean?" he asked. I didn't answer him. He was still standing there as we went up the steps and inside. It was early, and they were all sitting around the large dining room table in a room to our immediate left as we entered.

"Meithsor Prance," said Mrs. Gunnerson, waving at me. I stuck my head in the room. Mr. Oshman was absorbed in an effort to slurp his coffee off a pearl-white saucer. Mrs. Carreker was looking suspiciously at an egg that was left on a plate in the middle of the table.

"Mildred, can I see you a minute?" I asked. They all looked at me. Mrs. Gunnerson smiled and said something I could not come close to understanding. Babe Ruth was sitting across the table facing me. Her face lit up as she slid her chair back. "Come on up with us." Ginny and I went on up and Mildred Ruth silently followed. I unlocked my door and we went in. Mildred came in behind us. "Shut the door." She did. I rummaged through the bottom drawer of my dresser until I found the .22. I handed it to Ginny who slid it into her purse. Mildred Ruth made a noise of surprise and delight at the sight of the gun.

"Yes?" she said so softly it could have been the radiator hissing.

"I have an important job for you," I said. "Miss Calvert and I have been summoned for a dangerous mission. Do you understand?" She folded her hands and looked around the room with barely subdued awe. "This is a crucial part of our mission and we need your help."

"Mine?" she said.

"Yours," I said. "We need you to come up here once a day — no more, no less — and feed this cat and make sure it has water." I walked to her and put my arm around her shoulder. Our faces were only inches apart. "It's very important."

"Is it dangerous?" she asked breathlessly.

"I won't lie," I said. "It's a job only for someone brave and stouthearted. Are you brave and stout-hearted, Mildred?"

"Yes," she said.

"Will you take care of this animal as if it were your own?"

"Yes," she said. "I will, yes." I patted her on the shoulder and told her we'd be back in a couple of days. I stuffed some clothes in a bag and we got ready to leave. I gave Mildred one of the two keys I kept to my room. On my way out the door, she touched my sleeve, and I stopped.

"Does it matter if I . . . ah . . . confiscated something?" she said softly.

"What, Mildred?"

"I was the one who stole the Trivial Pursuit game," she said.

"Your motives were pure," I said, "and my lips are sealed."

We went down the stairs quickly and then back into my car and toward a motel I knew halfway to Athens, a pretty college town where the University of Georgia is located. I knew the manager, having spent some time there with a variety of well, clients, back when I was young and I knew what in the hell I was doing.

"I'm sorry about school," I said. She had dropped out of her classes for the quarter and did not know if she would start again. I had brought nothing but misery to her. Well, almost nothing.

"Oh hell, I don't mind it so much," she said. She pushed her auburn curls back from her face. "The only thing I think I'll miss is Faulkner."

"I have an idea," I said. "When this is all over, why don't we drive over to Oxford and put a flower on his grave? We can get a bottle of bourbon and sit there and I'll read you 'The Bear' and you can tell me what the italics mean in *The Sound and the Fury*."

"Oh," she said, looking out the window away from me and thinking about it, "what a lovely thought." She went silent and I let her. There was not much time left. It was a complicated plan, and if it all worked together, we might just make that trip to Faulkner country, and perhaps I could be the New Sage of Yoknapatawpha myself.

When I got to the motel, the other man was already there. I recognized him by his regulation-issue ferret car, a dark blue Oldsmobile. I also recognized him because there was no other car in the lot. I'd crossed several streets before I'd left Atlanta to make sure we had not been followed. For some reason, nobody was around this morning. A good sign.

The Blaze Motel was usually below industry-standard occupancy because the rooms were never held more than two hours at a time. It was not one of your tonier joints. It consisted of two cinder-block wings painted an appalling yellow, with a gravel courtyard in the middle. The office was in front of the building on the right. I parked and went in and took Ginny with me. Huel Toomey was the proprietor, and when I got inside, he was standing on the cluttered desk, holding a copy of *Stockman's Journal* and trying to squash a spider that was scuttling frantically across the low ceiling.

"C'mere, you little son of a bitch!" he yelled. "I pay twelve goddamn dollars a month for this place to get sprayed, and here we are after three goddamn frosts and the place's still like an outhouse crawling with the goddamn things. Shit!" He slammed at the spider and then looked at the paper. It was finished. He tossed the paper into the corner and climbed down off the desk. "Oh," he said when he saw me, "it's you." He was wearing a bright orange jumpsuit, which was straining to release his ample belly. Huel must have been nearly seventy, but he looked years younger, and when I had called him from Ginny's house early that morning and told him what I needed, he only said "Cash in advance."

"Hi, Huel," I said, "nice to see you."

"You ever seen a thing that turns your stomach like a big fat goddamn spider?" he asked.

"Not a single thing," I said.

"Your friend's already out there," he said, gesturing. He folded his arms across his chest and waited.

"I saw him," I said. I opened my wallet and took out seven tens and handed them to him. He looked over them, and at one point I thought he might bite them to see if they were really legal tender. He reached to a series of hooks on the wall over his desk and handed me the key to number 24, the last one in the building on the left, just as I had asked.

"You do anything screwy, and I'll call my good friend the sheriff," he said. He had been arrested twice for harboring prostitutes and three times for selling non-tax-paid liquor. I smiled. He smiled. I should have winked, but I just turned and took Ginny back out. I took her down to the room, keeping an eye on the ferret in the car. The room was bare and not very pleasant: no television, two double beds with Magic Fingers, a lamp made of some hideous pink plaster. There was a table. No Bible. The Gideons knew when they were fighting a lost cause.

"God," Ginny shuddered. "This is awful." She had brought two Faulkner books to read, *Light in August* and *A Fable*.

"Everything's going to be all right," I said. "You have to trust me on this. I know it sounds complicated, but it will work." I kissed her on the lips.

"How long will you be?"

"Maybe a couple of hours, or three if everything goes okay."

"What if it doesn't?"

"Then you'll have to figure out Faulkner's italics for yourself," I said. She nodded bravely. "The man outside won't bother you. He's just there to keep an eye on things."

"Why didn't you let Shuler do this part, let one of his men do it instead of me?" she asked.

"Like I told you," I said softly, "I don't know if I can trust anybody right now unless I have all the cards. Doing it this way, I do. If Shuler set this up, he'd get put away. This way, I think I can clear him and set up the guys who did it."

"Why do you want so badly to do this?"

"Because it's right," I said.

On my way out of the lot, I drove by the ferret and looked in his window.

"You know what to do," I said. He nodded and touched his right eyebrow with his index finger in a salute. And I was gone, driving too quickly back toward Atlanta. The fog still hung around the top of Stone Mountain as I passed it, making it look like a majestic, slowly swimming whale, swallowing up countryside as it inched forward.

"From hell's heart I stab at thee," I said to the white whale. It felt good to be so smart. I drove into town and toward Buckhead, one of the city's most affluent suburbs, where the women were women and, sometimes, so were the men. I parked three blocks from Rebecca Sanderson's house on Martin Circle. She would still be there. I knew it. I had a sixth sense about such things, developed from years of hanging around watching people. I walked to my bench across the street from her house and watched for a while as I read the sports section of *The Constitution*. It was still before noon, and her car was in the driveway. Before long, I saw a movement in the broad open front window. She was home. No other cars. No point in waiting.

I walked quickly back to my car, got in and drove into her driveway, jumped out over a few potholes and went to the front door. No one was around. The air was still, and the birds had gone silent. The fog seemed to be settling lower rather than burning off. I tried the door handle. It was unlocked. I opened it quietly and stepped inside. I had on my London Fog raincoat, open at the waist. I would have cinched it, but it made access to my gun difficult. There was a living room to my right. It was piled with suitcases. Straight ahead was a hall running to my left and right. The living room was full of fifties furniture, cheerless. I was thinking about furniture when she came into the den from the hall, arms over her head, combing her hair.

"Surprise," I said. She backed up against the wall and tried to think of what to do. Scream? She couldn't scream because then the cops would come. She did not want the cops to come. Fight? I was a foot taller and a hundred pounds heavier. She was wearing a dark blue dress. Her face was full of lines. She looked tired.

"Who are you?" she finally asked.

"Get your coat," I said.

"Who are you?" She was flat against the wall, breathing too hard. "Are you going to hurt me?"

"Of course not," I said. "But I am going to have to detain you."

"Who are you?" She shuddered. I thought she might cry.

"Get your coat. Now." I said it with some force. I followed her to the bedroom where she got an expensive coat from the closet. She dawdled putting it on, and I helped her, then took her by the arm, turned on a couple of lights, took her phone in the bedroom off the hook and locked the front door behind us. No one was around. She did not scream. She got into the car with me without a word and I drove off toward the Blaze Motel.

Halfway there, she began to shake, and then she sobbed, tears rolling down her cheeks. When we passed Stone Mountain, the fog had come down completely and the Great Whale had majestically disappeared back into the deep.

"I told him it was all crazy," she said rhetorically, staring through the brine straight ahead of us.

"Jack?" I asked.

"Who are you?" she asked. She turned in her seat. "If you are going to kill me, I at least have the right to know who you are."

"I told you that you won't get hurt," I said. "Oh, you'll probably go to jail." I thought of Tony. I thought of Sherrill's eyes staring at me. "And somebody in jail might kill you. But I won't."

"It doesn't matter." She sniffed. I hadn't let her bring her pocketbook, and she needed a tissue.

"In the glove compartment," I said. She opened it and took out a roll of toilet paper. "I know it's not very elegant, but I'm prepared for total war." She tore off a piece and blew her nose.

"So who are you working with?" she asked. I thought about it for a moment.

"I'm working for myself," I said.

"For yourself?" she said. "I know who you are. Jack told me about you."

"Aha," I said, "then you *do* know Mr. Railsback. This is a clue. Do you mind if I look you over with my magnifying glass?'' She was a nice-looking woman, but gone a bit on the far side of paradise.

"You don't know what in the hell you're getting into," she said acidly.

"Another clue," I nodded. "Uses big words and complex sentence construction. Probably went to Vassar."

"I have money," she said quietly, looking down now.

"Is willing to bribe for freedom," I said. "Perhaps went to Weasel University instead of Vassar. Keep talking."

"I . . . I have some money," she said. "I could get it for you."

"I don't want money," I said. "Money corrupts. Absolute money corrupts absolutely. There you have it. Lord Prince's Axiom. What do you think?''

"You're a fool, and you're going to regret this, I promise you," she said.

I didn't have anything else to say to her. We drove to the Blaze Motel without further incident, though she did pout, which really showed a sense of restraint since she'd just been kidnapped. This was my first kidnapping. If it went well, maybe I could take it up as a profession. Later, I could get a grant and go all over the country and teach it to out-of-work hoods.

When I got out of the car and took Rebecca Sanderson with me, she still didn't protest, though when I took her arm, she pulled it away from me. We went inside. Ginny was standing not far from the bathroom, holding *Light in August* in one hand and her gun in the other.

"What ho," I said when we came in. "What light through yonder slum breaks? It is the east, and Ginny is the sun."

"You bastard," said Rebecca Sanderson.

"Poetry doesn't stand a chance in a world like this," I sighed. Ginny stared at her. If they had been cats, their neck fur would be standing up, and they would be circling each other by now. I introduced them and told Rebecca that she would be staying here a while and that there would be no problem as long as she didn't try to get away, since Miss Calvert had a gun and so did the man outside. Rebecca lay on the bed and stared moodily straight ahead. Ginny came out on the breezeway with me. A car had pulled in front of one of the rooms in the other building, and a man and a girl were going into a room, laughing, holding a bottle of whiskey by the neck. It's the stuff of poetry, I tell you.

"I will be back by dark," I said "and we all can have fun. I'll bring some food. Just keep an eye on her. She has no place to go. If the man outside tries to come in, tell him no." We looked over at the car. He was still sitting there, reading *Hollywood Wives*. His lips were moving while he read. She nodded. We had been over it all, and she knew the risks. I kissed her lightly on the lips, got in the Buick and drove back to Atlanta.

I wanted to call Sandy Marcello, get him down here and wrap up the entire gang of flotsam and jetsam in one neat net. I had thought for a long time of calling him and trying to trick him, somehow, into coming down. But it would have to wait. For now, I wanted one man, and I would have to use another to get him.

It was raining now, a slow, steady rain. I put in a Frank Sinatra tape, the good Sinatra, before age finally caught him as it does us all. I listened to Sinatra sing slow songs as I drove to Tony's office downtown. The traffic was terrible, but I found a spot not too far away in a dollar lot next to the Georgia Pacific Building. I got to the Marshall Center Building and climbed on the express elevator with a woman who wanted to be President of the United States within eight years. She wore a wool skirt, wool jacket and a wool tie. I could almost hear her "baa" when she got off at 26. I watched her walking down the hall as the doors closed. She walked with her knees too close together. Tight dresses have ruined the normal gait of some American women, a disaster of unspeakable magnitude.

They had still not changed the lock on Tony Browning's office. Nobody cared anymore. He'd probably paid the rent for a year in advance. No one cared if the office were vacant. I let myself in and closed the door. The heat was still set on 68 and the room was whisper quiet. I went into Tony's office and closed the door. I sat behind Tony's big desk and tried to think of what it would be like to have a normal life, to have a prosperous business, a secretary, a membership in the spa, a Kiwanis Club pin. I'd had a bad ingrown toenail one time. I figured the sensations were so similar I need not go shear a flock of sheep for my upstyle clothing.

I looked up the number of Jack Railsback's office in Decatur and cleared my throat as I dialed the number. I whistled. I felt good because I was steering things now, and soon it would all be over. Soon. His secretary answered. I remembered her when I heard her voice. She was a good secretary.

"This is Mr. Steed," I said. "I have a matter of urgency to discuss with Mr. Railsback." She said nothing for a moment, not expecting the intensity of my voice or the formality of my diction.

"Yes," she said. The phone went dead for a moment and Jack came on.

"Hello?" he said. I had thought about using the Marlon Brando voice, but it might be a little risky, so I settled for a Mickey Spillane rasp.

"Hello, Jack boy," I said.

"Who is this?" he asked. There was an edge to his voice. He was breathing funny into the phone.

"I just want to see if you'd like to make a small deal," I said. Something wasn't right. Yeah. I needed a cigarette, so I lit a Camel.

"I asked who this is," he said.

"The hell's your problem, Jack boy?" I said. "I said I got a deal. You want to talk, or do we do something bad with Miss Sanderson?" He made a noise of surprise and horror, just a syllable or two, unrecognizable as English words, but full of meaning.

"What are you talking about?" he choked.

"Jack," I said patiently. "Jack boy. I have something you want and you have something I want. Would you like to deal?"

"What did you say about Miss Sanderson?"

"I have her, Jack boy. And you have something of mine." I let him think about it for a minute. If he were allied with Steed, it would make no sense to him for Shuler to want the cross. They had set Shuler up, after all. With the confusion, I was almost giddy with the thought of how I could mess up the heads of these gutless little twits.

"What?"

"A good name, Jack. I am calling for your friend Jake Shuler. He is not a happy man, Jack boy."

"I don't know what you're talking about." He didn't

hang up. He knew what I was talking about. Hot damn, I was right.

"Jack, today is what, Wednesday?" He didn't know what to do.

"Yeah," he said weakly.

"Okay, you have Steed meet with me on Friday and I will let you have Miss Sanderson back," I said. For a moment I was lapsing into a little Brando, maybe something from *One-Eyed Jacks*. "Otherwise, I will kill her and dump the body on your front steps."

"Don't hurt her," he said. His voice was shaking and wet. He had not set this up; he had been a pawn for Steed or he would have been thinking more clearly on his feet.

"Good job, Jack boy," I said. "There's one more thing."

"What is it?" he cried. I had ruined his day. Awww.

"We meet in room 412 of the Baker Motel on Cheshire Bridge Road," I said. "I'll bring the girl and you have Lt. Steed come to talk." He inhaled sharply. I could hear him fall back against his chair. It was suddenly clear that he had Big Problems, and he was thinking about what he could do: Not much.

"I don't know if he will," Jack said. I had damn done it, and I was so elated I wanted to do my Donald Duck impersonation, a few back flips and shoot off a Roman candle while drinking a glass of bourbon on the rocks. I had the bastards.

"He'll do it or she'll die," I said. "Friday at three o'clock at the Baker. You screw this up, and you will die, too." I slammed the phone down. I could hear him calling Rebecca, finding the line busy, then driving over there. He would discover he had no choice, no damn choice at all.

I savored my victory for only a few minutes. In every plan, there is a crucial time when it all could collapse in a sorry heap. Now was that time for me. It was time to call Sgt. Paul Tenhoor of the Narcotics Division of the Atlanta Police Department.

14

MET PAUL TENHOOR ON A CASE WHEN I
first moved back to Atlanta. My client suspected his
brother was involved with narcotics and wanted me
to find out. The brother was selling nickel bags,
nothing worth slobbering over, but the man who
finally arrested him when the time came was a young
cop named Paul Tenhoor.

I'd seen him dozens of times on cases, sometimes in
bars talking baseball or politics. He was a Democrat. I
don't understand party politics, and told him so. If
Adolf Hitler ran as a Democrat against God as a
Republican, the Democrats would find lots of nice
things to say about the Führer.

The phone rang, and a receptionist at APD
answered it. There is also a receptionist's factory, probably adjacent to the one that molds waitresses, the one
that made Treena for the Primate Haus. I could almost

see the serial number stamped on this one's forehead.

"I'd like to speak to Sgt. Paul Tenhoor," I said. She didn't say "thank you" or "one moment" or anything. She just punched hold and rang the call through. Surly bitch. I was sitting there trying to think of how to phrase the request when he came on the line.

"Tenhoor," he said gruffly.

"Paul," I said softly. "It's Hank Prince."

"Hey, hotdog," he said. "You still out of jail? We must be falling down on the job." He wasn't much older than me, but he treated everybody as if they were younger. It wasn't one of his most winning character traits.

"I need to talk to you," I said, "now."

"Me?" he said. "You getting confused, Prince. What you need to talk to is a lawyer. I know one, name of Carnelli." He laughed. I could hear him chewing on a cigar. Carnelli was Atlanta's ultimate ambulance chaser. Sometimes he got on the scene before the police.

"It's the most important thing you'll ever hear," I said as urgently as I could.

"You're moving!" he said.

"It involves police corruption and murder," I said. "Please." He sensed it, finally, in the tone of my voice. He cleared his throat and coughed. I could hear him turning to spit in the trash can.

"So tell me now," he said.

"Meet me in half an hour at the zoo," I said.

"Is it that important, Hank?" He had lapsed out of his pose, and I had stopped being a smart mouth. I love being a smart mouth, so it took some effort on my part.

"Paul, there's a few lives hanging in the balance on this one," I said. "Meet me in front of the cat house."

It was a perfect setup for a snappy comeback, but I knew he wouldn't take it.

"I'll be there." He hung up. I took a deep breath and rubbed my hand over my face. It was about 3 p.m. and things were moving. It was easy to keep telling myself this was going to work because I have the ability to convince myself of many improbable things. But I knew I'd never done anything remotely like this, and I was worried, mostly about Ginny Calvert.

The Atlanta Zoo is starting to get better. I remembered coming here as a child and being awed by the elephants. I thought it was awesome when the lions paced endlessly in their cages, knowing nothing, in my childish zoological pursuits, about neurotic behavior in wild animals. The zoo had fallen on hard times, but I still had a thread of affection for it and construction was under way all around the park.

I got there in fifteen minutes and paid and went on in. The rain had stopped. It was cool, and a light breeze ruffled the low clouds. Almost no one was there. I saw one old man wandering around looking for his youth, but he would not find it here. You never feel the same. Sometimes I try to go into movie houses and remember what that old theater was like back home, the sticky floors, seats strung with strips of duct tape.

I walked on up to the cat house, which is at the top of a hill. I had been standing there for five minutes when I saw Tenhoor coming up the hill wearily, like it was hard for him, even though the grade is not difficult. He was wearing a gray raincoat and no hat. His red hair came back from his brow in a series of twisting waves. He held a cigar between his teeth and its ash glowed red like the avenging eye of God. He started talking when he was twenty feet from me.

"This is a hell of a day, ain't it?" he said.

"A hell of a day," I echoed.

"Let's go inside," he puffed. He threw his cigar down in a puddle and we went on inside. There was no one in there. Down in the heart of the cages, some keeper was singing something by Hank Williams. It sounded mournful. We stopped in front of a magnificent male lion with a huge black mane. It sat placidly and stared at us. I leaned on the rail. "Now what in the hell is going on?"

"Paul, I know who killed Tony and Sherrill Browning, and why," I said.

"Yeah, me too," he said. "Jake Shuler had it done. We're going to grab the fucker here soon and it's going to be nasty."

"He had nothing to do with it," I said. Tenhoor straightened up and stared at me.

"What are you talking about?" I sighed and folded my arms over my chest. I had to say this right. No screwing around. If I lost Tenhoor, I lost the whole thing.

"This will sound like lunacy to you," I said, "but you have to trust me. I didn't believe it either. It was set up so perfectly that he must have been planning it for a long time. It's the smoothest thing you'll ever see. And the chances of it unraveling must have seemed remote to him."

"To who?" We were standing close together now. I felt my hands shaking badly, so I put them in the pockets of my raincoat. I was scared.

"There are several people involved, all over the damn town," I said. "But the person who set it all up was Adam Steed." He had been nodding slowly as if trying to understand what I was saying. When I said Steed's name, he started smiling. Then he smiled more. Then he started laughing, a low, gut-shaking laughter that started out silently and then increased in volume until he was doubled over the rail in front of the lion cage. The lion sat and watched the comedy in front of him and barely twitched. When Tenhoor finished laughing he shook his head and turned and walked outside. I followed him and grabbed his arm smartly.

"Get your damn hands off me," he said, turning angrily. A mist had started to fall. The zookeeper inside was now singing "Homesick Blues" at the top of his lungs. "I ought to take you in right now."

"Paul, it's true, damnit," I said. "You owe me to hear what happened."

"I don't owe you jackshit, pal," he said. He started walking down the hill.

"I'll give you $100 just to listen to my story," I said. That stopped him. His tongue moved around inside his mouth. He looked down and then up at me.

"You want a beer?" he asked. My heart was beating so fast I thought it would fall out right there in front of the elk cage.

"Yeah," I said. I followed him to a small bar just off I-20, and we slid into a booth. The waitress brought us each a large frosted schooner. I took a bill out of my wallet and slid it across the table. He looked down at it and let it lay there.

"Talk," he said.

"Don't you want the money?" I asked.

"Just talk," he said. He did not touch the money. I told him everything. At first he kept getting confused and asked the same questions over and over, but by our third beer it was all falling into place for him, and he shook his head a couple of times and stared out the window. It took an hour for me to tell him the story. He wanted another beer, and so did I. He still had not touched the $100 bill, but our waitress was doing everything but sitting on my lap each time she came back.

I explained my plan to him. He started shaking his head again.

"You realize what you're asking me to do?" he said. "Cut my damned throat?"

"But I'm not wrong," I said. "Hell, they'll probably promote you to general."

"But it's all on your word," he said. "All I have is your word."

"Look, if Steed doesn't show up, you haven't lost anything," I said. I had only told him that I had something Steed wanted. I did not tell him I had kidnapped Rebecca Sanderson. He knew better than to ask me what I had. He had been around, too. I told him it would be easy. I had set up the meeting in the motel room so it could be wired. Tenhoor would set up wiring the room.

"Shit," he sighed. He looked out the window. It was only about half an hour until darkness, and I needed to get back to Ginny. He looked back at me.

"Please," I said. "It's the right thing to do." He nodded and kept nodding.

"Okay," he said. "But if this goes up, it's your ass, Prince."

"I understand," I said. He picked up the $100 and folded it once and handed it back to me. I knew what he was doing, and I took it without saying anything. He sighed heavily. About the middle of the afternoon, the sun had briefly considered coming out and then given up, and now it was raining.

"I'll get it done tomorrow. I'll set it up near the lamp between the two beds. There's always a lamp," Tenhoor said. "And I will have to talk to somebody about this. It's going to have to be Singleton." I knew it would be this way. Raymond Singleton was a major, up the administrative ladder, a fair man, like most Atlanta cops, who could be trusted. I trusted Tenhoor, and he trusted Singleton. "Or maybe I'll set you up, hotshot. How do I know you didn't kill Mrs. Browning?"

"Because you know," I said.

"Yeah," he said. "Get lost. I need to think about this." I got up and went outside. My car was sitting there ready for action on the highways of Our Land. I drove first to a liquor store and bought a case of Molson Golden, then I went by a chicken place and bought a bucket or a barrel or a whichever the hell is the biggest one. Maybe they should measure chicken in furlongs or something. Then I stopped by the local K-Mart and bought a small portable AM/FM radio. Hot damn. I was all set.

When I got back to the Blaze Motel, night had come hard. The parking lot was nearly full. The weasel car was gone, but in the back of the lot was another dark Olds being indifferently managed by a ferret. I pulled up next to his car, and he looked at me and nodded. God, it's wonderful to be a celebrity. I got the beer and the radio and went to the door. I'd go back for the chicken. Only the necessities of life first. I knocked on the door with my elbow, the curtain on the front window went back and I saw Ginny's face. She opened the door and let me in.

"Oh God, I thought you weren't coming back," she said. She took the beer and hugged me. She was not holding her gun, and Rebecca Sanderson was lying under the covers smoking a Virginia Slims and reading a copy of *Hollywood Wives*. I knew where she had gotten it.

"You talked to the guy in the car?" I asked.

"Yeah," she said. "It was boring as hell here. He went out and bought us some papers and books." I looked at Rebecca, who didn't look as if she were plotting her escape.

"Hi," I said. "I brought beer."

"You expect me to come kiss your feet?" she asked.

"You won't be able to resist me," I said. "They all break down sooner or later. In tough cases, I'll often charisma them into submission."

"Bullshit," she said. She got out from under the covers and took the case of beer and opened one for herself and one for Ginny.

"In that case, I have fried chicken," I said. "Can I use food to win you over?" She smiled sardonically. Ginny came out on to the breezeway with me. "Where's your gun?"

"She won't try anything," she said. "She's as scared as I am. She didn't want to get involved with this."

"She had her bags all packed," I said.

"She was running away from Jack Railsback," Ginny said. I got the chicken, and Ginny and Rebecca ate heartily, but I started out with a Molson Golden and never made it to the food. I watched Rebecca while Ginny got ice from the office to put in the sink for the beer. Through the wall you could head a bedpost banging against the plaster.

"What do you think they are doing in there?" I asked Rebecca. "May I call you Becky?"

"You may fuck off," she said.

"Look, nothing's going to happen to you other than a few years in the pokey, " I said. "This could be one of your last free nights. Why don't you eat, drink and be merry?"

"He used me," she said. Ginny came back with the ice. I took it and fixed the beer. I was feeling mellow and wanted to talk, to dance. I sat on the side of one bed and fooled with the radio until I got a station somewhere out there in the Greater United States that played stuff from the forties, all old songs, most of them slow. I lit a cigarette and leaned back against the headboard.

"How did he use you?" I asked.

"He made her spy on Tony Browning," said Ginny without much emotion. "Promised her he'd marry her, take her to Europe if she found out a few things." I smoked and thought about it.

"It was something Steed used to pressure Tony into cooperating," I said.

"How did you know that?" Rebecca Sanderson asked.

"Very good," said Ginny, impressed. "Steed is apparently quite a guy." I had told Ginny about the setup, that it had gone perfectly, and I think for the first time she believed me. Instead of feeling elated that Wednesday night, I felt melancholy. Maybe it was from the rain and the sounds of love through the thin walls. Maybe it was from drinking twelve beers.

We talked about it for a while, but I knew all the details. I opened another beer. I was feeling tired, beginning to know the sensation of losing control of things. I had Ginny now, but I could not keep her for long, and once it was ended, I was not sure I could keep her at all. The music was slow, and Perry Como came on singing a piece I did not know.

"Let's dance," I said to Ginny.

"Come on, Hank," she said.

"Dance with him," said Rebecca. Ginny got up and came to me, smiling softly. She shrugged and her body came to mine and the music went on and I held her to me, and we moved easily across the tile floor. Since I had known her, my whole life had been like a slow dance in autumn.

It was late, and without hesitation, Rebecca Sanderson stripped down to her bra and panties and crawled in the bed nearest the bathroom and rolled into a fetal position. Ginny and I undressed. I left the radio on. She lay close to me in the darkness, but I was too embarrassed with Rebecca in the room to make love. Ginny wasn't.

We moved so slowly that the covers barely moved above us, and I tried to control my breathing. I could not imagine what was going through Rebecca's mind, but I convinced myself she could not hear us, that the music was too loud, that the drone of the heater kept her from hearing the sounds we made three feet away. A slow dance in autumn.

The next morning, I left for Atlanta just as the sun was coming up. The clouds had faded to the south, and it would be a fine day. I didn't have much to do, so I would kick over a few more dominoes, put my shoulder behind things one final time before Friday and see what happened.

By now, Jack would have talked with Adam Steed at length. It would be easiest for Steed to have Jack killed, but that would be nearly impossible now, because of the fact that I had Rebecca Sanderson. I had committed a felony in league with a drug kingpin in an effort to entrap a police officer. When this was all over, I planned to enter a monastery and whelm myself before God and inactivity.

Atlanta was beginning to stir. The expressways were starting to clog, the parking lots of restaurants were filling, and the sun dazzled itself, shining back from the glass and steel that rises high above downtown. I like cities because they force everyone to face their limitations. But I like country, too, because it clears the sorry mass of humanity from your heart and allows you to see things with the simplicity of sunrise.

I drove to the Primate Haus where everyone is constantly facing their limitations. Treena was behind the counter as usual. I sat on a stool and ordered a coffee. The place was about half full, mostly of winos. The Primate Haus serves free drinks between seven and eight a.m., an idea that helps the drunks get hold of themselves. I thought about having a beer myself, but I didn't want to drink any more until Friday afternoon.

"So how's it going?" Treena asked. The carpenters had done a fine job of fixing the hole Bull Feeney had put in the wall after the second Duran-Leonard fight.

"I've been in San Francisco for a few days," I said, sipping my coffee.

"Yeah? How come?"

"I was inducted into the Lovers' Hall of Fame," I said. "It was an unexpected honor."

"Hah," said Treena, snarling happily so I wouldn't see her upper teeth. "You think you're good, huh?" She wiped the counter off in front of me. A wino to my left stared at me. He was about forty but looked twenty years older, wearing a tattered Robert Hall blazer, pink pants and a week's beard.

"I can see, sir, that you mistrust my assertion," I said.

"Hey, I don't want no trouble," he said. "You in the Hall of Fame, you in the Hall of Fame."

"Damned right," I said. Treena laughed and shook her head.

I decided to drive around for a while. My car had no objections. I had lately been ignoring the Big Guy, using him merely as a tool to get places rather than a way of life on wheels. I drove by Ginny's house and nothing looked different. I drove down past the Stadium, where the Falcons were scheduled to lose again on Sunday, toward Angel Jiminez' house of broken bodies, broken dreams. No one moving there, either. I drove out by Jack's office, but his Mercedes wasn't there yet. Maybe it wouldn't be there at all today. I needed to bother Jack a little bit more, so I stopped at a phone booth and rang up the trendy little bastard.

"Yes," he said. He was breathing wrong. He must have been up all night worrying about it all, trying to figure out how he could get Rebecca back, how he could extricate himself from it all. His night must have been terrifying. I didn't give a damn. I let him say "yes" one more time.

"Jack boy," I said in my rasp. I wanted to imitate Bogart and say "You're taking the fall, Jack. Somebody's got to be sent over and I'm sending you, you miserable creep." Then I would laugh like Bogart, and he would sit down, put his face in his hands and sob. What a scene that would be. I restrained myself. "So you got it all set up, Jack boy?" He cleared his throat. I heard the sound of a match lighting. He was smoking. That was even better. Maybe he'd take up swearing and carousing next. Fear corrupts. Absolute fear corrupts absolutely. Prince's Second Axiom.

"He won't do it," he said. I froze. I licked my lips. This was no time to equivocate.

"Then I'm going to have to kill Miss Sanderson," I said in a childish singsong. "Or maybe I could send her to you a finger at a time."

"Listen to me," he said urgently. "You've got to listen to me. I talked to him. He doesn't care if you kill her or not. You have to understand. He will let you kill her before he meets Shuler to talk. Can't you understand that?"

"Jack boy," I said, "then you must persuade him."

"How?" he cried helplessly. I thought for a moment I felt a twinge of sympathy for him, a familiar feeling of regret and sorrow. "I don't have anything on him. I'm the fool in this whole thing, just like Tony was."

"I don't give a damn, Jack boy," I rasped. "You have to think of some way you can get him to be there tomorrow." He chewed on the thought for a moment and was silent. I wondered if Miss Formaldehyde were dressing in her house down the way.

"Maybe," he began slowly. He exhaled in misery. "But then he'd kill me."

"You could hide," I said. "We could keep you up at my place." Now I was starting to feel like Vito Corleone. Maybe I should make him a deal he couldn't refuse.

"But then I could never stay here," he said. "He still might have me killed."

"Okay, " I said finally. "Tell him this. If he doesn't show tomorrow, then his wife is going to be pushing up daisies by Saturday." Pushing up daisies? I'd better take it easy on the rhetoric. Nobody talked like that. Still, I could tell Jack Railsback liked the idea.

"Yeah," he said, enlightened. "That might work. He worships her. He might even love her more than money." It was another one of those amorphous gut feelings, but I thought it would work, too.

"Make it work," I said. "Don't disappoint me." Then I slammed the phone down and walked out, hoping to Christ Steed would buckle and take the bait. It was nearly noon now, and I wanted to get back to the Blaze Motel to see Ginny and Rebecca.

The drive back was uneventful, but I was tense. Maybe I would break down and have a beer, after all. I was so scared already that I had to hold my hands tight on the steering wheel to keep them from shaking. One more day. One more damn day. When I pulled into the parking lot of the Blaze, I felt that familiar falling sensation: there were no cars there at all except for Huel's. No ferret car. No car for a traditional suburban quickie. Nothing. I pulled up in front of Ginny's room, leaped out and pounded on the door. No one answered. I took out my key and opened the door.

The room was empty.

15

RAN BACK OVER TO THE OFFICE OF THE
Blaze Motel, sick, and feeling my mouth go dry. If
anybody hurt Ginny, I would kill them. Despite the
consequences, despite any moral law, I would kill
them. The door to the office was closed, but Huel
Toomey was inside. Sometimes his brother would drop
him off for work.

"Where'd they go?" I asked as I came into the small,
hot office. A kerosene heater crackled in the corner,
and Huel sat in his chair behind the cluttered desk,
reading a copy of a tabloid. The headline on the front
said something about a man whose head had been
exploded by voodoo.

"Who?"

"The people in 24," I said with unsubdued hostility.
"They're gone."

"How the hell should I know?" he growled. "Maybe

they went out for lunch or something." I stared at him for a moment and then turned and went through the door. I ran back to the room and looked through it, but I could find no sign of a struggle, and everything we had brought in was gone, even the radio. I sat down on the edge of the bed where Ginny and I had slept the night before and tried to think.

She would not have merely left for some small reason. She knew better. The fact that Shuler's man was gone meant something. I knew, anyway, that one of two things had probably happened: Shuler had taken Ginny and Rebecca Sanderson or Adam Steed had. It wasn't Steed. Steed thought I was a hopeless drunk who had presumed Shuler's people had taken the cross. Steed was counting on my ignorance, not my intelligence. I was pretty sure Ginny had earlier been taken to Rebecca Sanderson's house when she was kidnapped, but now I knew who had her. Maybe I wasn't in such dynamic control of my destiny after all. I had counted on Jake Shuler keeping his word, just as I was counting on a lot of things.

Goddamn that Jake Shuler. I got in my car and catapulted out of the parking lot, spewing gravel and leaving twin streaks of rubber on the blacktop. I tried not to think or feel. I had practiced not feeling for so long that I was unsure I could, until I met Ginny. I drove through town, running lights and turning in front of people. I didn't give a damn. By the time I got to Shuler's place, I was so revved up that I could have probably won the U.S. Olympic boxing titles in all weight classifications on the same day.

I did not park across the street. I drove down the long driveway and parked right beside the gate the Samoan had escorted me through before. I skidded forty feet before I stopped and hit the ground running. Standing at the gate with an enormous handgun was a fat man.

"Prince," he said. He smiled. He had bad teeth. The gate was open, and I walked up to him and, before he had time to say anything else, dropped my left shoulder slightly and hit him square on the jaw with a right hook. He made a sick sound and then went down. I didn't even bother to take his gun. If he shot me in the back, I'd know.

I walked up onto the porch and into the house. A man grabbed me as I came through the door and slammed me into the ivory wall, and we fell to the white carpet. I hit him in the face with two short rights and blood came out of his nose. He didn't seem to mind. He was huge, and he waited until I had to take a breath, and then he brought his knee up into my stomach. It felt like a tree trunk, and I felt myself go faint.

He came up and dragged me with him and took my gun away and threw me sprawling into the living room. I landed hard on the floor and lay there, ready for the sudden impact of the bullet in the back of my head. Do you really never hear the one that gets you? But no one fired. There was a faint sound of something dripping. The man was standing over me, and blood from his nose was lazily dropping to the white carpet only inches from my face.

I looked up and saw Manny Fargo sitting there with his legs crossed at the knees. He was wearing a white suit coat and a green tie and looked like someone trying to impersonate Tom Wolfe. I got up on my elbows, and then I sat up.

"You a real pain," he said.

"You have them," I said. "Why does Shuler have them?" He got up and went to the mantel and opened a small Chinese box and took out a brown cigarette. I didn't feel like fighting anymore. I thought two ribs on my right side were broken. I held them as I stood up. The bouncer's nose was still bleeding. He smiled at me. I was starting to calm down. I could not demand to know a damn thing. "Two out of three falls?" The bouncer did not answer.

"What makes you think we have anybody?" said Manny Fargo.

"Look, you goddamn . . ."

"Okay, okay, it was just a question," he said. "I don't care what you know. You got to finish the job tomorrow. I just wanted to make sure you done it.

"You?"

"Oh, Mr. Shuler sometimes don't think too smart," said Manny Fargo. I felt my gorge rising, but I could not touch him here without getting pummeled into a jelly doughnut, and he knew it. "So I had them moved to a safe place. When you're finished with the job, then they'll both be let go. You got my word."

"Your word is shit," I said. He lit the brown cigarette and shrugged. He didn't have to do anything but wait, and I knew he had me. I would never find them. I would have to trust him.

"Nobody'll hurt them," he said. "We'll be around tomorrow at the motel to see what goes down. If it works, you get the girls back." I didn't have to ask what would happen if it all didn't work.

I got up and went out the door, staggering, feeling defeated and hurting like hell. The bouncer gave me my gun back, and I wanted to shoot him, but I just stuck it in my coat pocket and made it to my car, past the guy I'd smacked. They knew I was coming, or they'd have shot me when I came in.

I backed down the driveway as fast as I could, and when I got to the end I ran into a pillar at the front gate on which was perched a snarling concrete lion. The pillar fell over and the lion tumbled down and landed on the trunk of my Buick and stayed there. I screeched off and the lion fell into the street and shattered into a million billion pieces. *Sic semper tyrannis.*

I was consumed with rage but had to remain calm. It was a situation to test my patience, maturity and problem-solving ability, so I drove to the nearest liquor store and bought a quart of Evan Williams Black Label Sour Mash Bourbon Whiskey. I had to make the time pass until tomorrow and then hope for the best. I drove to Ginny's apartment and sat in front of it and sipped on the bourbon. I don't know what I was waiting for, maybe for her to come home, wearing a gingham dress and tall boots, carrying a bag full of French bread, Chianti and the makings for spaghetti. Or maybe I was waiting for maturity to find me sitting there.

"Here am I, Lord," I said out loud. Then I toasted the words. I was seized suddenly with a fear of being alone, the great void staring at me, almost yawning, beckoning. The void was death, madness, loneliness. I headed for Shelleen's, and when I got there, I felt no better, but at least I was there with other miserable beings.

I ordered a bourbon and water and sipped it and smoked as I sat at the bar. The bartender was a lovely woman not yet old enough to curse the mirror each morning. For now, she would notice a wrinkle or two, a wayward gray hair, but nothing of the wretched advance of age, not for years.

"What is the meaning of life?" I asked her. It was not yet dark, and the place was as busy as the inside of a coffin. She was tall, maybe five-ten, with long red hair and a green pantsuit. Her nose was too pointed and her lipstick was too red.

"Love thy neighbor," she said. She had a whiskey-hoarse voice that immediately changed her from mildly attractive to the object of every man's lust.

"Where'd you pick that up?" I asked morosely, staring down into my drink. She didn't answer, and it was just as well. I was only another drunk hanging on the bar, no more to her than any other, even though I was incredibly handsome and full of witty repartee. Or maybe I was lying to myself again. I did not want to think about Ginny Calvert, about crosses, about anything. I wanted to take a journey, a crusade in search of something worthwhile on this godforsaken ball of earth and rain and winds.

I had four more drinks. I felt like challenging the team of Einstein, Picasso, Beethoven and Leonardo da Vinci on *College Bowl*. Some time later, long after darkness had gulped the town whole, a woman wearing a long brocaded gown sat down next to me. Her gown was dark green and seemed to be made of terry cloth.

"You could use that dress as a towel if you ever got caught in a shower," I said pleasantly. She got up and went to the other end of the bar. Some people have no sense of humor. The world is a wonderfully ridiculous place, full of hidden meanings, secret gardens. I had the futile idea that if man is not basically good, he is at least worthy of charity and pity.

"You have no charity or pity," I said to the woman after she had moved. She looked away, and presently a tall, good-looking man with a gold chain and neatly creased trousers sat down beside her and they seemed happy to be together. His teeth looked like they were made by the same company that makes toilet bowls.

I had a couple or four more bourbons. Another woman came in and sat down beside me. She seemed glad to see me. Perhaps we were related, maybe even married. She would take me home to a house in the suburbs, 2.3 children, a poodle and Friday night with my brother-in-law playing canasta or some other idiotic game. It might take me years to get out of it gracefully.

"Hi," she said.

"You can keep the house and the poodle, but I want the *Reader's Digest* condensations," I said. She laughed. Maybe later I would do my impersonation of Ed Sullivan and introduce her to Topo Gigio, my friend the Little Italian Mouse.

"What's your name?" she asked. The red-haired bartender brought her a Tom Collins.

"Aren't you going to ask me my sign first?" I asked. I noticed that several consonants gave me trouble. I didn't give a damn.

"What's your sign?" she said. She smiled wickedly. Or maybe she only smiled; by that time, I could no longer separate illusion from reality.

"It used to be Scorpio," I said, "but I changed it."

"How can you change your sign?" she asked seriously.

I leaned close to her and whispered conspiratorially, "I found out that my mother was really my aunt and that my aunt was my mother, and her husband was my uncle and my mother's husband was the Duke of Earl." She sipped her drink.

"What does that make you?"

"Or maybe it was Duke Ellington. Or Duke Snider. I forget."

She suddenly looked like somebody I didn't want to know. I paid my bar bill and staggered toward the door. I was as drunk as I had been in weeks. I came outside and stood in the doorway and lit a cigarette. I did not want to drive anywhere because I did not want to be anywhere; I only wanted to disappear into the maw of the Great City, to fold myself into it like a beaten egg into cake batter, come out something else on the other side. So I started walking.

I never, in my extended youth, thought I was built for failure. I had been good-looking and popular in school and smart as a whip, particularly in English, which was a paradox I encouraged people to see: the tough man of action who knows literature and the finer things of life. Like books. Wines. Women. Stumbling drunk in the neon glitter of cheap streets. Now it all was going to collapse on me tomorrow, and they would never give Ginny and Rebecca back, maybe kill them, and if I were lucky I could spend the balance of my days and ways painting license plates in the state prison in Reidsville. Maybe they would recognize my special talents and let me buff the vanity plates or road-test the warden's new car.

I was standing under a street light trying to light another Camel when a hooker appeared out of the corner of some dive and threaded her arm through mine. She looked about fifty, face fallen from grace, desperate for money if not for love. Maybe the money meant more to her than the body she held indifferently there in the night.

"You need a friend," she said.

"Your mother's going to be mad when she finds out you stayed out past curfew," I said. She threw her head back and laughed harshly, like a character from a Dickens novel or a Hogarth engraving. I felt my skin itch from her presence, but I knew as I stood there with the cigarette dangling from my lips that I was no better. I started running. I don't know why I did it. The ashes from my cigarette fell on my shirt and burned me, but I ran and ran and ran like I could escape Death there on the street.

I finally stopped running and walked into an alley to take a leak. When I got in there, I suddenly felt more tired than I ever had in my life, the kind of fatigue that wraps around your bones and hauls you down. There was someone else in there. He was squatting down in his rags, watching me urinate. I put my hand on the wall to steady myself and finished.

"Cold night coming," he said. His voice was deep and kind.

"Yeah," I said. "It's already cold."

"You down on your luck?"

"Yeah. You?"

"Been for my damn whole life." His voice was full of unspilled laughter. "Ain't never had no luck. Wouldn't know it if I seen it." I stumbled out of the alley and tried to walk back toward my car, but I had turned around and did not remember from where I had come. I walked and walked until I found myself in a small city park. I did not know what time it was. I sat in one of the swings and started moving back and forth, looking at the branches of a tree moving above me then away, above me, then away, above me, then away.

I got out of the swing and lay down under it in the sandy ditch dug by the feet of days and days of swinging children. I curled up. The sand felt warm. I slept.

I dreamed about being chased by a ferocious dragon. I wore a suit of armor and poked at the charging beast with a twenty-pound broadsword. I was standing at the edge of a vast lake when the dragon came upon me, and I had no escape. Just then, a huge swan came gliding out of a clot of reeds and spoke to me, saying, "Climb upon my back and we shall escape the beast." I recognized the swan and wanted to spend long hours talking in swan to it, but the dragon was upon us. I climbed upon the swan, and we had moved out into the still waters when the dragon came swimming alongside and began to lick me on the face with its long, forked tongue. I awoke.

The morning sun made diamonds dance upon the limbs over me.

"Damnation," I said. It was Friday, the day it all went down, and I had spent the night sleeping outside in the cold. I tried to stand but my ribs were hurting with a pain I had never felt, except when I hurt my Achilles tendon one time. I groaned and made it to a spreading oak tree before I got sick. I stood there a long time.

"Never again," I thought. I had made the promise before. I had made plenty of promises before. I felt better now and I walked back to the street across the way and found out that I was right across the street from Shelleen's and my car. I got in and sat there trying not to shake, but I could not help it. I wanted to cry, for some reason I still don't understand, but I held it in me; I usually held it in me. A smart mouth, a clever fellow who always held it in him. I thought of Ginny Calvert, and I went ahead and cried. Then I felt better.

I started the Buick. Its power cheered me, as it always did, and I patted the dashboard and moved out slowly. I needed a shower and some new clothes. I probably needed to have the ribs taped. I drove back to Mrs. Gunnerson's. *This thing was going to work. I would make it work.* When I got there, they were all in the parlor waiting for Mrs. Gunnerson to finish breakfast. I knew I looked like hell, but not as bad as their eyes said I did.

"Hah!" said Dicky Thacker happily. "You look like something the cat drug in." Mr. Oshman had his mouth open.

"I have a list of clues for you," said Mrs. Carreker. She opened her purse and handed me a folded piece of paper, careful not to get too close to me, and she reached out and then withdrew.

"Thanks," I said.

"I hope you find the thief," she said.

"Me, too," I said. Mildred Ruth stared at me with, I thought, great affection and I nodded at her and then went upstairs and showered. I came back and lay naked on my bed for a while, staring at the picture of Wanda Mankowicz above my dresser with the knife through her forehead. I wondered how she and Mr. Encyclopedia were getting along. My ribs were hurting like hell, but I no longer felt sick. Benjy the cat sat on the table and stared at me.

I slipped into my pants, but I knew I needed some help with the ribs, so I went out into the hall and called Mildred. I could almost see the others looking at her and wondering if she and I had something going on. She came into my room, and when she saw me naked to the waist, saw the huge mass of bruises, she drew in her breath sharply and put her hand over her mouth.

"What happened to you?" she cried. She was not pretty, but she had the kind of soft vulnerability that men with real taste can always discern. I did not know why she had never married.

"It's a dangerous business," was all I said. I got the tape from the medicine cabinet. "I need for you to wrap this around me, around these ribs." I was a foot taller, and she had to put her thin arms completely around me to put four strands of tape on. I winced as she wrapped the tape, but I did not cry out. She expected me to be brave and strong. I would be.

When she finished, she stepped back and a strand of her hair had come loose from where it was moored with a barrette and she was looking over her handiwork. I stretched my arms and moved a bit, and it helped, though I felt vaguely like Boris Karloff. Maybe if I had some bolts implanted in my neck I would feel right at home.

"Does it feel better?" she asked.

"Much better," I said. "You are a wizard, Mildred." She blushed and licked her lips, then she went and rubbed Benjy, who seemed glad to see her.

"Are you going to tell Mrs. Carreker I stole the game?" she asked.

"I have a plan," I said gravely. "I don't want you to say a thing. I'll spring it maybe tomorrow or Sunday. Trust me."

"I do trust you," said Mildred Ruth. She went downstairs. I put on a fresh shirt. The day was clearing and cool, a fine day for rescuing fair maidens and stopping, for one brief shining moment, the evil that men do.

16

THE FIRST THING I DID WAS DRIVE TO THE
Rich's at Lenox Square and buy a nice slouch
hat, for $85, then stroll with it on by Buttons 'n
Things. It was open for business as usual. They
didn't know where Rebecca Sanderson was. They
didn't care. Then I stopped at a phone booth not far
from an IHOP and dialed Tenhoor.

The same factory-made receptionist took my call
and put me through.

"Yeah," he said. "Tenhoor."

"I have it all set up," I said. He paused for a
moment.

"It's ready," he said curtly. "We'll be there."
He slammed the phone down, but the sound
of the receiver was a symphony. Now if Steed would
only do his part. The day had risen perfectly, one of
those spectacular fall days with the high blue arch of

heaven overhead.

I tried to think of what I would say, how I might get Steed to tell the truth about what he had done. If he merely denied it all, I was sunk — and so was Rebecca Sanderson and Jake Shuler. And Ginny Calvert. I drove around trying to kill time.

The two hundred miles I'd seen on Jack's odometer that night were clear to me. He was the one who had driven, probably on Steed's order, to Shuler's hideout and shot at the house. Steed knew everything there was to know about Shuler. Only two things fouled up his plans: Tony Browning ran away, and I didn't just wander home and get drunk again. Take either one away and he would be lying in bed fondling the French cross.

Without Steed's confession, I had no proof that any lawyer could hang a case on, and though I knew Tenhoor must be concerned with entrapment, I think he knew I was right.

But there was more. Tenhoor did not like Steed, and from the time I found out that Steed was involved, I knew Tenhoor might be the man who would help me tidy things up.

I do not know if I was really in love with Ginny then, but love has many guises, and I had shucked most of them enough to know that what I felt for her was far beyond either passion or friendship. If I made this work, perhaps she would stay with me.

The Baker Motel was built twenty years ago, before the area was littered with condos and stores every six feet, and it had lately been making a valiant stand against commercial growth. It consisted of two stories of brick rooms, and the owner had added a painted twenty-foot-high figure of a baker out front, complete with apron, cap and bulging belly. I drove by it one time in the late morning but nothing looked out of place.

By two, I had used up a tank of gas. My car loves gas and uses it as an intoxicant, sniffing the highest octane available through its carburetors and then shouldering its way proudly through a world of dwarfs. By now, as I stood under a sunny autumn sky, I felt my hands wet on the pump handle as the gas sloshed into the Buick.

I paid the attendant $31, a small price to pay for fast driving, one of the true pleasures of the flesh. Then I drove over near the Baker Motel and parked at an auto parts store two hundred yards away and walked slowly along the highway back to the motel. It was 2:15 and I was early, but I needed to be early. I had my sunglasses on and my hat slouched down and my jacket collar up. I felt like a pervert looking for a perversion.

There was a van at one end of the parking lot with a small circular antenna on top. I wondered if it were the good guys; I hoped so. I went up the stairs two at a time to room 412, which was on the end of the second floor. For some arcane reason, the numbers on the first floor were all two hundreds and those on the second floor were four hundreds. Let's hear it for marketing strategy.

I took the silvered knob in my hand and turned it, and it opened, just as it was supposed to. I went on inside and turned on the lamp between the beds and then went and sat in the black naugahyde chair in the corner. I wanted to look out between the curtains, but I knew that would be a mistake.

I was jumpy but confident. I got up and looked at myself in the mirror. Not bad. The sunglasses were reflectors. I snarled. Hmmm. I'd have to work on the snarl, perhaps taking lessons from Treena. I went to the lamp between the bed and sang a few lines of "Feelings" for the boys in the truck. You could have tattooed "false bravado" on my forearm, and it would have fit me like my own name.

I looked at my watch: 2:45. The gun was heavy since I was wearing my shoulder holster instead of the hip clip. I hoped I wouldn't have to use it at all. In a place like this, all manner of mayhem could come from the use of a firearm.

I did a few deep knee bends but soon quit because my ribs reminded me that such exercise is a poor idea when the rest of your body is falling apart. I licked my lips. It was 2:46. How in the hell could only one minute have passed? I daydreamed. I thought about my grandfather for some reason, how he used to put a worm on the hook with his thick, work-cracked fingers when he took me down to the lake, patient as sunrise. How long had he been gone now? Twenty years?

The knock was so soft I did not hear it at first. I was shocked, and when I looked at my watch and saw that it was straight up 3 p.m., I thought the adrenalin rush would make me jump up and break through the tar and gravel roof and cruise around Atlanta for a while. He knocked again.

I got up and walked to the back of the room and stood facing away from the door.

"Come in," I said. My voice sounded like it was coming from Andy Hardy. The door opened. I turned halfway around, my heart thumping, skipping beats, flailing at my ribs as if it wanted to get out and bounce away. It was Adam Steed, and he, too, was wearing sunglasses. "Close the door." He closed it and looked at me, cocking his head as if I looked familiar. I wondered which one of us would take off his sunglasses first.

I did.

"Guess who?" I said.

"Prince," he said with a mixture of disbelief and disgust. He took off his glasses and squinted at me. He looked terrible. His eyes were bloodshot. Maybe he wasn't as smart as he thought.

"I know what you're thinking," I said. I wanted to say, "Did he fire five shots, or was it six?" but this was no time for my Clint Eastwood impersonation. "What in the hell is a nice guy like me doing mixed up with a scumbag like Jake Shuler?"

"I don't know what in the hell you're talking about," he said. The room was warm, and he loosened his tie with his left hand; his right hand was in his coat pocket, something I did not like.

"The hell you don't," I said. I was getting mad again. "You're here because Jack Railsback told you what he'd never get back if you didn't come talk to Shuler. If you weren't in cahoots with Jack, you wouldn't be here. You set up Tony and Sherrill Browning, and you set me up. You got the cross back. That was pretty smart, Adam, but I'm probably nearly as smart as you are. I know it was you who shot those two men on Ponce de Leon. And I know it was you who set it all up."

He licked his lips and started smiling and nodded lightly.

"Prince, I didn't think you had it in you," he said. "Working with Shuler. You must have really gotten desperate to go to work for such a piece of shit."

"I'm not working for him," I said. His mouth twitched at the corners.

"Then who in the hell are you working for?" he asked.

"The same person I was the last time I saw you," I said. "Sherrill Browning."

"Well," he said. "It doesn't matter anyway." I knew it was a signal but I could not reach inside my coat quickly enough. He jerked out an automatic, and he pointed it at my heart. "Give it to me, butt first." He was sweating heavily. I took my gun from the shoulder holster and handed it to him. I sat on the bed.

"Shall I say the prosecution rests?" I said. He put my gun in his coat pocket.

"Say whatever you want to," he said. "You tell me what happened, you know so much."

"Gee, where shall I begin?" I asked. "With your brother-in-law Sandy and the cross? With Edvard Johannsen and the cheese import business in Atlanta? With Jack Railsback and poor Tony Browning? With the two men in the parking lot where you shot them dead?" His face fell in disbelief. "Or should I begin with Sherrill's body where you blew her brains out, where you slaughtered that sad, wayward, harmless little girl? Did you know I once loved her, you piece of garbage?"

"Shut the fuck up," he said. He licked his lips again. "Do you know what it is like to be a collector, Prince? No, of course you don't. To admire something of beauty, to really want it so badly that nothing in this world can make up for it? When I was a fifteen-year-old kid I had a Guiana One Penny Black, the rarest stamp in the world. But the cross. Now that was something that went beyond everything. It was perfection. It was God to me, everything. And I knew how to get it. I knew how to set it all up. I made a mistake relying on other people. Jack told me that you would lead us to Tony. He was right. He was wrong about you in every other respect, however." He seemed to be enjoying it, icy as always.

"Jack is a congenital idiot," I said. If the bug were working I had nothing else to do. I had done my job. Anyway, it was starting to look like I might not be alive to enjoy my triumph. He held the gun steadily on me. I knew what he had in mind, shooting me and then claiming he was trying to bring me in. Then he'd tie me to Tony as a drug dealer, and he would be safe. Wrong. Steed had failed to account for something: I may be a drunk, a rotten detective and one of God's prime failures, but I have never forgotten the difference between right and wrong.

"I just want to know one thing. Why did you kill Sherrill?"

"Tony called her and told her what had happened, and she confronted me," he said. "I didn't want it to happen."

"You bastard," I said.

He stood closer to me, the gun closer to all my vital organs. There was a sound outside. I waited for Steed to pull the trigger but he hung there, deciding what to do next, eyelids working like mad. He came over to me, and I weighed my choices: I could dash for the door and hope he wouldn't fire. I could try to disarm him. Or I could just wait, do whatever he wanted and make a move later. I decided to wait. He came close to me, put the barrel of the pistol on my right temple and then his left arm around my neck. My heart was missing beats and I felt as if it were swelling in me. My skin went cold, then hot, then cold again.

He moved me toward the door. The barrel was pushed so hard into my skull that it hurt considerably. I kept thinking now, now, now. But he did not fire. Would I hear it anyway? Probably not.

"Open the door," he said calmly.

"Okay," I said. I reached carefully down and opened the door, and we walked with baby steps out onto the balcony. I could see men running down below, hear their footsteps, leather on asphalt. "Now what?"

"To your car," he said. "Where is it?"

I heard the crackle of a bullhorn. A voice below us said, "Come on, Lieutenant. Let him go. You can't go anywhere." He looked below us and saw the police everywhere and softly said "My God," and it was then he realized what had happened to him. "A block, that way," I said, gesturing with my head. "You can't get away with this. Your pal Jack Railsback is going to sing like Tina Turner, and as you can see, the room was wired." He made a sound in his throat.

"Go down the stairs."

We edged downward. I know how to disarm a man, but I could not see his finger. If it were snug on the trigger, a light trigger, the least jar would kill me. The police would not shoot Steed as long as the gun was pressed to my head, though by now he was surely in their sights.

We made it to the parking lot.

"Adam, this isn't going to work," I said.

"Be quiet," he whispered in my ear. I could feel his breath on my neck. I could hear cops changing positions, moving with us like wind through a field of wheat. When I saw my car, I felt suddenly as if I had little choice: to save myself I must do something before we got there.

My life did not flash before my eyes, only my options. I had to assume that they had Steed sighted. I had to make a move.

We were thirty feet from my car, then twenty-five. I sucked in my breath. I felt my muscles go taut, full of fire and pulsing like a hose.

"The cross," I said, "is a fake." He hesitated a moment and his grip relaxed only a little, but it was enough. I went limp as a petulant child, arms up over my head. Then there was the sound of gunfire. I looked up and saw Steed hanging against the autumn sun, blood pouring from a hole in his lower chest. He touched the blood and looked at me, puzzled, one motion, one second. Then there was another shot, and Steed fell straight down on top of me, eye to eye, blood spurting out a huge wound in his neck. I lay there breathing hard, scarcely hearing the footsteps around me. Steed's blood spilled slickly over my face. I pushed him off and stood, fighting off arms trying to help me.

"Are you hit?" a uniform cop was asking me.

"No," I said. I tried to say something else. "No."

There were sirens, then men. I could feel the pulse in my temples, pain where the barrel had pressed, and for the first time in what seemed like years, I really thought of Sherrill. I told them about Jack Railsback, and they went to pick him up. I told them to go to his house. He would be holed up there, not at his office. I did not tell them about Ginny Calvert or Rebecca Sanderson. I had to believe Shuler's men were in the gathering crowd and that they knew what had happened. If they did not know yet, they soon would. I could only hope they would keep their word, as I had mine. They had nothing to lose.

We went back downtown, and I was grilled by everyone from Narcotics to Homicide to the top administrators, including Raymond Singleton. They all came to the main office on Decatur Street instead of dragging me all over town to where each operated. Just after 11 p.m., they let me go for the night.

Tenhoor and I walked outside at about the same time. My car sat there in the parking lot beside his.

"Mrs. Steed's taking it real hard," he said. We both lit cigarettes and I nodded. Her husband and her brother. "Newspaper and TV folks all over the place downstairs while we were talking. Most coverage Steed ever got."

"He was a bad guy," I said.

"More stupid than bad, at first," said Tenhoor. "But then he decided the cross was worth more than some people's lives."

They had come crashing into Steed's home just after he had been killed, seven or eight detectives, and in only twenty minutes they had found the cross, hidden in a box under his desk with some papers. The Sûreté was already on its way with investigators.

The Atlanta Police Department had arrested Edvard Johannsen, and while we had been talking at about 8 p.m., a faceless cop had stuck his head into the door and said the Philly boys had picked up Sandy Marcello.

"He was bad all along," I said. We walked down to the cars. The city was just starting to get moving for the night. Traffic was not very heavy.

"Yeah," said Tenhoor. He looked tired, but he knew that he had scored a coup with the break in the Browning murder. He would get a commendation and maybe a promotion. I felt like I was getting a one-way ticket to Palookaville.

I got in my Buick and drove off, not knowing exactly where to go. I did not feel like going to Mrs. Gunnerson's that night. I wanted a drink so bad I could barely stand, but I did not stop for one. I put in an Andy Williams tape. I could drive up to Jake Shuler's, but my ribs still hurt, and I did not want to get beat up again. I had to trust them to find me.

I drove over to Ginny's house but no one was there. No one was at Rebecca Sanderson's place, either. Jack Railsback was in jail. They had found him at his house, on his knees, wringing his hands. He would tell them about Rebecca soon enough, but I knew he was scared for her and would not talk for a long time. When he did, she would, I hoped, be in jail, too. Shuler would be gone, and Tenhoor would, sensibly, not have charges pressed against me.

I drove by the Waffle House and got a tall coffee to go and went back to Ginny's and sat in the car sipping my coffee and listening to the National Public Radio jazz show. I was in no hurry. I listened to Wynton Marsalis play his horn for a long time.

What would I do next? Reopen my agency. I had no choice on that one. I'd get a small office somewhere and start back on the divorce cases, the missing moms and daughters and sons and fathers. I would become what I had always been. Always, always, like the wind coming back, I was finding I could not escape who I was. There was no escape in the bottles or the miles I had put between this poor drunk and that uniformed boy of summer standing out there bright-eyed, waiting for the next fly ball.

I slept. I did not dream. When I awoke it was light outside, and my ribs hurt so bad that I could barely move. I reached up to turn off the radio and found that I had done it sometime in the night. I thought I heard a car engine running and was just about to get out and look around when I saw a black glove throwing itself onto the window two inches from my face. I opened the door, and Manny Fargo was standing there. Behind him and to one side was Ginny.

"Hank," she said, and she came to me. To hell with the ribs. I got out of the car, and Manny stepped aside and I took Ginny into my arms and held her there as the sun began to yawn over Atlanta. She clung to me and cursed at Manny, who did not seem to care.

"Are you all right?" I asked.

"Yes," she said. A weasel and a ferret took all of her things and set them down on the porch in front of her door. Manny was in a great mood, clapping his hands against the cold. He wore an expensive overcoat.

"Where is Rebecca Sanderson?" I asked.

"We did our duty and turned her in to the police," he said. He smiled, and you could tell it was going to be a great day for him. He reached inside his coat. A breeze scattered leaves down St. Charles Place. He took out a white envelope with nothing written on it and handed it to me. Ginny did not let go.

I opened it, and inside were five one-thousand dollar bills. It would be enough to let me live a life of indolence for weeks. I took the money out and held it aloft and stared at Manny Fargo, who couldn't have been happier. Then I threw the money up into the air and the wind blew it off down the street.

"Why'd you do that?" asked Manny. I turned to Ginny, and we headed up the stairs.

"Love thy neighbor," I said. When we got to the top of the stairs, I turned to and saw him scuttling down the street like a crab after the money, and that was the last time I ever laid eyes on Manny Fargo.

17

J UST BEFORE WE WENT TO BED THAT MORN-
ing, Ginny cut the tape off my ribs. Every tug of
the strands, every snip, reminded me of what they
had done, what all of them had done, and, finally,
I felt more sad than exultant. As we lay down, I told
her so.

"Is it all over now?" she asked wearily. They had
taken both women to a house down near Sugar Barvano's gym, and she had not slept much during the
long night.

"I think so," I said. "I'm just sorry that you got
mixed up in all this. I didn't mean for it to happen this
way."

"I know," she said.

We spent the entire day in bed, sleeping at first,
until late in the afternoon. I was lying there watching
the sun escape over her windowsill, wondering what I

should do next, when I felt her stir next to me. She rolled over and snuggled up to me, still half in love with her dreams. It was then that I realized I did not know her, because you don't know anyone if you don't know their dreams. I stroked her hair gently.

"Hi," she said.

"Hello," I said. "The Clean Books League would like to present you its gold medal for never having read *Ulysses*."

"I have read that," she said.

"Drat," I said. "How about *Tropic of Capricorn*? You haven't read that, have you?"

"I'm afraid so."

"Then you'll have to accept the prize for most beautiful woman in the bed," I said. She kissed me. I didn't notice the pain in my ribs until an hour later when we were taking a shower together. But the pain would pass, as it always did.

We ate at the Primate Haus and then went over to Mrs. Gunnerson's. Ginny was anxious to get Benjy and start her life over. I didn't blame her. And I knew that a new life probably didn't include me, though she protested she hadn't even thought about it. All she had thought about was going home to her parents' house for the holidays.

"So you don't want to go see Faulkner's grave?" I asked as we pulled up in front of Mrs. Gunnerson's. She was beautiful. The autumn light was escaping west, and it came through the window on to her face, illuminating it like a Rossetti painting.

"Oh, Hank," she said. "I just want to get away from this town, to go home for a while. I do feel something for you, but I don't know what it is. I just need to go home and think things over." I wanted to tell her that life is too short to search for meaning. Life is a series of gestures and sighs and kisses and losses and gains, and you never understand what happened last or what comes next.

"Okay," I said. "You've been special to me, but I know I'm not the kind of guy who appeals to everybody."

"It's not that," she said. Through the window I could see Mildred Ruth staring at us. "It's just that I've always lived inside books, and now I've lived outside them, and I don't know which one is better."

"Neither is better," I said. There was nothing else to say so we went inside. Mrs. Gunnerson grabbed me by the arm as I came through the door. The others were standing in the parlor looking at us with large bright eyes.

"Yrdey ina pyepers be fimyas!" exclaimed Mrs. Gunnerson. She held up a copy of that afternoon's *Journal*. I didn't want to read it. Mr. Oshman came up and shook my hand, his long arm moving like a seaweed in a stormy wave. Mrs. Carreker shook my hand, too, and her hand felt like a shard of peanut brittle. Dicky Thacker was still at work, I guess, but Babe Ruth was looking adoringly at me through her thick glasses.

"Mildred, you have done a splendid job," I said.

"What?" cried Mrs. Carreker. "What are you talking about?" There was a grumbling growl out front, and I knew Dicky Thacker had come home.

"Yeah, what has Mildred done?" asked Mr. Oshman. Ginny went on upstairs to get Benjy and a few of her things she had left. I walked to the mantel and held it. The front door flapped open, and Dicky Thacker came swaggering in, covered with grease.

"Meithsor Thackery," said Mrs. Gunnerson, "Meisthor Prance as bick." Dicky looked at her with great resignation.

"What has Mildred done?" asked Mrs. Carreker.

"You people probably don't know that Mildred Ruth is one of this city's great detectives," I said. Mrs. Carreker's mouth fell open in disgust. "While I was gone, I gave her a list of the clues of your stolen game. And she has located the game, using time-tested methods of deduction. Isn't that right, Mildred?"

"Yes, Hank," she said. She looked triumphantly at Mrs. Carreker.

"It seems that when the game disappeared, all of you had motives to steal it," I said. I started walking around the room with my hands behind my back, looking at each of them as I passed. They all started staring at each other suspiciously. I needed a swagger stick and a magnifying glass. "You, Mr. Oshman." I looked at him. "Or you, Mrs. Carreker." She curled her lip and backed up a couple of steps. "Or you, Mrs. Gunnerson." She smiled and nodded. "Even you, Dicky." He laughed and lit a cigarette.

"You are, of course, stating the obvious," said Mrs. Carreker. "But I don't see the game anywhere." I smiled, the smile of Buddha, Voltaire's Smile of Reason, the smile of a hundred shallow triumphs.

"Mildred," I said, "would you get the game, please?" She nodded and went up to her room, passing Ginny who was coming down, a bag under one arm and Benjy, limp as a sock, under the other.

"You need to get his litter pan, Hank," Ginny said. I nodded. Mrs. Carreker was looking around at everyone trying to discover who might have been the thief.

"What you all need to remember," I said, "is that a kind word turns away wrath."

"I read that somewhere," said Mr. Oshman. He started softly humming "Danke Schoen."

"And that now is the time to forget and forgive whoever took the game and start over," I said. "Life itself is but a series of beginnings. You can begin to hate or be suspicious, but it is far better if you begin to forgive and to forget." Mildred came down the stairs bearing the Trivial Pursuit game on her outstretched hands like a communion platter. "Detective Mildred Ruth at your service."

Mrs. Gunnerson started clapping, and Mr. Oshman picked it up and even Dicky Thacker clapped a couple of times spastically before he realized it was not cool. Mrs. Carreker had a sick smile on her face.

"Let's play a game," said Mr. Oshman. "By golly, I feel lucky today." He took the game to the coffee table and started setting it up. Ginny went on out to the car and I went up and got Benjy's litter pan. I stood in my silent room for a moment and looked around. I liked it here. Maybe I would stay.

I got to the bottom of the stairs and Mildred Ruth came out onto the porch with me. It was windy, and her hair blew around her face, and she pulled it back. I set the litter pan down and gave Mildred a big hug.

"You did have a plan," she said. "You made it look like everyone might have done it."

"Just a trick," I said.

"I'm going to tell them I did it," she said, raising herself up a little. "I feel strong now." I nodded and grinned at her.

"Here's looking at you, kid," I said.

I got the litter pan and put it in the trunk and took Ginny Calvert home. I hated the drive because it was full of silences. The next few days would mean plenty of talking to us by the police, but nothing would come of it. There was no one left to try for much, and it would take weeks for everything to be put together. My name was in all the papers, on TV, but I wouldn't talk to any of them. It had something to do with pride. It might be a year before I was through with Adam Steed. Ginny would be through in a couple of days.

And that's exactly how it happened. We talked. The police talked. Jack Railsback and Rebecca Sanderson talked. Sandy Marcello talked. Edvard Johannsen did not talk. He wasn't the type. The cross had been stolen by a man who had since disappeared, supervised by Sandy Marcello, who had been in France for it. He took it to Denmark, where it was flown across, just as I had figured. Within weeks, it would be back under glass and tighter security. Jack was involved in a massive insurance fraud, and Steed had found out and was smart enough to blackmail Jack into helping him. Steed's brother-in-law, Sandy Marcello was stinking rich with drug money.

A week before Christmas, she told me she was going home for a month or so. She would start her school over winter quarter at the University of Georgia in Athens. I could come over and see her, and we would have some grand times, she said. But we both knew that the future held no certainties for us, that we were only drifting through time, and no one could say when or where we might be together again.

It was bitterly cold. I took her to Le Chat Noire, a wonderful French restaurant, dark and quiet and with the best trout amandine in town. She was leaving early the next morning for home, had already moved a load home with a U-haul trailer. The only things left in her apartment were a suitcase and the sheets on the bed. When I had picked her up, the room looked lost and sad, as all empty rooms do. No more fuzzy slippers, no more bottles of Chianti, no more smells of spaghetti. Not even Benjy, whom she had taken to her parents' house. And no *Portable Faulkner*.

We sat in the restaurant and ordered drinks, she a margarita, a bourbon and water for me. I was wearing my best suit, a smashing three-piece gray pinstripe. I wanted to make a summation to the jury and then loosen my tie and go visit some trendy watering hole and talk about my golf score. Ah, the good life. We ordered our food and waited. You wait a lot in restaurants, and our waiter was distracted because, as he told us, he had been in a car accident earlier in the day. Ginny felt sorry for him but I thought he was fishing for a tip. Who can account for human nature?

"So you got the office opened?" she asked. She had saved one dress for this special night, a blue Indian-print number with a high collar. Her hair was rolled perfectly and she wore dangly earrings with small stones in each.

"Yeah, and I even have a phone now," I said. "When you get bored going to school over in Athens, you can ring me up and we can talk of cabbages and kings." She smiled beautifully. "Or maybe Flem Snopes."

She had helped me move in a desk and a couple of filing cabinets two days before. My office was on the south side in a neighborhood that the yuppies would call downscale. Actually, it was in the midst of a slum. It was in an old house, on the second floor, but the place was clean and big enough for both me and my dreams. And on clear days, I could see Atlanta Stadium across the way and muse, as I would, about baseball.

Our waiter came. He looked very sad.

"Have you been to a doctor?" asked Ginny.

"I had to come to work," he sighed. "Maybe I'll go tomorrow. Another drink?"

"One more for each, and then bring us a bottle of Chianti," I said. "And if you'd like, I'll hammer out your fender when we leave." Ginny kicked me under the table. The waiter looked at me the way Treena looks at me and went away.

"That wasn't very nice," Ginny said.

"You have so much to learn about human nature, my dear," I said. I raised one eyebrow. Charles Boyer should have been as good as I was.

"I know it," she said, looking down. "But you could take a few lessons now and then yourself. You know, why people do things and all."

"Yeah?"

"Well, for instance, you might have asked me why I was so attracted to you from the beginning," she said softly. "You might have asked me that."

"I thought it was my knowledge of Faulkner and the finer points of the Kama Sutra," I said.

"Oh Hank, I couldn't tell you," she said. "Not earlier. You wouldn't have understood. Maybe you will now."

"I'm listening."

"My grandfather was the sheriff of Branton County," she said. "I adored him. He was this tall, lanky man with big hands, and he loved me more than anything. He and my grandmother lived in the country, and I would go visit them in the summer, run barefooted for days. He was a stronger man than my father, and I compared them. My father is not the strong, silent type. He loves to grow roses. Anyway, when I was twelve years old, my grandfather was indicted for embezzling funds from the sheriff's department. It was all over the papers. Everyone was sick, but it was more to me. I felt he must have had a reason. Before he could tell anybody why, he killed himself in the loft of his barn."

"My God," I said.

"And since that day I've wanted somebody to tell me the real difference between good and bad, right and wrong," she said. "You awakened that in me, Hank. You took me back to my grandfather's arms, before he lost sight of the truth. Maybe we can't return to innocence, but if we're lucky, we can have a little faith in the people we love. That's what this has meant to me. How about you?"

I thought about it for a moment. I knew things that were so seamy they would curl your toes, but I had forgotten most of what she knew with every fiber: home, heart, loving, forgiveness.

"I'm going to miss you," I said softly. "That's what it's all about." She slid her hands across the table and took mine. We didn't say anything else, just stared into each other's eyes until the waiter came back again.

"Just wait," she said. "Maybe things will work out for us."

Late that night, we got back to her place. It was cold and as we stood on the porch, I could see her breath. I did not want to go back inside, and she knew it. She leaned on me, putting both her hands against my chest.

"Do one thing for me," she said.

"Okay," I said. "I promise."

"Don't ever be anybody but who you are," she said.

"Crap," I said. " I was thinking of being Joe DiMaggio for a while."

"You know what I mean," she said.

"Yeah," I said. "And you do something for me. Something special."

"What?"

"Remember."

"I always will."

"I will, too."

Then I kissed her and walked down the stairs for the last time and got into my car and drove away. I drove by Shelleen's but did not stop. I wanted to be at work early the next morning, ready to answer the phone, to right wrongs, to salvage marriages, to look at women through my binoculars. Okay, so I was a degenerate in some ways still. But at least I knew in which ways.

The night was lovely, the sky, when you could see it, full of stars. I wanted to see the stars, so I drove out I-20 about thirty miles until I was in the country. I pulled off the side of the road and drove down this country lane until I was really alone then got out and lay on the hood of my Buick where it was warm. I looked up at Orion. I was, I knew, hopelessly old-fashioned in many ways. But fashion fades just as eyesight fades, and the residue is often merely sadness.

"Love," I said out loud, "doesn't fade."

I drove home and went up to my room and lay on my bed. I felt like smiling, so I did. My room wasn't so bad. I had the Hotpoint burners to make coffee on, a shower and a place to sleep. What more was there to life?

Rather than spend the next night alone or slumped on a barstool, I looked for something else to do and found out about a Christmas trade show for publishers being held in an annex to the Atlanta Civic Center. I hadn't read a good book in a while, and maybe I could get some for gifts. And maybe I would meet someone. I think Ginny knew we both would meet new people, laugh, love, while always reserving a special place for each other.

I shaved and showered and put on dark blue slacks, a brown military-style field shirt with epaulets, and a light blue corduroy jacket. My ribs were feeling better. The day had been good at work, as I got three calls, one developing into a job. A developer thought one of his employees was stealing from him. He didn't flinch at paying $150 a day plus expenses. He had seen my name in the papers. Apparently, many people had.

The city looked beautiful. Even the most humble business had a wreath or a strand of holly for the yuletide, and colorful lights sprouted everywhere. Christmas is the best time of year to be in a city. I felt full of good cheer.

I went to the Civic Center once with a woman named Joan Lowell to hear *La Traviata*. The singers raved and ranted for a long time in Italian and then somebody got killed.

I paid two bucks for parking to a woman whose rear looked like a sofa cushion. Perhaps it was only vanity, but I thought that among the tawdry and everyday vehicles lined up nearby, my car shone. I patted it on the door when I got out.

I walked up a long set of steps and onto a broad patio that separates the auditorium from the other building. A banner was slung over the building that said "Publishers Christmas Show and Sale." A good crowd was milling around inside. The walls are mostly glass, and I could see people. It was quite cold. I went on inside.

I wandered slowly around the concourse, picking up a few biographies, notably one on Ted Williams, a hero for our times if there ever was one. I turned a corner and right there, set up neatly, was a display for World View Encyclopedias. Behind it, sitting in a ladderback chair, was Wanda Mankowicz.

Our eyes met. She was wearing a frilly blouse and her eyes were the same transparent blue they had always been. Her mouth dropped open slightly.

"Hello," I said pleasantly. She looked better without my Rapala fishing knife through her forehead.

"Hank," she said. "I've been meaning to call. I read about you in the papers."

"Where's Mr. Encyclopedia?" I asked.

"He's in Sarasota," she said unhappily. "He had a regional conference to go to." Nobody seemed interested in buying a set of encyclopedias for Christmas. "I really have been meaning to call you." She smiled and arched her eyebrows hopefully.

"You're looking well," I said.

"I don't know what in the hell I'm doing here," she said. "I need to take a break." She got up and slipped on her suit jacket and walked across the room to an uncrowded corner, sure I would trail right along. I did. She leaned against a wall and looked demure while taking out a Virginia Slims. She waited for me to light it. I lit mine and then hers.

"So the old boy's taken off for Florida and left you stuck here," I said. "And this is the Christmas season. Where's the charity? Where's the pity?"

"You look good," she said. I looked at my reflection in the glass wall.

"I do, don't I?" I said.

"Michael won't be back until Sunday," she said. She stared deeply and with great meaning into my eyes. "It's just all so depressing about what happened to the Brownings." She tried to look sad. "I feel so alone. This place makes me feel so vulnerable."

She was beautiful. Classic features. A fine body that I knew so well.

"Really?" I asked.

"I just feel like getting drunk and staying in bed for a couple of days," she said. She ran her tongue over her upper lip slowly. "I feel so lonely." I smiled. She smiled. I still had time to have a couple of drinks and call Ginny Calvert and wish her season's greetings.

"Frankly, Wanda," I said, "I don't give a damn."

I paid for my books and went outside and looked up at the star-spangled floor of heaven.

"Sleep in heavenly peace," I said. I wasn't sure who it was for, but I had to believe that somebody was listening.

ABOUT THIS BOOK

Slow Dance in Autumn was designed by Paulette L. Lambert, typeset by Typo-Repro Service of Atlanta, Georgia, and printed by R.R. Donnelley and Sons at their Harrisonburg, Virginia plant. The typeface used in the book is Palatino.